TOLLING BELLS & DARK SPELLS
A SOUTHERN PARANORMAL COZY MYSTERY

A DARKLY SOUTHERN MYSTERY
BOOK ONE

TAM LUMIÈRE

MAGNOLIA HOUSE PUBLISHERS

Copyright © 2023 by Tam Lumière

All rights reserved.

No part of this book may be reproduced in any form or by any electronic or mechanical means, including information storage and retrieval systems, without written permission from the author, except for the use of brief quotations in a book review.

For Dennis, Will, and Ava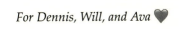

CHAPTER 1

"Are you sure this is right?"

My ears reverberated from the thunderous humming of the airboat as I stepped onto the brown planked walkway and tried to ignore the murky green water below the gaps. On my head, my big floppy hat—one that I had worn to countless poolside soirees and garden parties—was now a drooping, shapeless mass. I brushed down my white jumpsuit and cursed my lack of forethought in choosing my attire for the day. A relaxing *boat* ride I was expecting. A choppy *air*boat ride? Not so much.

"Yes, ma'am." The boat operator grinned broadly. "Darkly Island."

My fashionably messy bun, which had taken my stylist two hours to create, was undone in less than twenty minutes; it now stuck out all over my head as if a family of swamp rats had moved in and redecorated. I tried to tuck some of the stray chestnut brown hairs back into place, gave up, and plopped my ruined hat back on my head, protecting my pale skin from the blistering sun. The earthy smell of wood rot and wet grass hit my nose, along with an undercurrent of something sweet and delicate, perhaps honeysuckle, or frangipani. A thicket of bald cypress trees ran along the shoreline surrounded by tall swaying cattails. Beyond the dock, a few low-growing palms swayed next to a gravel path.

As I looked around my new home—contemplating returning to the boat and hightailing it back to New York—the boatman set my designer trunk and matching vanity case on the dock. With a flourish, he tipped his hat and hopped back onto the boat, sliding deftly behind the air shield. The engine cut on with a roar, and I threw a hand on top of my hat, waving hysterically with the other.

"Wait! Aren't you going to help me with all these bags?"

The man waved back, gave one last toothy grin, and spun the boat around, heading back the way we came.

I stomped one high-heeled boot in frustration. Without the rush of air from the boat ride, the Louisiana heat smothered me in its heavy cloak. Within minutes, my whole body felt hot and sticky, and I wondered how I would ever get used to living in this devilish heat.

With a sigh, I heaved my tote onto my shoulder, swatted at a dragonfly trying to hitch a ride, and grabbed both pieces of luggage. Never one to overdramatize things—and I mean that quite sarcastically—I stomped my foot one last time for good measure and was repaid with a booming crack as my heel crashed through the rickety dock. I toppled sideways, over adjusted, and then fell forward, butt up in the air. I clutched my precious bags beneath me, not daring to move an inch. My ruined hat slid from my head and lodged itself in the cattails lining the shore.

I shook my head. "Oh, for Pete's sake!"

"Need some help, chère?" A smooth Southern voice called to me from the shore.

Leaning against the willow tree was a tan, blond man in khaki pants and a short-sleeved silk shirt. He appeared to be in his thirties, like me, and held himself with a laid-back assurance I desperately craved at that moment.

I might never get accustomed to this blazing heat, but I could definitely get accustomed to Louisiana gentlemen, especially if they call me chère and happen to be as movie-star attractive as this man.

"Yes, please. If you would."

"You must forgive Char," he said as he ambled over to inspect my intertwined luggage and legs. "To his detriment, being in that wretched boat every day has left him almost completely deaf."

He pulled his hands from his pockets and bent over until he was at my eye level. "You're going to need to let go of these bags if you want me to deposit them safely on terra firma."

Once I had relinquished my hold, he easily untangled my luggage. Without launching either of us into the marsh, I might add. He then picked up both the trunk and the case, deftly skirted the gaps in the dock, and deposited the bags next to the gravel path.

He sauntered back to the dock and crouched down, examining my foot dangling above the muck. "Looks like you've got it stuck tight."

I nodded my head. "It won't budge." I pulled and shook my foot, but no matter what I did, my ankle remained lodged in the planking.

"Sorry to tell you, darling, but that boot's gonna have to go," he said with a commiserative shake of his head.

"Can't you just—I don't know—cut a hole in the dock?" I cried, panic rising in my voice.

His smile was back. "I could. But do you really want to wait here in that position—as adorable as it is—while I try to find someone with the tools to cut out a piece of this dock? And who knows if they'll even be able to do it without cutting off a chunk of your foot?"

"Oh fine," I said. "Do what you have to do."

Levering the heel of my boot up against the dock to hold it in place, I tugged and wiggled my foot as I grasped the man's arm. After a few minutes of twisting and pulling on my foot, it finally popped out, as my sweaty hands slipped off the man's arm and I tumbled backward into the green waters below.

My butt hit the water first, and I splashed and sputtered as I tried to find my footing on the slimy mud bottom. The soft, warm water swirled around my legs as I finally stood and squelched my way to the shoreline. To his benefit, the man neither laughed, nor ran away. He simply extended a hand to me through the cattails and pulled me to dry land.

"Sorry about that, dear," he said in his soft, Southern twang.

I waved a hand and a dripping cluster of duckweed flew off and slapped me on the forehead. "Not your fault. You have just witnessed the past three months of my life condensed into a brief thirty-second vignette."

"C'mon, let's get you to town," he said, chuckling. "By the way, I'm Chase Abernathy-Wyatt. My husband Lorenzo de Zavala and I own the Spells & Gels Salon right up the road."

I looked down at the wet, brown mess that had once been my trendy jumpsuit and sighed dismally. Was the universe trying to tell me something?

"Are you staying at the Green Gator Tavern or White Hart Inn?"

"Neither." I hobbled down the walkway, tiptoeing as best I could in one stiletto boot and one bare foot. "I own a house here in Darkly."

Insecurity getting the best of me, I stared down at the gravel path. I was uncomfortable with being willed a house from someone I didn't remember ever meeting.

He stopped and raised an eyebrow. "Well, bless my stars! Are you Windsor Ebonwood?"

"I am," I said, extending my hand. "But most people call me Win."

Chase shook my hand heartily.

"Minta's granddaughter! It's wonderful to meet you, Win." His voice dropped its jocular tone. "I'm terribly sorry about Minta, dear. She was a hoot, and we all miss her."

I didn't know what to say to that, so I remained silent, continuing to hobble and drip by his side.

"Do you have a ride to Fernwood? It's not far, but with all this luggage and only one boot, it might take you awhile," Chase said.

"Fernwood?"

"Fernwood's the name of your new home, hun."

"Oh. Right. Yes, my grandmother's attorney will pick me up. Mr. Hathaway, I believe."

At the end of the gravel path, a paved road passed over a stone bridge, where it changed into cobbles, then curved through a row of two- and three-story brick buildings, with iron scroll balcony railings and overflowing flower boxes.

I gasped. This was not at all what I expected.

Chase smiled proudly. "Yep. Our little town does have quite a bit of charm."

Just then, a white Jeep passed us, swung around, and screeched to a stop.

∼

"Hi, Chase." A brown-skinned woman with a platinum blond pixie-cut waved.

"Hey, Tzazi."

The woman turned to me. "Are you Windsor Ebonwood?"

"Win," I said.

The woman hopped out of the vehicle and strode to where we stood. As she drew closer, tattoos of black and red roses twirling up and down her arms caught my attention. Huge diamond studs decorated her ears, and I envied the light cotton dress and sandals she wore. I looked down at myself again—yep, I still looked like a mess—and cringed. At least the heat was now bearable.

"I'm Tzazi. Tzazi Strangeland, an attorney at Hathaway & Strangeland. Mr. Hathaway is tied up with a client, so he sent me in his stead." She shook my hand, giving me an up and down look. "Whatever happened to you?"

Chase snorted, picking up my bags and placing them in the back of the Jeep.

I ignored him.

"My heel crashed through the dock, and I fell into the swamp," I said.

"Char really needs to fix those docks. C'mon. I've got a blanket in the Jeep." Tzazi turned to Chase. "Will I see you at the Gator tonight?"

"You bet, mon amie," he replied. "See you around, Win."

Chase waved, slid on his sunglasses, and strolled up the lane toward an old man selling poppets from a metal pushcart.

Tzazi removed a midnight blue quilt from the back of the Jeep and wrapped it around me. I climbed in, carefully placing my foot on the floorboard. The skin burned where it had scraped against the wood, and it felt good to take the pressure off my raw ankle.

Tzazi frowned as she turned onto the lane and pointed at my foot. "Do you need to see a doctor for that? And what happened to your other boot?"

"It's only a scrape." I frowned. "And the boot's found its final resting place at the bottom of the swamp."

Tzazi laughed. "That swamp has taken in more designer duds than a harpy on a bender."

"Huh?" I had never heard that one before.

"Nothing," she said, waving a hand. "Would you like a quick tour of Darkly, so you can get your bearings and see a little of our town? Only take a minute."

I nodded my acceptance and off we went.

As she drove, Tzazi pointed out various shops and buildings on the main thoroughfare, Tataille (pronounced Tah-tie) Street—such as the butcher, the grocery store, and her law office—along with a few notable residents, like the mayor, whose bushy red hair I wouldn't easily forget, and Mr. Sugarloaf, the owner of the sweet shop. At odds with its name, I found Darkly to be a lively town with window boxes full of showy ferns and bougainvillea. The sidewalks, shaded by the balconies above, bustled with townspeople, who smiled and waved as we drove by.

"What kind of law do you specialize in?" I asked as we turned next to the tavern called the Green Gator, and the road ascended a small hill. A Tudor-style mansion with an expansive, green lawn appeared outside my window, and I craned my neck to take it all in.

"Well, in a small town, we do a bit of everything," she said. "Contracts. Divorces. But my favorite? Criminal Defense. Dewey —Mr. Hathaway— says I'm like a shark smelling blood in the water. That might not be the nicest thing to say about an attorney" —she shrugged— "but it did get me into the Top Forty Under Forty list this year. I don't enjoy seeing good people being pushed around."

"Is there a lot of crime around here?" I asked. We drove past several small homes, long and thin, painted vividly in greens, yellows, purples, and reds. Shuttered windows stretched from floors to ceilings.

"Not really. I usually end up going out to Strawbridge or Wychwood. Those towns are a little larger. Here, the worst we get is too much drinking on Solstice. I'm guessing you do something in books?"

I laughed. "Good guess! I'm a book conservator. Taught at a university until, well, things fell apart recently."

"That sounds like an excellent story to be told, and listened to, with a glass of wine. I've got a few of those stories myself."

After we turned around on the outskirts of town (She was right; it did only take a minute!) and drove down the hill back into Darkly, Tzazi stopped before one of the taller three-story buildings in the center of town. While this building shared the distinct brick walls and cast-iron decorative railings of the others, no bright awnings, nor overflowing window boxes, graced its front. Instead, stained-glass windows rose from sidewalk to roof, split by an arched wooden entryway. The building was flanked by

Dianthe's Oopsie Daisies and a shop with the odd name of Besoms & Britches.

"This is your bookshop," Tzazi said with a flourish. "Mr. Hathaway has the keys. He'll be in touch with you in the next few days. He wants to give them to you himself."

"My bookshop." An overwhelming urge to reach out for the structure overcame me, and I placed my palms longingly on the car window.

The building appeared regal, almost cathedral-like, and I felt a strange bond the moment I saw it. The stained-glass pieces in the windows portrayed various life scenes—like a shepherdess and her herd, birds in flight, and a spectacular castle with spires and flags. There were hundreds of them, each one depicting a completely different scene.

I startled, Tzazi's voice drawing me out of my reverie.

"Maman's coffee shop." She pointed at the corner building only a few doors down from the bookshop, one with an outdoor seating area and a colorful sign written in fancy script: The Magic Cup.

"Maman also serves the best tea and scones in town," Tzazi said.

She hesitated for a moment and then pointed across the street to an imposing metal entryway. An intricate wrought-iron fence, embellished with winged demons and openmouthed gargoyles, ran alongside the property. Beyond the entrance, a path threaded through lush green foliage and twined around oak and magnolia trees. In the distance, a stone bell tower stood tall in its center like Tolkien's Treebeard.

"This is Darkly Cemetery," she said softly. "When you're ready to visit Minta and your mom."

I pushed back the sudden onset of sadness and found that I could only nod.

Tzazi watched me for a few moments.

"You ready to see Fernwood?" she asked.

Despite the emotions threatening to overpower me, the thought of seeing my family home raised my spirits.

I smiled and gave Tzazi a thumbs up, not trusting myself to speak.

As we left town, the cobblestone street soon gave way to a dark asphalt road, which we drove on for only a few minutes. Turning right next to a Herculean oak, one that looked to be over five hundred years of age, we passed through a gateway with a simple metal sign: "Fernwood." The Jeep rolled onto a curved driveway laced with terracotta pavers.

I gasped as the home came into view.

Tzazi reached over and patted my arm reassuringly. "Welcome to Fernwood."

CHAPTER 2

Fernwood stretched out before me like a lazy yellow cat in the sun. The French Colonial-style house sat on raised brick pillars, with a wide veranda and seven shuttered glass doors spaced evenly across the front of the house. The center entryway featured adornments of intricately carved molding, along with stained-glass images in greens and blues.

Tzazi parked the Jeep under a magnolia tree covered in gigantic white blooms. As we passed through the wrought-iron gate, a giant hibiscus bush trailed its deep green leaves down my shoulder and frangipani bells of pink and orange swayed in the warm breeze.

Ahead, purple passion vine coiled around a lamppost, its rich red fruit plump to bursting. Behind it, a pair of white staircases led to a covered porch where a trio of ceiling fans lapped lazily in the heat. I ran my hand through a rosemary bush, its powerful scent following me up the stairs to the front porch.

Tzazi met me in front of the double doors. "Here are your keys," she said, placing a metal key chain into my hand. She stared at my flushed face for a moment. "It's a lot to take in, I know. And I don't just mean this house. We'll get you some water from the icebox."

As I inserted the key in the lock, my heart raced, and I had to agree. Never had I felt so excited and terrified at the same time.

Still, I bore up, took a deep breath, and turned the key.

As the door swung open, all I could do was stare.

"Yes, it's quite remarkable," Tzazi said, stepping into the cool foyer. "Your ancestors built Fernwood over two hundred years ago, but as you can see, Minta wasn't a doily and afghan kind of lady. Fireplaces and ceiling fans in every room. All the modern conveniences. A/C. Heating. Plumbing, of course."

Inhaling the fresh scent of lemon and wood polish, I clomped along behind Tzazi on deep brown hardwood floors, finding myself in a room full of plump velvet sofas and tufted chairs. A flatscreen TV, no less than six feet wide, hung at an angle above the large, elegant fireplace.

"This is your sitting room," Tzazi said.

"Oh, I like this room," I mumbled, brushing my hand against a small round table, meant for storing knitting materials. The room was homey, and relaxing, and I could see a person spending a lot of time here.

Reluctantly, I followed Tzazi out the back door, where I found myself on a narrow, screened-in porch, running along the backside of Fernwood.

"The dining room and kitchen are separated from the main house by this screened-in walkway," she explained. "Shows you how old this house is."

Pushing through the door in front of me, I discovered an opulent dining room. The ornate wooden table easily accommodated a dinner party of ten, but how they'd be able to see or speak to each other through the three silver candelabras, I couldn't imagine. More shuttered glass windows overlooked a dense forest on one side, and a swampy pond with a small tropical courtyard on the other.

"Minta liked dinner parties," Tzazi said. "Do you cook?"

"Not really," I admitted.

She shrugged. "Me neither. C'mon. I'll show you the kitchen anyway."

We passed through a set of double doors and into a bright kitchen leading to a back deck with wooden railings. Black-and-white tiles crisscrossed on the floor, edging up against stainless steel appliances. I was relieved to see that what Tzazi called an icebox was a state-of-the-art refrigerator, with an ice and water dispenser.

"I stocked the kitchen for you this morning. Of course, I didn't know what you'd want, so I got you all my favorites." She shrugged and handed me a bottle of water from the fridge.

Tzazi walked to a thin pantry in the corner and withdrew a tube of antibiotic and a large first aid bandage. Handing them to me, she said, "Your housekeeper, Hilde Orso, has her own place above the kitchen. She's visiting family, but she'll be here Monday."

"Thanks," I said, accepting the items. "Orso? That name sounds familiar." I climbed onto a stool placed alongside a center island to examine my injured foot. The scraped area on the top still stung but had already begun to heal. I applied the ointment and bandage. Much better.

"Yeah, Hilde has worked for the Ebonwoods all her life, and her parents did the same before her. Minta promised her a job with the family for as long as she wants it. Your grandmother was like that. Hilde took it hard when she died."

Tzazi glanced at her watch. "Ooh. I'll let you get cleaned up and settled in. I've got court this afternoon."

As we passed through the sitting room, she pointed out the door leading to my bedroom, and the ones opposite, which opened to the library. Afterward, I followed her back to the foyer, where she opened the top drawer of a narrow cabinet.

"Almost forgot. In here are Minta's will, along with all the house keys. Oh! And be on the lookout for Pyewacket. He's been very upset since Minta's death."

"Don't tell me my grandmother had a boyfriend!"

Tzazi laughed. "Pye is Minta's cat. They were inseparable. I'll get the rest of your bags. Be right back."

I wandered around the room until I paused in front of a small, tarnished hand mirror, propped up next to a photo of an elegant woman wearing a string of white pearls. She cradled a tiny baby in her arms; I recognized my grandmother and myself immediately. Next to us stood a woman with long, wavy hair and a bright smile. My mother.

I replaced the photo on the sideboard as Tzazi rushed back in with my bags and set them down.

Giving me a quick hug, she turned to leave and then hesitated. "Do you want to come with me to the Green Gator tonight? Casual, Southern comfort food. Just what you need on your first night in Darkly."

As tired as I was, the thought of sitting down to eat by myself in that large dining room wasn't appealing.

"Sounds wonderful!"

She looked at me wistfully.

"You know, you remind me of Minta. I think it's the stiletto. See you tonight."

After Tzazi left, I lugged my bags into the bedroom and squealed with delight. Decorated in soft creams, the room was a haven of delicate French provincial furniture, including a gorgeous, beveled mirror and matching dresser. Most of all, it was the giant four-poster bed that really grabbed my attention. I desperately longed to burrow into its soft comforter for the rest of the day. Instead, I shed my smelly jumpsuit, tossed it into the hamper, and then stepped into a much-needed shower.

Feeling refreshed afterward, I threw on a comfy tank-top and jeans and unpacked the rest of my clothes. I threw the last of my PJs in the drawer and then rebandaged my foot. Now it was time to go exploring.

Interestingly, the house contained no hallways connecting all the rooms, unless you counted the outdoor porches running along the front and back of the house. My bedroom linked to a small study, with a kidney-shaped wooden desk and a blue-and-cream Persian rug. Stepping into the next space, I found an airy music room, with a white grand piano and several potted palms. On a small side table rested an old phonograph with an LP still lying on its turntable. Paintings of ballet dancers graced the walls. The next doorway led me back to the entry foyer, and I grinned like a silly schoolgirl as I turned to the library.

Tingling with excitement, I threw open the doors and—to my delight—found the most magnificent personal library I had ever seen. Barrister bookcases made of glossy walnut wrapped around the entire room. I lifted one of the glass doors, slid it back into the bookcase, and pulled out a few of the volumes inside: Shakespeare, Lumière, Keats, Rowling, Dostoevsky. All first editions. All in impeccable condition. All with that wonderful, bookish smell.

I probably spent an hour that first day, pulling out books and breathing in their heavenly scent. Finally, I collapsed into a cozy chaise lounge in the corner, immersing myself in *Wuthering Heights*, a book I hadn't read since high school.

By the time I left Heathcliff and Catherine on the moors, the sun was low on the violet-tinged horizon. On an end table, I found a ceramic vase holding a variety of bookmarks. I used one to mark my chapter before placing the book on the back of the chaise.

Heathcliff would have to wait until another day.

Before Tzazi arrived to pick me up for dinner, I wanted to take a quick stroll around the grounds and gardens. Behind the house, visible from my bedroom windows, swamp waters covered in white water lilies, rippled softly, while outside the guestroom windows on the other side, lay the woodland forest I had spied from the dining room. I knew little about forests, and even less about swamps (except that they were teeming with alligators, snakes, and who knew what else). I decided to hike into the forest for my first quick jaunt around the property.

Pulling on a pair of low-heeled boots, I grabbed a papaya from a fruit bowl in the kitchen, my umbrella from the coat stand, and stepped out onto the porch. Dark clouds were gathering in the distance; however, they were far away, and I didn't plan to spend much time in the trees anyway.

The droning of the cicadas followed me as I pushed open the metal gate. A well-trod trail led through a field of tall grass and wildflowers between me and the forest. A warm breeze ruffled the stalks, as a large blue and black butterfly zig zagged through the blooms alongside me.

The forest immersed me in a cool, earthy shadow the moment I stepped under its branches. Birds raucously chirped and tweeted around me, while leaves rustled in a breeze blowing through the canopy above. I found a path and followed it deeper into the trees. At one point, I heard the crunching of leaves, and when I turned, glimpsed a deer with a mouthful of green leaves before it scampered into the brush.

The forest was alive, and I found the chatter of small animals and whisper of falling leaves unexpectedly calming. I'd finally decided it was time to turn back when I saw a flash of movement in front of me. Peering through the branches, I saw a woman, her long hair flowing wildly. She wore a black, flowing dress and spun in a circle, arms stretched wide, until she fell to the ground, laughing (or crying, I wasn't sure) hysterically.

"Hey!" I yelled.

The woman turned toward me. Without a word, she raised her hands in my direction and disappeared.

I hurried to the spot where the woman had sat only moments before and spun around myself. I stood there for a few seconds, dumbfounded. Where had she gone? Had I imagined her?

Deciding it was best I got myself out of this forest and back to the house, I looked around for the path I had traveled. I hadn't walked far from it when I thought I saw the woman. I studied the ground, hoping to retrace my steps, but all I saw were leaves, fallen branches, and twigs.

I pulled out my phone. No signal, of course.

As a raindrop plopped on my forehead, panic rose in my throat. What was I thinking coming out here on my own?

I took a deep breath, calming myself, and examined the area. I thought I recognized a curiously bent tree I had passed earlier, and so I warily set a path in that direction.

The forest was growing dark, and I was aware of forest sounds —small animals creeping, water drops on leaves, the hoot of an owl. Somehow, it was comforting to know I wasn't alone.

A break in the canopy gave me a peek at the sky. The sun hadn't yet set, but storm clouds were indeed pushing in. A flash of movement caught my eye—something large flying over the trees—and that was when it began. A deep, guttural howling erupted all around me.

Taking a few hesitant steps, the hairs rose on the back of my neck as a low growl issued from somewhere directly to my right. Without daring to look, I turned and ran. Shrieks, howls, even cackles filled the air, driving me on.

Somehow, I found the path again, and following it at full speed, I glimpsed the lights of Fernwood in the distance. As I grew closer, I could see a figure standing at the edge of the trees. Tzazi! I'd never been so happy to see someone.

Upon approaching the clearing, I slowed. Lights from the house backlit the figure, preventing me from seeing her clearly, but I knew something wasn't right. The arms were extraordinarily long, fingertips grazing the knees. The body hunched forward, pulsing with the tempo of its erratic breathing. I stopped. The person stepped forward a few feet and I screamed. Jagged teeth protruded from a snarling, grinning mouth, oozing saliva.

Yelping, I thrust my umbrella in the beast's direction and

rushed back into the forest. The creature howled once, then loud footsteps plowed into the brush after me.

Daring to glance back, I almost stumbled in surprise when I saw a gigantic black dog—perhaps even a wolf—instead of the hunched figure I had seen earlier. Whatever it was, it was the size of a refrigerator and coming at me fast. Hot breath huffed against the back of my legs, and the dog yipped and nipped at my boots, almost playfully, like it was just having some fun. It gave a small leap and snapped its jaws at my face.

A few yards ahead stood a tall oak, its large, gnarled branches curving and spreading along the forest floor. When I reached it, I leaped over a low branch, hoping to put some space between myself and the dog. A flash of light through the brush caught my attention, and I strained to focus on it. My burning lungs threatened to burst. I dashed through a thick curtain of leaves when I saw the light again. Safety! Wait, maybe not. What if the dog lived there? What if the dog's owner lived there? Forget that. What if Freddy Krueger lived there? I didn't see how I had a choice, and so pointed myself toward the fiery glow.

CHAPTER 3

When I burst through a tight band of trees and vines, I found myself in a green glade. Smoke puffed from the small chimney of a rustic wooden cabin set back at the rear of the property. Before me, a fire blazed in a bonfire piled high with old wooden chairs, bits of broken lumber, and was that an outhouse on top?

I hurried to the safety of the fire, then turned toward the tree line, my breath rising and falling in jagged peaks. The rumbling footsteps and eager pants of the beast had subsided. Had it given up? I stood quietly for a few minutes, not daring to move a muscle, as I struggled to catch my breath, studying the tree line for the slightest of movements. Nothing. Somewhere between the tree and the clearing, I'd lost the mutt. Score one for the city girl!

In my celebration dance, a kind of wild flailing, my arm came down on a solid object, and I turned around to find a leering hollow-eyed animal skull resting on a spike. Screaming, I spun around and whacked it hard with my umbrella, screaming again as the skull flew. It landed with a thump on the ground. I felt a light tug on my sleeve and swung my umbrella again, when the umbrella suddenly stopped in mid-swing, as if halted by an invisible hand.

"You'd do well to wait," a soothing voice said. "He's not gone. Tricky devils, they are!"

Standing before me was a tall, thin, dark-skinned man, with grey wisps of hair atop his head and on his chin. He wore brown pants, no shoes, and a long white tunic. His bony hand wrapped around a wooden cane covered in tendrils of dark, ashy smoke.

I had no reason to trust this man, other than that he looked like someone's sweet grandpa—but his voice was calm and lilting, soft like a song.

"I could help you hide from him, if you care to venture back into the forest," he said in that reassuring voice. "However, they have extraordinary olfactory senses. He would find you through your scent."

His bright green eyes stared me down for a moment. "Do I know you, child?" He tilted his head.

"Probably not, sir. My—"

He let out a raucous guffaw. "None of that 'sir.' Friends call me Mizizi."

I nodded, smiling back uneasily.

"You probably knew my grandmother, Minta Ebonwood."

He hesitated before saying, "Ah. You're Genevieve's daughter. You're Windsor Ebonwood."

Turning toward the cabin, he beckoned with his free hand, and I followed.

"You knew my mom?"

"Knew?" He glanced back at me. "Yes, I knew your mom."

We circled around to the far side of the blaze, where comfortable seating lay scattered about—plump sofas, fuzzy poofs, a couple of rockers, even a throne-like chair with a fringed roof above it. How were they not soaked from the storm? Come to think of it, the entire glade looked as if it had not seen a drop of rain that evening.

"Please have a seat, Windsor," he said, pointing to the nearest sofa, one covered in a multitude of fluffy pillows.

"Mizizi?" I said, drawing his attention. "Were you friends with my mother?"

Mizizi shushed me, pressing a finger to his lips, before climbing the steps, and entering the cabin.

He returned quickly with two mugs, aromatic steam drifting from each, and sat in the cushioned chair next to mine. He handed me one of the steaming mugs, and I took a careful sip. A warm rush of comfort flowed through me as the flavors melted on my tongue—nutmeg, cinnamon, and a flavor I couldn't quite place.

"Turmeric and honey," he said with a smile.

Did he just read my mind?

Mizizi gave a chuckle. "It is good you found my cabin. Those who wish to cause harm are not welcome."

I pointed to the heads and nodded.

Leaning in, he said, "Just between you and me, they're fake."

"I can't tell you how relieved I am to hear that," I said.

Mizizi chuckled and relaxed back into his seat, crossed his long legs in front of him, and took a long sip. The fire blazed warm and high as it licked the bottom of the outhouse. Between the tea and the fire, I almost forgot about the dog, out for my blood somewhere back in the forest. Almost. But not quite.

"Why do you ask me about your mother?" Mizizi asked as he stared into the fire. "Did your father not speak of her?"

His questions surprised me. "You knew my father?"

He dipped his head slightly. "I've met your father. A very interesting man. We debated at length the effects of Stoker's *Dracula* on Victorian society the one time I met him."

I laughed. That was Dad alright. "He could never pass up a literary debate, especially if it concerned the supernatural. You know that was his specialty, right? He was a university professor. Just as I was."

My voice trailed off as I lapsed into silence and stars began flickering on in the sky above, the murmur of crickets filling in the lull.

"Dad refused to speak of Mom," I finally answered. "I guess

talking about her stirred up painful memories. But now that he's gone, I wish I'd tried harder to get him to talk to me about her."

Mizizi nodded. "Genevieve was…" he began, but then stopped and cocked his head, listening.

Through the crackle of the fire, I heard heavy footsteps pushing through the brush. I picked up my umbrella and held it at the ready. I could do a lot of damage with the pointy little tip of an umbrella. Mark my words.

"Now what do you intend to do with that, lass? Poke me in the eye?" The voice at the edge of the clearing was powerful and incredibly sexy, Scottish sounding in its lilt.

Mizizi produced a pipe from his shirt pocket as a man stepped into the clearing.

"You should keep a stronger leash on your dog, Bain." Mizizi spoke softly, but I knew the man heard.

"That was your dog?" I snapped. "I could have been —"

He stepped closer to the bonfire, and I closed my mouth with a click.

My heart nearly fluttered to a stop. I was gazing at the most gorgeous man I'd ever set eyes on. Dark wavy hair curled around his ears, tumbling onto broad shoulders. He was tall, with tattoos cascading down taut, muscular arms, and he strode toward us with a confident swagger that sparked a sudden thrill in my chest.

Chocolate brown eyes took in the surrounding scene, wincing slightly as they passed over the animal heads on spikes. As his eyes locked on to mine, he came to an abrupt halt. I felt a shiver pass through my body as his full lips opened in slight surprise. I almost felt dizzy, as a strange desire to wrap myself in his brawny arms and caress the sides of his gorgeous face suddenly overcame me.

What the heck did Mizizi put in that mug?

I pushed the ridiculous emotions aside as the man shook his head and strode around the fire. "First, he's not a dog. Second, he doesn't belong to me —"

Mizizi paused in the middle of stuffing of his pipe and grinned. "Wellll —"

"— and third, he wouldn't have hurt you anyway!"

I pointed my umbrella at him.

"First," I said, stalking toward him, wielding the umbrella before me like a fencing foil. "That thing was most certainly a dog … or maybe a wolf!" Did he honestly think I didn't know I was in danger when I clearly was? "And second, if that was YOUR dog …"

Before I could spew further indignation, my toe caught the edge of a metal glider and I face-planted into the lawn at his feet. A loud pop sounded through the clearing, and I rolled to my side as a sharp pain exploded in my right ankle.

"Bring her into the cabin," Mizizi ordered, and the man picked me up as easily and carefully as if I were a newborn kitten. "And summon Ileana."

I bit my lip to keep from crying out, as he strode across the glade with me in his arms, my head resting on his shoulder. I couldn't help but breathe in his scent. He smelled of the forest—earthy and wild—and despite the pain, I felt the strangest compulsion to run my hands through his hair.

Mizizi stood on the porch of the cabin. "Yes, yes. You are welcome here," he said, when the man hesitated for a moment on the steps.

It took my eyes a moment to adjust to the darkness inside the cabin. Candles flickered and sputtered on every surface, allowing mere glimpses of the items in the room. One side of the home was clearly a living area, containing two rocking chairs in front of a stone fireplace, a small sofa, and a well-used dining table. The man carried me to the opposite end of the cabin and gently placed me on a rectangular wooden table with a bench pushed up next to it. Jars, bottles, books, and herbs cluttered every shelf and countertop. Shadows loomed heavily in the corners of this area of the home, and a chill ran down my spine as they appeared to writhe and dance along the walls.

The man helped me onto the table, then stepped out the front door as Mizizi removed a sharp-looking pair of shears from a drawer behind him. I looked away as he cut down the side of my leather boot and gently lifted my foot out. Two pairs of boots in one day. Gone!

Climbing up a wooden ladder, Mizizi retrieved an onyx jar from a top shelf. He placed it on the table and scooped out a handful of green liniment. When he massaged it into my foot and ankle, the pain vanished.

"Who's Ileana?" I asked, as the numbing ointment seemed to relax my entire body.

"Ileana is the village healer."

"A doctor?"

"A doctor, yes."

The door suddenly banged open, and the man jogged back into the cabin.

"She's on her way," he said.

I pointed at the man. "And who is that?"

Mizizi tipped his head in my direction. Without looking up from my foot, he said, "Keir Bain, may I introduce Windsor Ebonwood? Win, this is Keir Bain."

An adorable grin lit up Keir's face as he said, "Ah. You're an Ebonwood." He suddenly frowned. "You don't look much like an Ebonwood."

Okay. Not that adorable.

"Well, if your dog hadn't attacked me, maybe I'd look a little more presentable!"

"That's NOT my dog!" He shook his head. "Hold up! He's not even a dog!"

"Whatever," I muttered. I waved a hand dismissively as I snatched a small branch out of my hair, which had chosen that very moment to fall into my face. I had to admit, I probably looked a fright.

Mizizi cocked his eye and stifled a grin.

Keir ambled easily around the cabin, picking up various

objects, examining them, then setting them down. He moved with a simple casualness that I envied, as if he knew his place in the world and it was right where he wished it to be. I tried my best to stare at the dark wooden floor beneath my dangling foot, but I felt my eyes moving to track his whereabouts, especially after I noticed him cutting his eyes at me when he thought I wasn't looking.

I felt a flush of heat and tied my long thick hair into a knot on the top of my head to circulate some cooling air. The skin on the back of my neck prickled, and I knew he was staring at me. I turned in his direction as he moved next to me and nodded toward his cupped hands. Between leather bracelets, circling tan wrists, he held two large blue-green eggs with brown splotches.

"Black vulture eggs."

"How beautiful," I said, releasing my hair, and reaching out a finger to stroke the larger of the two. The egg was warm and smooth and delicate as a broken heart.

Keir nodded. "They mate for life, you know. Just like wolves." His voice was soft and sexy.

I was saved from replying by the sudden whoosh of the front door as it opened. A petite, spritely woman hurried to my side.

My ankle had now swollen to twice its normal size and was a lovely shade of eggplant. Mizizi's balm was wearing off, and the throbbing was almost unbearable again.

"I'm Ileana Sorrel," the woman said as she entered the cabin, her long white gown dragging the floor behind her. Her feet were bare, and her wavy hair pulled back in a long braid. "Now let me see that ankle."

She was young, yet she spoke with the authority and confidence of a much older woman.

Ileana slathered the green salve all over my foot again, bringing immediate relief.

Then placing her hands around my foot, she cocked her head as if listening intently, and gently pressed along my ankle, the area above, and my Achilles tendon.

Ileana nodded once. "Honey, you've got yourself a nasty sprain. Which is great news, cos broken bones are much harder to mend." Turning to Mizizi, she pointed to the corner. "May I?"

"Of course, Ileana," he said. "Whatever you need."

She moved to the corner of the room, appearing to speak emphatically with someone. Her arms gesticulated wildly, and then she smiled, put her hands together in a gesture of thanks, and returned to me at the table.

I furrowed my brows. What was that about?

A soft movement stirred the air at my side and—to my astonishment—sitting on the table next to me were a translucent jar containing a brown sparkling substance, a white tube, a couple of dried purple flowers, and a thick metal bowl. I hadn't even seen her place them there.

Ileana removed the stopper of the translucent jar, and an acrid scent pervaded the room. "Don't worry," she said, as I covered my nose. "Stinging nettle puree always gives off a powerful scent before it stabilizes."

She poured the contents of the jar, a thick tarry substance, into the bowl. With her back to me, she pulled out a black mortar from under the cabinet and began grinding the flowers into a fine powder.

"What about an X-ray?" I asked.

"Don't need one."

"What if it's broken?"

"It's not."

"Okay, how about if —" She twirled around.

"Honey, if you don't shut your trap, you may end up with a propagation liniment for warts rather than a fine-fettle elixir for sprains. And I guarantee you don't want that."

Keir laughed, still examining the various items crammed in the room.

I directed my best evil eye in his direction.

"Keir, dollface," Ileana said, "be a dear and hand me one of

Mizizi's empty vials. He keeps them over there next to the dung beetle balls."

Keir retrieved the vial and flung it in her direction. Without missing a lick, her hand flew up and caught it.

She laughed. "Gotta do better than that to catch me out."

Keir grunted and resumed dallying around the room.

"You know, you don't need to stay," I said when his meandering took him close to the table where I was sitting.

He crouched to browse through some books piled on the floor, then looked up at me through long, dark lashes. He grinned, and my stomach somersaulted.

What is going on with me?

"I have nothing better to do."

I cocked my head. "Really?"

"If you must know," he huffed. "I told Mizizi I'd help you get home. In case the, uh, dog's still out there."

"Oh." Of course. Why would a drop-dead gorgeous man like that be sticking around because he wanted to? I was surprisingly disappointed.

"Alright, dear. Your elixir is ready." Ileana approached me and lifted my chin. She looked at me for a long second and smiled. "I want you to drink this now and at bedtime for the next three nights, beginning tonight. You'll be much better in the morning."

Before I could argue that last point, the front door banged open and a tall man, so gaunt and pale I thought he was a skeleton, strode into the room. Dressed all in black, the man had a gun holster slung around his waist and a five-pointed star pinned to his chest. A black cloak billowed around him as he approached the table. Pointing one long, thin finger at me, he demanded in a hissing, guttural voice, "Hand over the intruder!"

CHAPTER 4

I scrambled to the back of the table, as Ileana stepped in front of me, her legs spread wide, hands on hips. For such a tiny woman, she projected quite a presence.

As I peered over her shoulder, she yelled, "Boddy Grim, how dare you act that way to our newest resident! I'm about to take that blasted star and pin it where the sun don't shine!"

Boddy scowled at me with wide eyes but seemed to lose some of his swagger because of Ileana's furious outburst. Now that I had a better view of him, he was indeed thin, with joints jutting out at odd angles, but scarcely looked like a skeleton.

Mizizi patted the cloaked man on the back, drawing his attention. "Bodderick, I would like you to meet Miss Minta's granddaughter, Windsor."

Boddy's eyes brightened slightly, then faded, as if a fire inside the man had been tamped.

"Windsor, meet Bodderick Grim." He turned to the man. "Now let's you and I go outside for a bit and let Ileana do her job."

Mizizi held the door open and waited. Boddy Grim glared at me one more time, then glided out the door.

"Good grief!" I said. "What did I ever do to him?"

Ileana patted my arm reassuringly. "Don't you pay him no mind, honey. His bark is worse than his bite."

What is it with dogs around here?

She placed a vial in my hand. The liquid inside bubbled and hissed.

"You're kidding, right?"

"Nope. Down the hatch. And best if you do it all at once. Cuts the bite. But then again, there are some who like the bite," she said with a wink.

I ignored Keir's laughter behind me.

Putting the bottle to my lips, I threw back my head and swallowed as quickly as I could. The thick, nasty liquid slid down my throat. I coughed and sputtered as I tried to keep it down.

Ileana gently rubbed my back, while the elixir spread its warmth throughout my body. I extended my leg and gasped as my ankle shrank in size.

"Ileana, your medicine is amazing!" I said, wiggling my toes.

She shrugged. "It does what it's supposed to do." With a flourish, she spun around on her own toes and added, "But thank you for saying so."

"Wait a minute," I said. "That was you I saw in the forest earlier, wasn't it?"

Keir replaced the book he was examining and stood, a slight frown on his face.

"Hmm," Ileana replied and appeared to be thinking about the question. "Nope." She twirled and dipped toward my face with a grin. "Not me."

What an odd woman. It had to have been her that I saw, didn't it? I mean, how many women around here live in a forest and like to spin around?

None of my business, I decided. Although I did wonder why she would lie.

Mizizi came back inside. "How's our patient?" He smiled warmly.

"I'm good," I said. "And ready to go back to the house."

I slid off the table, dabbed my foot to the ground, delighted to find I could walk on it with only a tiny bit of discomfort.

"I wouldn't suggest doing that," Ileana said. "You should stay off that foot as much as possible for the next hour."

"I can carry you to Fernwood," Keir said. "I promise I'll be gentle."

My face reddened. "That won't be necessary. I'll be fine."

I didn't understand the intense attraction I felt whenever Keir was near me and until I sorted that out, the less I was close to him the better.

"Then I will walk with you instead," he said. "I insist."

At Mizizi and Ileana's urgings, I agreed.

I promised Mizizi I would return for a visit once my ankle had completely healed and tucked three bottles of Ileana's elixir into my bag. Ileana surprised me with a quick hug, then Keir and I set off back through the forest.

KEIR SLIPPED on a pair of Ray Bans, parting the dense brush with his leg. A narrow white stone path came into view.

"Now that you have been to Mizizi's, this path will always be here for you," he explained.

"Wasn't it here before?" I muttered.

"It was."

Okay?

Feathery ferns grazed my face as Keir helped me maneuver through the brush protecting Mizizi's clearing.

"You really don't need to walk with me," I said.

"I told Mizizi I would, so I am. Besides, following this path will take us straight to Fernwood. It's not far. Here—" he crooked out his elbow "—take my arm."

I sighed. "I told you. I don't need your help."

Keir released his breath in a huff. "Are you always this difficult?" he asked.

"Fine," I grumbled and took his arm, causing my heart to leap into my throat. As much as I hated to admit it, I wanted his help just as much as I didn't want it. Moreover, the forest undergrowth was thick in areas and despite Keir's assurances, I wasn't convinced the beast was not lying in wait. I'd be easy pickings with my injured foot.

As we made our way down the stone path, he chatted amiably, pointing out the various trees and birds that made the forest their home. We saw tiny squirrels playing circle tag around tree trunks, and golden chanterelle mushrooms sprouting next to water oaks. I nearly jumped out of my skin when we disturbed a great blue heron, his agitated squawks resounding through the trees. With each gesture Keir made, each description of the local flora and fauna he gave, I found myself more attracted to him. It didn't hurt that the arm I clung to was as muscular and defined as a Greek god's.

As I hobbled next to him, Keir suddenly put a finger to his lips, signaling me to stop. The warm breeze rustled the leaves above, as he crouched down next to a bright green fern spreading along the forest floor.

He lifted a few fronds, and I gasped when a mother skunk waddled out into the clearing. Four babies toddled behind her.

The mother nuzzled Keir's outstretched fingers. He drew a walnut from his jacket pocket and cracked the shell in his palm. The sound momentarily startled a few of the kits, then they rushed forward to join their mother.

He popped the fleshy meat from the shell and offered tiny bits to the mother and her kits.

"Oh, Keir," I whispered. "How adorable."

"Come here," he said with a grin, those dark eyes sparkling. "Just walk slowly."

I nodded. What's the worst that could happen? I get sprayed by a skunk? Wouldn't be the worst thing that's happened to me today.

I barely breathed as I padded forward until I stood next to

TOLLING BELLS & DARK SPELLS

Keir. After lowering to the ground and steadying myself against his arm, I cautiously held my hand out to the mother.

Without hesitation, she waddled closer and stuck her wet nose in my palm. Keir handed me some walnut bits, which mama skunk quickly devoured. I giggled in awe as the tiny soft kits scrambled into my lap, clamoring for some walnut bits of their own.

After a few minutes, we stood, and I watched as mother and babies shuffled back into the safety of the fern.

Keir pointed out the white stone path and slowed down for me to catch up.

"Keir, that was amazing!" I gushed. "How did you get her to trust us like that?"

He tossed the last pieces of the shell into the forest.

"I spend a lot of time out here," he said, inspecting the bark of a tall oak, before stepping back next to me. "In the forests."

"Camping?"

"Sometimes."

When it was obvious that he wouldn't say more, I sent the conversation in another direction.

"Did you know my grandmother well?"

He nodded, holding back a large pointy frond before it walloped me in the head.

"Better than most, I guess," Keir said thoughtfully. "We were Town Elders together. Minta was tough. She always knew what she wanted and let nothing stand in her way."

"I didn't know she was a Town Elder. She sounds rather intimidating."

"She was. But probably not in the way you're thinking. Here, let me lift you over this log."

As his hands wrapped around my waist, a tingle ricocheted throughout my body, as if I had just been zapped by electricity. Keir inhaled deeply, then stared at me for a second, and I wondered if he felt it too. But as my feet gently touched the ground, he stepped back and offered his arm. No sign he had felt anything peculiar. Definite one-sided zapping.

"Minta cared for Darkly Island and everyone who lives here." He let out a quiet chuckle and smiled. "Your grandmother wasn't afraid to bump heads with anybody. Elder meetings were never boring."

"Are you afraid to bump heads?"

Where did that come from?

He surprised me with a deep laugh, one that was both warm and genuine. "Let's just say I try to be the peacemaker."

I snuck a look. Not only was Keir ruggedly handsome, with his long dark hair and broad shoulders, but he was also intelligent, charming, and, obviously, a nature lover. Completely different from my ex-fiancé, Lucas, who was attractive in a snobby, academic way.

We walked in silence for a few minutes until a breeze suddenly kicked up and rattled the leaves overhead. As we stepped from the trees into the wildflower field, I could see a white Jeep parked under the magnolia.

Tzazi waved from the front porch and met us at the gate.

Her eyes darted back and forth between Keir and me, stopping at the top of my head. I reached up and found several small twigs still embedded in my hair.

"Are we still on for dinner? Or have your plans changed?"

"No," Keir and I said at the same time.

With a crooked little grin, Tzazi shrugged and raised her eyebrows.

"I've got to go," Keir said. "How's that foot?"

He crouched down, gently running a finger over my ankle. A thrill ran up my spine, and I gasped as I jumped backward, knocking his hand off my skin.

Tzazi's eyebrows raised even higher.

"I'm fine. Thank you for helping me home, Keir," I blurted.

"Anytime," he said, giving me a wink. "See you, lawyer lady," and with a wave he headed off down the gravel road.

"Wait! Don't you need a ride?" I yelled.

He stuck a hand up in the air. "Nah, I'm good." At the next curve in the road, he was gone.

"Tell me everything," Tzazi began, but then sniffed and backed away. "Ew. But first go take a shower because you stink to high heaven."

CHAPTER 5

By the time we entered the Green Gator, the place was packed with customers. Still, Tzazi found us a spot in the corner of the dark-paneled tavern. As we scooted into the booth, I glimpsed Keir standing at the bar, on the other side of the room. A greasy-looking older man in a black suit and dark sunglasses laughed harshly as he clasped Keir's shoulder. Keir grimaced and picked up a pitcher of beer from the bar counter. Together, they walked out of view.

"Looks like the whole town's here," I said, as a bubbly woman with a notepad and a swinging red ponytail approached our table.

"Hi, Tzazi," she said, reaching over and giving Tzazi a hug. "So glad you're here."

She set down silverware and turned bright blue eyes on me.

"And who is this?"

I introduced myself, and her eyes widened.

"Well, bless your heart! Minta's granddaughter! I'm Jessamin Wilde. So nice to meet you, hun! Now what can I get you ladies? The special tonight is Creole rib roast crusted with rosemary and mustard. One of my favorites."

"Thanks," I said, "but I'll just have a salad with a side of raspberry vinaigrette and a glass of sauvignon blanc."

"Oh, no, no, no," Tzazi huffed. "You must try our Southern cuisine."

"Our chef Phenny Guthrie is an excellent cook," Jessamin said. "You wouldn't be disappointed."

"Fine," I laughed. "I'll have the special with a glass of cab."

As Jessamin turned to Tzazi, I glanced around the room. Despite the warm weather, a fire blazed in a stone fireplace to the right of our booth. An oil painting of an alligator with an open mouth—full of huge, razor-sharp teeth—hung above the mantle. To our left, a cushioned bench ran the length of the wall, with tables and chairs placed along it. Pendant lighting, along with the murmuring of voices, created a cozy, friendly feel.

Jessamin tucked her notepad into the pocket of a small apron. "I'll be back with your food in a few minutes."

Once she was gone, Tzazi placed an elbow on the table and relaxed her chin into her hand.

"What do you think of Darkly so far?"

"It's actually very nice."

"Yes. The name doesn't do it justice at all." She laughed, just as a man approached with our drinks.

He handed Tzazi a bottle of Corona, with a lime stuck in the top of it, and placed a wineglass in front of me.

"Jessamin tells me you've recently arrived in Darkly," he said. "I'm Carter Guthrie, owner of the Green Gator."

Carter was a large man with ruddy cheeks and a swooping mustache.

"Looks like business is good," I said, indicating the room.

"Exceptionally good," he beamed. "Especially during sporting events—soccer, football, tennis. You name it, we get the crowds."

Tzazi nodded. "Sports days are legendary at the Gator. Bet you and Phenny are making money hand over fist these days. Won't be long until y'all are starting on that dream home Phenny's always talking about."

Carter's smile faded.

"Right," he stammered. "Um. I need to get back to the bar.

Welcome to Darkly, Windsor. Pleasure to meet you." Carter rushed away from our booth.

"Did we do something?" I asked.

"That was weird, wasn't it?" Tzazi looked as puzzled as I felt. "I mean, everyone knows they bought property up by Darkly Falls. Wonder what's going on."

I shrugged and took a sip of my wine. It was delicate and delicious. After a day like today, it felt like an extravagance.

Tzazi pushed the lime wedge into the beer bottle and then, to my astonishment, put her thumb over the top and turned the bottle upside down so the lime wedge floated to the base of the bottle. She then carefully flipped it back over and leaned forward.

"Don't look, but Keir is staring at you."

"Really?" I snuck a glance in the direction Tzazi was looking and saw him gazing lazily over at me. I hurriedly looked away, smoothing my hair.

"And here he comes!"

I felt his presence even before he reached the table. A leather string held back his wavy brown hair, and he wore a long-sleeve white shirt rolled up to his forearms, tribal tattoos spiraling down to his wrists.

"Evening, ladies."

"Hi, Keir," Tzazi said brightly.

He took a sip of his beer and smiled down at me. "Fancy meeting you here, Windsor. How's that ankle doing?"

My face flushed hot, and I reached for my wineglass. In the booth behind Tzazi, I saw a woman in the group turn an ear in our direction. It felt like the entire bar was listening. My body tensed at the unwanted attention.

"Much better," I said. "I appreciate your help today."

The light tittle-tattle of the women in the booth resumed, and I cringed when I heard my name being tossed about.

"Anytime," Keir said. "You getting settled in at Fernwood?"

"Slowly but surely. I have had little time to get everything unpacked," I replied, "but I already love it."

"I knew you would," Tzazi interjected.

Keir's brow wrinkled. "Although with its seclusion, you should be careful out there—especially once darkness falls."

I glared, remembering my narrow escape from the beast in the forest. "Or one of your dogs will attack me again?"

Tzazi choked on her beer. "Sorry," she muttered, grabbing her napkin.

"Win, really! That wasn't my dog," Keir said, frustration creeping into his voice.

Suddenly, a hand snaked around his shoulder, each finger encircled by a large gold ring, and the man in the dark shades appeared at Keir's side.

"Keir, my man," he slurred as he swayed on his feet. "You haven't introduced me to Minta's granddaughter."

He hissed my grandmother's name in a derogatory manner. I took an instant dislike to this man. And who wears dark sunglasses indoors anyway?

"Dorian, this is Windsor Ebonwood. Windsor, Dorian Wilde."

"Wilde?" I asked, my irritation at Keir forgotten. "Are you related to our waitress?"

Dorian leaned down into my face as a string of coal black hair fell in front of his eyes.

"My brother's wife," he sneered. "Let me rephrase that. My dead brother's wife."

I picked up my wineglass and looked away.

"Don't you think you've had enough for tonight, Dorian?" Tzazi demanded, her disgust for the man apparent.

"C'mon, Dor. Let's get back to the table," Keir said, directing the drunk man in the other direction. Keir turned back to Tzazi and me. "Good to see you, Win. Tzazi." He gave me one last look and then led a belligerent Dorian across the room.

"Dorian Wilde is the worst kind of person," Tzazi fumed. "Stay far, far away from him." She slammed her Corona and waved her hand for another.

"Don't have to tell me twice. What is wrong with that man?"

"Too much to tell in one night!"

I sat back in my seat. That guy gave me the creeps, and I was going to stay well clear of him.

Jessamin brought our meals, along with fresh drinks. She slid everything onto the table and patted my arm.

"I am so sorry you had to see that. Dorian's not always that awful."

Tzazi guffawed as Jessamin scooted back to the bar.

"True," she said. "He's usually worse."

I took one bite of my meal and decided delicious didn't even begin to describe the Creole rib roast I'd ordered. The cook served it with roasted pumpkin and onions on a bed of arugula. The rosemary in the crust added a crisp lemon-pine taste that paired perfectly with the tangy mustard. If all Southern food tasted like this, I was going to gain twenty pounds just my first week here.

As I enjoyed my meal, Tzazi told me about herself and her family. Besides the time she had been in college and law school, Tzazi had lived her entire life in Darkly. She had two older brothers, who lived elsewhere, and a father who left their family when she was very young.

"Oh, Tzazi. I'm sorry."

She waved a hand. "Yeah, it was tough, but it just strengthened my relationship with Maman. She's my rock. If Père doesn't want to be around, I don't want him around." She stuck her nose in the air and took a swig of Corona.

I nodded. "My mom died when I was a baby, so I know how hard it can be. Just as you had your mom in your life, I always had my dad. Until he died a few years ago." My heart hurt at the memory.

A loud crash at the end of the bar suddenly interrupted our conversation. Every head in the tavern turned toward the noise. Dorian Wilde stood in front of a terror-stricken Jessamin, a broken stool on the ground next to him.

"And don't ask me again! Any rights you had died with Brychen!" he yelled, his finger inches from her face. His lips twisted in an awful grin as spittle flew from his mouth. "I owe you nothing!"

The tavern was dead silent as Jessamin, trembling and pale, took a step back. "You know what? It should have been you, Dorian. You should be the one who is dead."

Jessamin turned and, seeing all our faces pointed in her direction, covered her face, and ran back into the kitchen, followed by a stout woman in a ruffled apron.

Dorian smirked and fell back hard against the bar as the murmur of conversations started back up.

Tzazi jumped up from the table. "I'll be right back, Win." She zigzagged through the tables and disappeared into the kitchen.

What a jerk! No doubt Dorian's drinking contributed to his aggression, but I had a feeling that at his core, the man was basically a horrible person.

"Dorian Wilde has always been the scourge of this town." I looked up to see an elderly gentleman in a white seersucker suit standing next to the booth. He smiled gently and offered his hand.

"I am Dewey Hathaway, Esquire, and this beautiful lady is my wife of eighty years, Maybelle. I apologize for not meeting you at the dock." He patted his wife's arm. "We had an unfortunate emergency."

"Oh! I hope everything is fine."

"Yes, yes, dear. All is well," he said with a smile. "On a more professional note, I have some paperwork for you to sign and need to give you the keys to your bookshop. Is there a good time for me to call?"

We agreed to meet the next morning at the bookshop. As he turned to leave, his wife Maybelle smiled and said in a low, sweet voice, "Do you like stewed peaches, hun? If you do, I'll have Dewey bring you some."

"That would be very nice, Maybelle. Thank you."

Maybelle waved a white gloved hand at me and walked away with her husband.

A few minutes later, tornado Tzazi slammed back into the booth.

"I'm sorry for leaving. I just needed to make sure she's okay. Phenny's looking after her." She put her face in her hands. "I swear, I hate that man!"

Raising her head, she banged both hands on the table.

"She didn't deserve that!" Tzazi said, grimacing. "Ever since her husband died, Jessamin has been working her fingers to the bone just to keep her head above water!

"When Brychen died," she explained, "Dorian took everything they owned. Their house, their lands, their bank accounts. He is supposed to care for her for the rest of her life, but he doesn't. I believe he may give her a monthly stipend of some small amount, but it doesn't even give her enough to rent a house."

"What? This isn't the Middle Ages!" I exploded.

"Tell me about it. That man is despicable! But that's the way it is here—at least for some."

I set down my glass. "Why doesn't anyone help her?"

Tzazi shook her head and sighed. "We've all tried. I've offered her a place to live for as long as she needs, but she refuses. That woman is nothing if not prideful."

Tzazi took a gulp of beer. "Just between us, I believe she's living here at the tavern and bathing in the restroom every morning."

As Tzazi turned to converse with a woman in the booth behind her, I shook my head. How could Dorian treat someone in such a heartless manner, especially his own sister-in-law? And how could Keir be friends with that kind of person? I looked across the tavern, to where Keir stretched against the booth cushions, staring at me. His face was drawn with worry. Ignoring the revelry at his table, he quirked his lips and managed a weak smile in my direction. Even at a distance, his brown eyes sparkled, and I felt the same flutter in my stomach as I had during our walk through the forest.

What's wrong with me? Although Keir's friendship with

Dorian Wilde bothered me, I couldn't deny this absurd attraction I felt for him.

As tipsy patrons weaved their way through the packed tables, a statuesque dark-skinned woman with a large curly afro kissed Keir's cheek and then plopped down in the seat across from him. She threw her feet in Keir's lap and leaned back in her chair. Jessamin arrived and, laughing at something the woman said, set down an empty pilsner glass. To my dismay, Keir grasped the pitcher on the table in front of him and filled the glass, handing it to the woman, whose hands glittered with golden bands and bracelets. He then leaned forward and whispered in the woman's ear.

My heart squeezed, and the warm fluttery feeling from a moment before faded. Of course, Keir has a girlfriend! Why would I have thought otherwise?

I casually leaned to the side, hoping to get a better view of the woman. With any luck, she'd have a hideously deformed face, with eyebrows like Frida Kahlo and a jaw like Jay Leno. With a brilliant laugh, the woman leaned away from Keir and fell straight into the arms of a blond, muscular man sitting next to her. He beamed, pulled her close, and to my surprise, kissed her full on the lips! Astonished, my eyes turned to Keir, who cocked his head at me, lips twisting into an adorable smirk.

I sat straight up and turned abruptly to Tzazi. I was so confused!

As I tried my best to ignore Keir and the party at his table, Tzazi and I enjoyed our meal together. Her descriptions of the town and its citizens kept me laughing. Many of those very people stopped by our table to say hello to Tzazi and introduce themselves to me.

While I was talking to Mayor Mayór, his voluptuous wife Lilith, and their grown son, Jaime, a woman sitting a few tables away caught my eye. She glared in my direction as her dinner partner, a man in a floral Hawaiian shirt, chatted amiably. I did a double take. Without a doubt, she was staring at me.

The woman's skin was golden brown, as if she spent every day luxuriating at the pool. Swirling golden waves framed a sculpted face with dark blue eyes and full lips.

"Tzazi, who is the woman over there who looks like she wants to kill me? Do I know her?"

Tzazi looked around me and then raised an eyebrow. "Looks like you've caught the attention of Solara Nova."

"That's a name?"

"Solara is Keir's ex-girlfriend. The way she's staring daggers at you, my dear friend, means Keir is interested in you. Ex-girlfriends can always tell those kinds of things, especially crazy ones like Solara."

I laughed. "Solara's got it wrong this time."

Tzazi shrugged and stretched out in the booth, resting her head on the back cushion. "What a remarkable first day you've had! An enemy and a friend all in one day."

"Room for two more?" asked a voice in my ear.

I felt a bump against my leg. Grinning, Chase slipped into the seat next to me. Tzazi got out of the booth and let a handsome man with dark skin scoot in next to her. She slid back in and gave him a big hug. She motioned to me.

"Win, let me introduce Chase's better half, Lorenzo de Zavala."

"Hey! I resemble that remark!" Chase quipped.

Lorenzo and I waved to each other from across the table as Carter arrived to take drink orders and remove our plates.

After Carter left, Chase leaned forward.

"Sorry we're late. Ren cooked a heavenly chicken cordon bleu tonight." Chase winked at his partner. "What did we miss, ladies?"

Tzazi and I recounted Dorian's nastiness at our table and his rant at Jessamin.

Chase's mouth fell open. "No, he didn't." He turned to Lorenzo. "I told you. We always miss the drama."

"Why doesn't anyone do something about Dorian?" I asked. "Like the Mayor or someone."

"Only one person can keep that monster under control," Chase said. "Keir. That's—Ow!"

Chase's leg walloped against mine.

"Sorry, Win," he said. "Tzazi has a trick knee that kicks out randomly at the oddest of times." He pointed a finger at her. "I implore you to get that looked at."

"Why would Keir —" I began.

"Ren," Tzazi said abruptly. "Tell me about the new face glamours that are so hot at the salon right now."

"Our glamours have never been better or more long lasting," Ren began.

As the conversation flowed into a discussion of skin treatments and trending hairstyles, I snuck a peek over to Keir's table.

The muscular blond man was now sitting on top of the wood table, talking excitedly to a tattoo-covered man leaning back in his chair. Both Keir and the woman were nowhere to be seen.

I felt crushed, berating myself for even looking. I'd been in this town one day and only broken up with my fiancé six months ago. It was way too soon for me to be going all gaga over some guy I barely knew. I was startled when Chase nudged an elbow into my side.

"Earth to Windsor."

"Oh, sorry," I said. "What did you say?"

"Ren and I want to invite you to Spells & Gels for a day of pampering. I guarantee his massages will leave you calm and stress-free for the next month and my facials are the most transformative in all the Charm…," he gulped, "the world!" He finished with a grand flourish of his hands.

I laughed at his exaggerations. "You can't imagine how wonderful that sounds. I'll definitely take you both up on your kind offer."

"Perfect! But not tomorrow. That's my day off," Chase said.

The Gator was quieting down, as many tables cleared, and people headed home after their dinners. Keir's table, I noticed, was crowded and loud, but he was still nowhere in sight.

I stifled a yawn, and Chase put an arm around my shoulders.

"You've had a big day," he said. "Maybe it's time we all pack it in."

"Yeah, I am feeling a bit tired. Do you mind, Tzazi?"

"Of course not. It's getting late anyway, and some of us have to work in the morning!"

Chase rolled his eyes at her. "You shouldn't let Win see the mean side of you so early into your friendship! You'll scare her away!"

Chase extended a hand to help me out of the booth, just as two women approached us.

"Dixie-Dean. Mathilda. How are you ladies?" Tzazi said. "Have you met Windsor Ebonwood? Char brought her to the island today."

"I knew it!" one of the women exclaimed, thrusting out a hand. Large blonde curls bobbed and bounced around her head as she spoke. She turned to the woman next to her. "Didn't I tell you, Mathilda?"

Mathilda dipped her head once and smiled. "You did."

"I'm Dixie-Dean Poplar," the blonde woman said, turning her attention back to me. "I run Lyla and the Piggles, an animal sanctuary."

"Lyla and the Piggles?" I laughed. "What a delightful name!"

A huge smile spread across her face. "Isn't it? When I first opened the sanctuary, my first rescues were a mother pig named Lyla and her piglets so I named the sanctuary after them. You must come visit sometime. Lyla loves belly rubs."

"I'd love to, Dixie-Dean."

"And I'm Mathilda Bristlebroom," the woman next to her stated. "Dee-Dee here's my BFF, as you young folk like to say."

What a contrast in personalities! Where Dixie-Dean was bubbly and bouncy (basically a middle-aged version of Jessamin),

Mathilda came across as stern and serious. Even their hair was on the opposite ends of the scale. Mathilda's straight black hair flowed to her collarbones, interrupted only by a bright streak of white framing her face.

"I own the business next to yours," she said matter-of-factly. "Besoms & Britches. Come by and see me when you need a new broom and some riding pants."

What a bewildering jumble of items to sell in a shop, I thought, but thanked her for her kind invitation nonetheless.

We spoke to the two women for a few more minutes, then made our way through the jumble of people, many of them calling out goodbyes to us. As we passed through the door and back onto the street, I noticed a raucous dart game going on in the corner.

A woman with wild frizzy hair, wearing a tattered green dress, laughed victoriously, arms pumping in the air.

"Pay up, Victor!" she crowed.

Victor pulled out his wallet and handed over some cash to the woman. He shook his head. "I just can't beat you, Maenad."

"And you never will," she cackled.

Victor's friends chimed in.

"I'd give it up if I were you, Vic."

"How many losses is that? I don't think I can count that high."

The door closed on more laughter.

"Who was that woman?" I asked.

"Maenad Grog," Chase answered. "The old dear drinks too much, but she's a hoot to be around and honest to a fault. I really dig the old girl."

"She must be quite the dart player," I said.

"Maenad's good, but not that good," Tzazi said. "They lose to her on purpose to help her out. Dorian is the exception to this town, not the norm. Thank goodness."

We said goodbye to Chase and Lorenzo, then walked toward the corner where we parked the Jeep. As we drew nearer, I heard voices. One I recognized as Keir's, but who was the second person?

"Keir and Dorian," Tzazi whispered, leading me to a large oleander bush where we could eavesdrop. As we burrowed into the flowering blossoms, I heard Keir say in a calm, but firm, voice,

"It's stalking, Dorian."

Dorian laughed. "Dude, it was all in fun."

Keir sighed. "I won't let you treat people like that anymore."

Dorian's voice turned gruff. "Yeah, what are you going to do?"

"Dinnae push me, Dorian," Keir growled, his Scottish lilt becoming more pronounced.

Tzazi and I pressed our bodies farther into the giant shrub as footsteps sounded on the flagstones and Keir strode past. Dorian screamed an expletive at Keir's back and then his steps disappeared in the other direction. We huddled in the flowering bush for a few more seconds and then stepped out.

"There are some very interesting people in Darkly," I said.

"You have no idea, Windsor."

CHAPTER 6

As the headlights of Tzazi's Jeep swung into the driveway of Fernwood, I realized I'd forgotten to leave any lights on.

"Want me to come in with you?" Tzazi asked.

"Nah. I'll be fine."

We said goodnight, and I ran up the steps to the porch just as raindrops began to fall.

Thankfully, Tzazi kept the Jeep lights trained on me as I rattled around in my bag for the house keys and unlocked the door.

I waved to Tzazi as she pulled away from the house. Suddenly, I felt something bump against my leg. With a scream, I launched myself into the house, slamming the door shut.

I crouched perfectly still in the dark house. Why I crouched, I don't know. Smaller target, maybe? A steady rain fell, pattering against the roof. Other than that, I heard nothing else—no footsteps, no voice, no rattling of the doorknob.

Just my imagination.

I reached for the light switch but froze when I heard a sound.

There it was again.

A faint scratching, then suddenly "Mee-YOW!"

I jumped two feet in the air, before quickly realizing my mistake. My grandmother's cat!

As I opened the door, a tiny black cat pranced in. After I had hurriedly relocked the door and flipped on the light, the cat jumped on to the side table, purring loudly.

"So you're Pye," I said, petting him behind the ears. "Have you had dinner? Want something to eat?"

Pye meowed and ran to the back of the house.

I let us into the kitchen and then rustled around in the pantries for something a cat might like. I finally found a shelf full of catfood tins.

He meowed excitedly, swimming back and forth between my legs. As I set down his platter, he looked up at me and—goodness gracious—the cat only had one eye. Just a slit where the other one should be.

"Poor guy," I said, stroking his soft, sleek fur. "What happened to you?"

I'd often thought of having a cat for a companion when I was in New York, but my schedule was so disruptive I didn't think it would be fair. But here? Maybe here would be the perfect place to have a pet or two. Maybe I could even take Pye along to the bookshop.

Pye finished his meal, and I washed his platter. Setting it on the drying rack, I picked him up and carried him through the house.

As we entered the bedroom, Pye jumped from my arms onto the bed. By the time I showered and put on my pajamas, he had curled up in a ball on one of the pillows.

Opening the French doors to the porch, a balmy breeze, brought on by the rain, swirled into the room. I breathed in the warm, moist air. The buzz of crickets rose and fell, bullfrogs bellowing in reply. Uncorking the first bottle of elixir, I slammed it as quickly as possible, flipped off the light on my nightstand, and sunk into the soft sheets and fluffy comforter as soft rain pattered on the roof.

I was just about to drift off when my eyes shot open. Through the haze of sleep, I noticed a warm light glowing from deep within the shadowy swamp. The light piquing my interest, I crept from my bed and stood before the windows. Could someone be fishing this late at night? Come to think of it, I was certain there was a fish that could only be caught at night with a flashlight. Gar, I think it's called.

Satisfied with that explanation, I curled back up in bed, hugged Pye to me, and gazed out into the night. The rain slowed, a white fog swirling above the green water and through the mangroves and low growing ferns. The glow winked once and disappeared.

I WOKE to the smell of sizzling bacon and scrambled eggs. For a moment, I couldn't imagine who could be cooking, but then I remembered the housekeeper returned today.

Through the open doors to the back porch, the sky was a startling display of pinkish-yellows. A light breeze ruffled the sheer curtains, carrying with it the intoxicating scent of gardenia, but I knew it wouldn't be long until the humidity and heat set in. Reluctantly, I tossed back my sheet and closed the doors.

Dressing quickly, I re-bandaged my foot, then ventured out onto the open walkway, clutching Pye to my chest. As I entered the kitchen, he leaped from my arms, meowing loudly at the feet of a dark-haired woman who looked to be in her 50s. She was large, at least six feet tall, and solid. When she turned to glance at me, her dark eyes and broad nose made me think of an ancient Amazon warrioress, and I stumbled back a step.

"Well, bless my stars. You are here, aren't you?" The woman frowned when she noticed my bandage. "What happened to your foot?"

Without waiting for an answer, she turned back to the stove.

"Do you always sleep this late?" she demanded.

"Um... I... It's only half past eight," I stammered.

"Exactly! By now, your grandmother would have read her papers, drank four cups of coffee, and eaten a full breakfast. Go sit down in the dining room and I'll bring it in. Unless, of course, you'd like to eat down into the courtyard like she always did."

I told her I'd be fine in the dining room, and she turned to Pye. "I suppose you're hungry again?"

Escaping into the adjoining room, I pulled out one of the plush brocade chairs. I wasn't about to tell her I never ate breakfast.

"My name is Hildegard Orso," she yelled from the kitchen. "But everyone calls me Hilde."

Hildegard Orso? Did anyone in this town have a simple name, like Jane Smith?

The woman entered, plopped a large steaming mug in front of me, and returned to the kitchen. I took a sip and sighed. Well, at least she made a wonderful cup of coffee.

I settled back into the chair and gazed out the window. The swamp pond adjoining the courtyard still lay in a low white mist, but the sun was peeking over the distant line of bald cypress. A slight movement rippled through the water, catching my attention, as a large alligator slid to the surface, eyes and nostrils visible just above the waterline.

"Hilde. Hilde! HILDE!" I screamed and jumped up onto the table.

A crash sounded in the kitchen, and Hilde rushed into the room. Crouching in an aggressive stance, she swiveled her head left and right. The fierceness of her action surprised me, and I could have sworn she grew in size. It seemed comparing her to an Amazon warrioress wasn't off the mark. "Where?"

"There! There!" I pointed.

Hilde stood at her natural height and cocked her head at me. "Where?"

"In the water."

She looked out the window, back at me, and then laughed.

To be honest, I didn't think she could do that.

"That's just Greta Garbo," she grunted. "Harmless as a kitten."

Yeah, a five hundred-pound kitten with razor-sharp teeth.

"You scared the wits out of me," Hilde said, wiping her brow. "I thought … It doesn't matter what I thought. Have a seat and I'll be right back with breakfast."

Within seconds, she placed a piping hot plate of scrambled eggs, bacon, and something lumpy and orange in front of me.

Although, I was still nervous about Greta Garbo—eyeing me hungrily from the other side of the window—the smell of bacon had my stomach rumbling, and I had a hard time waiting for Hilde to reappear with her plate. I poked at the orange lump with my fork and frowned.

Hilde returned with a basket of biscuits and placed them in the middle of the table. "I'll be in the kitchen if you need anything."

"Have you already eaten?" I asked, puzzled.

For the first time that morning, she seemed at a loss for words.

"I eat in the kitchen."

"Why? Sit down and eat with me here."

She surprised me with a small smile. "Miss Minta and I took many of our meals together as well." She nodded. "I'll be right back."

When she returned, she carried a plate heaped high with bacon and eggs.

We fell into an uncomfortable silence, so I pointed at the lump on my plate.

"If you don't mind my asking, what in the world is that?"

"Those are grits," she explained. "Miss Minta liked hers with cream and cheese, so I made yours the same. Try it."

She gestured to my plate with her fork.

Tentatively, I scooped up a small bite. I smiled when the savory flavors hit my tongue. "Oh, my! Grits are delicious!"

"That's what we call Southern comfort food."

"Why aren't you having any?" I asked.

"Not much for vegetables," Hilde grumbled.

Cheese grits seemed to have broken the ice between Hilde and me.

"Tzazi told me you've worked for my grandmother all your life," I said between bites.

"Not just Minta. Our family has assisted the Ebonwoods for generations. When I was but a cub, Fernwood was the site of many outdoor balls and galas. The Ebonwood Ball held every spring was legendary."

"I'd love to have seen that!"

Hilde grunted in agreement, biting into a piece of bacon.

"They set a temporary floor up in the meadow next to the forest, and a jazz band played until dawn. Fireflies lit up the meadow like the sun at dusk.

"And you should have seen your grandmother! As a wee one, I snuck out to the porch on ball nights and fell asleep watching Minta swirl on the dance floor. She was never short of suitors."

"Was the whole town invited?" I asked.

"Not just the town. The entire island! Although back then, the population wasn't quite as large. People enjoyed the opportunity to dress up in fancy clothes and drink Sazeracs. Unlike today, where all we really have is the Gator, with its beer and rowdy clientele."

I thought for a second. "I had dinner at the Gator last night with Tzazi and met some of the townspeople."

"Don't get me wrong. I like the Gator just fine. It just doesn't have the refinement of the old establishments," she said wistfully.

"Be glad you weren't there last night," I said, describing Dorian Wilde's antics and his attack on Jessamin.

She shook her head. "That man is a sorry excuse for a human. Mean as a polar bear, he is. Poor Jessamin. That young lady doesn't deserve a bit of what's happened to her at the hands of that family."

Hilde stood and picked up our plates. "I'll take care of this," she said. "I understand you have a meeting with Mr. Hathaway this morning. While you're in town, would you mind dropping off our grocery order at Bosada's?"

"Of course," I said, glad to be useful.

"Stop by the kitchen before you leave, and I'll have it ready. And Windsor? Thank you."

"No problem." I couldn't help but grin as I returned to my room.

CHAPTER 7

I took the grocery list Hilde offered and slipped it into my bag.

"Hand the order to Mr. Bosada. He'll have his grandson deliver the groceries to us later today."

As I shut the door, Pye scooted out before it closed, pattering along next to me. I enjoyed his company, but it was strange the way he followed me around everywhere. I didn't know cats were like that.

After the coolness of this morning, the air was already heating up. Pye and I walked out to the main road. As I strolled farther into town, the friendliness of everyone in Darkly struck me. Well, most everyone. That man Dorian last night seemed absolutely horrid, and I wasn't too sure Solara Nova was pleased I was in Darkly. But besides those two, everyone had been accepting and kind. Very different from what I was accustomed to in the city, where everyone seemed to be either guarded or distrustful.

Mr. Bosada's store was tucked between Sugarloaf (I definitely wanted to check that place out) and a butcher's shop, The Cloven Hoof. As I entered, Pye hopped into a planter next to the door and sat.

"I'll be right back, Pye." I patted his tiny head.

Inside, I was happy to see our one grocery store was well-stocked and much larger than it appeared from the sidewalk. I found Mr. Bosada stocking bread and he promised to have his delivery boy bring out our items later that afternoon.

Chore completed, I stepped back outside and looked at my watch. I had about ten minutes until my appointment with Mr. Hathaway. That would give me just enough time to grab a chai at The Magic Cup.

Pye jumped from the planter and fell in line next to me, his tiny tail swishing back and forth. The line at The Magic Cup wound out the door. I groaned, hoping it wouldn't take too long, but I had to have my morning chai. It was kind of a ritual.

"Morning, Ms. Ebonwood," said a deep sultry voice at my back.

My pulse began to race before I even turned around. When I faced him, I found his brown eyes sparkling down at me.

"Morning, Keir," I replied.

His white graphic tee emphasized his chiseled pecs and biceps. A tangle of silver necklaces hung from his neck, and his brown hair flowed freely past his shoulders.

"Hey, um, I want to apologize for last night," he said. "Dorian's a jerk when he drinks too much. He didn't mean what he said about Jess."

I sighed, disappointed Keir was making excuses for Dorian's actions. "Sounded to me like he meant it. I know his behavior isn't your responsibility, but I don't understand why you'd want to be friends with someone like that."

We stepped forward in the line, and he said, "We're not friends. We're more like family."

"Family? In what way?"

He shook his head. When he did, I could see a small tattoo of a tooth, like a vampire's fang, on his neck. Good grief! Could this irritating man be any sexier?

"It's complicated."

"Well," I said, taking a step back. "He was terribly cruel last night. I just hope Jessamin is okay."

"Aye. As do I," Keir said, grimacing.

As we approached the counter, a beautiful dark-skinned woman with a red silk scarf tied around her head put her hands on her hips.

"Well, you must be Windsor Ebonwood," she said. "I'm Azalea. Tzazi has told me wonderful things about you. I'm glad to finally meet you."

She glanced over at my companion, flashing a sly grin. "I see you have found some worthwhile company, Keir. How are you? Keeping out of trouble?"

"Well as can be, ma'am. But as far as trouble, I'm sure Mizizi might have a thing or two to say about that."

Azalea laughed, her grin widening as she looked me over. "Now, what can I get you two?"

I chose an iced vanilla chai tea, while Keir ordered an extra-large black coffee.

"What are your plans for today?" he asked me, while Azalea moved away to prepare our drinks.

"I'm about to see my bookshop for the first time," I said excitedly.

He smiled. "That's great, lass. Do you have much experience with books?"

"I love books," I gushed. "Back in the city, I was a book conservator and a university professor. During the summers, I travelled around the world repairing books destroyed by catastrophes like floods, earthquakes, or people. So, yes, I'd say I have a lot of experience with books."

"That's impressive," Keir said, handing me my chai. "No, really!" he said when I rolled my eyes. "I guess it runs in the family."

"I guess so." I tried to hand Azalea my credit card, but she waved it away.

"On the house," she said. "My 'Welcome to Darkly' gift."

I thanked her, and we stepped back onto the sidewalk. The heat and humidity were back, and I fanned my face in a useless effort to move some air.

"Well, um, I guess I need to head to the shop. I don't want to keep Mr. Hathaway waiting," I laughed nervously. "At least not on my first day."

"Oh! Yeah, right. Okay. Well, I'll see you around, Win."

With a parting wave, he turned and jogged across the street. I realized I still hadn't asked what he did for a living. Probably something in construction, I thought, with a body like that. Oh, hush already!

Glancing down the sidewalk, I saw Mr. Hathaway standing in front of the rounded doors of the bookshop. Such a quaint Southern gent—today he wore a light blue suit, with a straw boater atop his head. He nodded as I approached.

"Good morning, Ms. Ebonwood," Mr. Hathaway said brightly, handing me a large old-fashioned key on a metal hoop, with several other keys hanging below. "Did you sleep well last night?"

"I did, Mr. Hathaway."

"Good, good. Well, dear, let's take a look at your shop, and I can answer any questions you may have."

As I inserted the key into the lock, a stained-glass image above the door caught my eye. Unlike the other still-lives of city and country life, this one was simply the image of a book with wings, soaring through the clouds.

Mr. Hathaway followed my gaze. "The winged book is the symbol of the bookshop. Quite fitting," he said.

I turned my attention to the door, took a deep breath, and turned the key. Mr. Hathaway pushed open the door, and I stared into pitch blackness until he reached in behind me and flipped the light switch on the wall. As the lights blinked on around the building, I covered my mouth, in awe at the scene in front of me.

An ornate wooden fireplace presided over one side of the room, while a long dark counter, much like a bar, ran down the other. Thick carpets covered the floor, interspersed with plush sofas and chairs, pointy-leaf palms, and delicate side tables, reminding me of a comfortable old manor house. A set of curving staircases at the back of the building led to a second-floor gallery overlooking the area below. From there, a winding staircase spiraled its way to a stained-glass dome above. Multiple galleries, stacked one on top of the other, seemed to go on forever, each walkway stuffed chock-full of books.

"You have four keys," Mr. Hathaway explained. "The antique one, as you know, provides entry to the store. The silver one opens the cabinets under the checkout desk." He pointed to the long counter on the left. Then strode to the back and disappeared behind the stairs.

Dazed, I followed and found him standing next to a wooden door.

"That blue one opens the door to your conservation lab."

I drew out the key and quickly opened the door, eager to see my work area.

Inside was a sizable airy room, well-equipped and clean, with a door on the far wall leading to a small, covered parking lot.

"Occasionally comes in handy," opined Mr. Hathaway.

A black rectangular worktable took up the center of the room, piled high with books. Various storage units along the stone walls contained rolls of book cloth, stacks of board, and a wide range of paper. Arranged at either end of the worktable were a book press and a guillotine. I felt like I had just won the Super Bowl. Look, mom! I'm going to Disneyland!

"What about this key?" I asked, holding up a golden key.

"That one, my dear, I can't help you with. Minta never told me. I assume it unlocks something precious and important to the Ebonwood witches. Important enough that Minta kept its purpose to herself."

I examined the key closer. It was of the large, old-fashioned sort with no special markings or engravings on it. Unlike the other keys, it appeared well-worn. The dull tone of the metal emphasized the scuffs and scratches marring its surface. "How odd."

He smiled. "Minta was very generous with her time and commitments, but she was also a very private person. Hence, the remoteness of Fernwood and, of course" —he pointed at the gold key— "that key.

"And now," he said, "if you have no further questions, please sign these documents and the bookshop is all yours."

"Thank you, Mr. Hathaway," I said as I signed and handed him the papers.

"Of course, my dear. Please don't hesitate to contact me if I can help you with anything. Anything at all. Minta was a dear friend, and I expect with a little time, you shall become a dear friend as well. Ta-ta, dear. Oh, and Maybelle sends her best."

Once his footsteps had retreated, and the bell on the front door stopped ringing, I fell to my knees on the floor. Today held promise that twenty-four hours ago I couldn't even imagine.

"Thank you, Grandmother," I whispered, as I dabbed my eyes. I felt a now familiar bump against my side and scooped Pye into my arms. "And thank you, Pyewacket." He meowed and rubbed his head up against my cheek.

Now more than ever, I felt the urge to visit the cemetery, properly thank my grandmother, and visit my mother. Next to the lab, I found a restroom and freshened my makeup as best I could.

Locking up the shop, I stopped at Dianthe's Oopsie Daisies next door, where I bought two large sprays of daffodils and pink tulips. The yellow and pink flowers reminded me of the beautiful sunrise this morning, an appropriate tribute.

The main entrance to the cemetery lay catty-corner to The Magic Cup. I was thankful cars in Darkly were few, as Pye and I darted across the street. A drip of perspiration trickled down the side of my face and I swiped it away as we approached the gate.

I hesitated, gaining my bearings, when a large Irish Wolfhound suddenly bounded down the sidewalk, turning right at the next corner. I stared for a moment, then reached out and unlatched the lock. Pye, it seemed, had no such qualms. When the gate opened, he scampered in and disappeared amongst the monoliths and tombs. I called his name, but soon gave up. Looked like I was on my own.

Cool shade and the light fragrance of frangipani hit me when I entered. Large, gnarled oaks stood like guardian sentinels, bending their graceful arms to the ground. A hot breeze wafted between the trees, setting the Spanish moss aflutter.

I stopped to admire a gravestone, pink marble with carved cherubs—the grave of a cherished wife, perhaps. Farther ahead, a black granite monolith rose twenty feet in the sky. Right next to it, a bright white obelisk rose only about five feet, with purple clematis blooms twirling up its base. In the distance, I saw two crypts. One appeared to be made of a transparent green stone, while the other was a kaleidoscope of oranges and reds. Coffins were visible inside each.

I wound through the cemetery—scanning surnames on tombstones, searching for my own—when through a break in the trees, I glimpsed the brown, stone walls of the bell tower. I had already made it to the center!

A sudden burst of hot wind nearly knocked me to the ground. Thrusting my arms down by my sides, I used the bouquets to keep my dress from flying over my head. A strange thud resounded throughout the cemetery, and I looked around for what could have caused such a noise.

Just as quickly as it came, the wind subsided. I heard a familiar meow and looked down to see Pye back by my side.

"What just happened?" I asked him.

He stared at me with his one eye.

"You don't know either, huh? C'mon. We might as well head home. I won't find the family plots on my own."

Instead, Pye dashed around a red tombstone in the shape of a shooting star, his tail in the air, and disappeared into the bell tower.

Inside the stone structure was a wooded stairway, which

coiled up the sides of the tower. Scrambling up the spiral stairs, the only place Pye could have gone, I finally reached a stone floor leading to a wide opening in the tower. Through the gap, I could see the tops of green leafy trees, below blue skies. I bet the view was gorgeous from here, but I wasn't about to step any closer to that ledge.

Pyewacket paced around the edges of the room, until I scooped him up. As I did, I realized the stone floor was soaking wet with shallow puddles, gathered in areas where the floor was uneven.

"Bad kitty," I admonished, running back down the stairs.

As I reached the last step, the cat bolted from my arms.

"Pyewacket! You are so in trouble!"

I ran after the little black cat once again, skidding to a stop before a shiny white obelisk, rising high into the air. My eyes followed the column up to its sharply pointed cap—where, to my horror, I could see a body! A man, impaled through his back on the sharp point of the gravestone. Blood ran down the sides of the pinnacle and puddled around its base.

I stifled a scream. Thin blue pieces of plastic rained down around my head, as the tower bells rang out in a sharp warning. Pulling one of the fragments out of my hair, I impulsively placed it in my pocket. That was when the dead man's head flopped to the side.

It was Dorian Wilde.

CHAPTER 8

By the time I reached the town sidewalk, my screams, along with the harsh toll of the bells, had alerted the townspeople that something was amiss. Many were standing outside of their shops. I ran to Tzazi's mom and clasped her hands.

"In the cemetery," I rasped. "It's Dorian Wilde. He jumped from the tower."

Azalea's eyes widened. She sat me down at one of the tables outside of The Magic Cup and handed me a cold drink that bubbled and popped, reminding me of Ileana's ankle elixir.

"With a measure of something to help the nerves," she said.

I nodded my thanks as the crowd in front of me grew larger. Keir arrived across the street with Mayor Mayòr and glanced in my direction. For a second, I thought he was going to come over, but then they both dashed into the cemetery. Next to the brick wall, Jessamin, the red-haired server from the Gator, stood wide-eyed, watching the lively activity surrounding her. She twisted the hem of her serving apron nervously in front of her.

Setting down my drink, I stood, pushing my way to the front of the crowd. I was about to step back into the cemetery when a hand stopped me.

"Are you sure you want to go back in there?" Tzazi asked.

I nodded.

"Then I'm coming with you."

We linked arms, and I led her down the same path Pye and I had taken just moments before. As we passed the red monolith, I drew in a quick breath. Tzazi's grip on my arm tightened.

"It really is him," she whispered.

We watched for a few minutes as Boddy drifted around the scene, confiscating items he discovered on the ground, meticulously examining the body with his strange red eyes. Keir, however, was nowhere around.

Tzazi gasped and pointed to the base of the monument, where under the thick splatters of blood I could barely make out the words:

BRYCHEN SEVILLE WILDE

PERFECT SON, PROTECTIVE BROTHER, LOVING HUSBAND

IN MY HEART FOREVER

Tzazi and I walked back to the patio in front of Azalea's shop, where I crumpled into a chair as her mom handed me a fresh drink. The patio and street were now packed with people milling about, chatting, and waiting around for updates about the unexpected death.

"Someone pushed him," said a woman behind me. "And you know Boddy Grim will never figure out who did it, because it could have been anyone."

"I don't know," the man standing next to her countered. "I'd bet he jumped."

"Pfft," his friend said. "Dorian was too much of a coward to do anything as honorable as that."

After about ten minutes, Boddy Grim strode out of the cemetery and up to our table.

"Windsor Ebonwood," he said in his deep, whispery voice. "I have some questions for you pertaining to the death of Dorian Samiel Wilde."

I didn't trust this man one iota, not after my first run-in with him. I turned to Tzazi, who nodded and reached for my hand.

I pursed my lips. "Fine."

His red eyes seem to pierce through my very soul as he asked, "Did you kill Dorian Samiel Wilde?"

"What? No!"

"How well did you know Dorian Samiel Wilde?"

"Not at all," I said. "I only met him last night. We only spoke for a few minutes."

His weird, sunken eyes stared into my own, and then he nodded.

As he turned in Tzazi's direction, his head dipped a bit, his eyes lingering for a second on her face. "Miss Strangeland," he whispered. With a flash of his cloak, he was gone. My head whipped around. Where did he go?

"Let's get you home," Tzazi said quickly, grabbing my arm.

"Will you be okay, Mum?"

Azalea rushed over and wrapped her daughter up in her arms.

"Of course, love. And one for you too, Win," she said, enveloping me in her silky soft caftan.

"I love your mom," I said to Tzazi as Azalea returned to her shop.

"Yeah, her brews will do that to you," she laughed.

We stopped by the bookshop, so I could make sure the lights were off and the doors were locked up tight.

"I want to get a few bottles of wine first," I said once we had stepped back onto the sidewalk. "This night definitely calls for it."

"Does it ever," Tzazi agreed.

Mr. Bosada's Grocery was busy—everyone was gossiping and talking about Dorian, both his life and his death. Dorian wasn't going to be missed, and despite my sentiments about him, I still held some pity for the man.

The wine section of the store was exceptionally crowded, but I managed to wriggle my way in and pick up a couple of bottles of red. I lifted them high to show Tzazi, who was across the aisle in the produce section.

"How's this?" I asked.

"Perfect!" she replied, holding up bags of oranges, lemons, and green apples. "Sangria!"

As we walked together to the checkout line, a teenage boy burst through the doors.

"Grim's gone and arrested Jessamin Wilde for Dorian's murder," he yelled.

The crowd broke out in exclamations of surprise and murmurs.

"Evon!" Tzazi signaled to the boy. "Come here!" He trotted over to where we stood.

"Did you just say Boddy arrested Jessamin?"

He nodded. "About five minutes ago. I saw it with my own eyes. He's taken her up to town hall."

"Listen, would you do me a favor?" Tzazi handed him a green note. "I'll be over at Win's this evening. Would you let me know when you hear any updates on Jess?"

He agreed and ran back out the door.

"I don't know Jessamin well," I said as I set my purchases on the conveyor belt, "but I don't think she would kill Dorian."

"She wouldn't," Tzazi agreed. "She's not that kind of person. Besides, if she were going to do it, she would have done it a long time ago."

"Like when her husband died?" I asked, then remembered something. "Dorian was impaled on his own brother's gravestone, wasn't he?"

Tzazi nodded. "That's the strangest, isn't it? It's like Brychen got revenge from the grave."

"Revenge for what?"

Tzazi pointed at the wine bottles. "That's a story for later."

TAM LUMIÈRE

~

As we approached the front door of Fernwood, Pye sat on the doormat, tiny tail swishing back and forth. I scratched him behind the ears, while a clap of thunder rumbled across the sky.

"Looks like we have another storm on the way," Tzazi said.

"Why don't you stay?" I suggested. "You don't need to be out alone at night anyway. Not until Dorian's murderer is caught."

Tzazi shivered. "Good idea. Do you have jammies I can borrow?"

I laughed. "Plenty of jammies you can borrow."

I unlocked the door just as the rain began to patter on the roof.

We rushed into the house as another rumble of thunder rocked the sky—closer this time. I could feel the house shudder in response.

"Land sakes! What is this?" Hilde stood before us, hands on her hips, looking like a mother who had just caught her daughter out past curfew. Then, to my surprise, she broke into a smile.

"Tzazi Strangeland! I haven't seen you for ages. How are you?"

She wrapped Tzazi in her arms, then held her at arm's length to look at her. "I like what you've done with your hair. Short and sassy. That is you, dear. That is you."

Maybe it was only me that brought out the grumpies in my housekeeper.

"Thank you, Hilde," Tzazi said, giving the woman a quick peck on the cheek.

"Tzazi's staying tonight, um, if it's okay?" I said, overcoming my shock.

"Fernwood isn't my house, honey. It's your house. But of course it's okay with me."

What the tarnation is going on here? Did she just call me honey? Forget that – did I just say 'tarnation'?

"I didn't think it was safe for her to walk home alone," I continued. "What with…" My voice trailed off.

Hilde nodded. "With a killer on the loose? I heard about that. But I really don't know if we all have anything to worry about. I mean, it was Dorian Wilde that died. Whoever killed Dorian Wilde did this town a big favor! Now let's get these groceries into the kitchen."

∼

Hilde got Tzazi set up in one of the guest bedrooms, and by the time we had both showered and put on some comfy pajamas, Hilde had prepared a quiche Lorraine using the leftover bacon from breakfast. We all gathered around the dining table and watched the rain fall as we ate and talked. Pye even got his own little slice.

From my previous exchanges with Hilde, I never expected to see this side of her. She amused us with stories of herself and Tzazi's mother Azalea, who had been close friends since their days in diapers. I could totally see Hilde hiding behind an oleander bush and scaring her calculus teacher to get them out of taking a test.

But when the talk turned to Dorian, everyone grew somber.

"That man was pure evil," Hilde said. "I've known him all my life, and I could tell you stories about Dorian that would give you nightmares."

I shivered at the thought, while Hilde cleared the table and then brought in a gigantic pitcher of sangria.

"Made fresh just for you girls," she said, setting it on the table, along with two glasses.

"Hilde, thank you!" I said, pouring us each a glass, as a long rolling thunder resounded over the house. "You won't have any?"

"You're welcome, dear," she said, even giving me a pat on the shoulder. "But no. I'm off to bed now. If either of you should need me, call. I'll hear you."

I didn't see how that could be true in such a big house, but I nodded, happy to stay on her good side.

We all said goodnight, and I watched through the windows as she ascended the covered stairs leading to her apartment over the kitchen.

Tzazi and I moved to the sitting room, where we each sprawled on a velvet sofa and swathed ourselves in blankets and pillows. We had been sipping our sangrias in silence for only a few minutes when a rat-a-tat-tat sounded at the front door.

"What the—" Tzazi exclaimed.

As the storm boomed all around the house, we creeped to the dark foyer. The porch lights blazed, framing the silhouette of a person within the cotton panels of the French doors. Either a woman, or a short man. I couldn't tell.

I inched the panel to the side, then chuckled.

"It's Evon, the kid from the grocery store," I said, opening the door and inviting the teenager inside.

"You have news," Tzazi said, approaching the door, her eyes wide.

Evon nodded. "Boddy released Jessamin from jail. Don't know who, but someone posted bail for her. They're saying Boddy didn't even have her for an hour."

"Thank goodness," I said, letting out a breath I didn't even know I'd been holding.

Tzazi handed the boy another greenback for his trouble, and before I could stop him, he disappeared into the night.

"Shouldn't we have had him stay until the storm lessens?" I asked, as Tzazi shut the door.

"Nah," she said, padding back into the sitting room. "You moved here during our hurricane season. Those of us who have lived here all our lives are used to it. Besides, I'm sure a carload of teenagers was waiting for him in the driveway."

I watched the rain blowing through the covered walkway and pelting the French doors of the sitting room, sliding down the glass. The pond was only visible in slices of lightning, stabbing through its murky darkness. Thank goodness Jessamin wasn't sitting in jail on a night like tonight.

"Tzazi?" I asked, once we had settled back on to the sofas with our sangrias.

"Mm hmm?"

"What is the deal with Boddy Grim? There's no evidence Jessamin had anything to do with Dorian's death. Yet he arrested her."

She rolled into an upright position on the couch and took a big sip. "That's hard to explain right now. Boddy was great at his old job. Not so good at this one. But until we find someone else, he's all we've got."

"What is his job?"

"I guess he's like our sheriff."

"'Like' your sheriff?"

"Well, he doesn't exactly have a title. He just does the job. But I guarantee he's got this one wrong. I can tell you who did it," she concluded, flopping back onto the sofa.

"Really?" I sat up. "Who?"

Just then, there was a loud boom, and the lights went out. The darkness was so complete, I could barely see my hand in front of my face.

"Tzazi, you okay?"

"I'm fine," she said, from across the room. "Just getting some matches from the foyer. One sec."

I heard a whoosh as the match lit. Tzazi slowly circled the room, lighting candles.

"Thanks, Tzazi."

"No problem."

Pulling the blanket tightly around me, I glanced out the windows. Flashes of lightning softly backlit the trees beyond the pond, reminding me of Keir's warning.

"You were about to tell me who you believe killed Dorian," I prompted, ignoring the flickering shadows filling the corners of the room.

"Fernando Mayór."

"The mayor?"

Tzazi nodded and poured herself another drink.

"Why him?"

"First, Fernando and Dorian never got along. Dorian believed his newfound money and so-called position in society gave him the right to be a jerk. He was always sticking his nose in city business, especially Fernando's duties as mayor. Minta had trouble with him as well, but she was too smart to fall for his shenanigans."

She reached in her cup, grabbed a piece of apple, and popped it in her mouth. "Second, Fernando hated Dorian with a passion. You've met Fernando's wife, Lilith, right?"

"The one with the big—" I cupped my hands about a foot out in front of my chest.

Tzazi laughed. "That's the one. Dorian and Lilith had an affair. Quite torrid by all accounts. Lilith let Dorian know when her husband would be gone by placing a single red rose in the window. And get this. I heard Fernando caught them in the act in his own bed."

"Ick! And Lilith is so pretty!"

"I know, right? I'd say Mayor Mayór had two huge reasons to want Dorian gone forever," Tzazi said, cupping her hands in front of her chest.

We both fell back onto the sofas, shaking with laughter. Once I caught my breath, I refilled our glasses and curled back up in the velvety blankets.

"When I picked you up from Char's dock, you mentioned you worked at a university. What'd you do there?" Tzazi asked.

"Professor," I replied as the storm continued to boom around us. "I taught courses on the book—its history, structure, technology. Plus, I took care of the university's rare book and manuscript collections and travelled to restore books for other institutions."

"Well, isn't that interesting? Books. Just like all the Ebonwoods before you."

For as long as I could remember, my life revolved around books. First as a kid hanging out at the library, begging the librarian for just a few more minutes at closing time. Then, as a college student, who so profoundly couldn't imagine a life without books that she made them her career.

"So why did you leave? It sounds perfect for you," Tzazi asked.

It was. Wasn't it?

"Well, a few years ago, my boyfriend Lucas asked me to marry him," I answered. "I said yes, but we never seemed to find the time to set a date."

"Hmm. Maybe you didn't set a date because deep down you knew he wasn't right for you," Tzazi offered quietly.

I shrugged, a deep sigh falling from my lips.

"Maybe," I said. "But it sure hurt like hell when I found out he was having an affair on the very same day he turned down my request for tenure. All that hard work, down the drain."

My voice quivered. I couldn't tell if I was talking about my relationship or my career.

I turned to face Tzazi. "When Mr. Hathaway called, I was more than ready to leave that life behind me and start a new one."

"Win, I'm so sorry. I didn't mean to pry," Tzazi said.

I waved a hand, pasting a smile on my face. "It's okay. And you're right. He wasn't the one for me. What about you? Anyone special in your life?"

"There was someone once. But it didn't work out." She stood up suddenly. "Bathroom break. Be right back."

Had I touched a nerve?

As the storm continued to blast the night, Tzazi and I talked for hours in the sitting room. At one point, Pye joined me, curling up in a tight ball on the back of the sofa, his tail whacking me in the face every few minutes. But by 10 p.m. the sangria pitcher finally emptied out, and we were both yawning every few seconds.

I made sure Tzazi had everything she needed in the guestroom and said good night. After blowing out the candles, I gathered up Pye and plodded into my bedroom, collapsing onto the bed. I downed that evening's bubbling and hissing dose of elixir and then fell into a deep sleep with Pye softly purring in my ear.

CHAPTER 9

A noise woke me around midnight. I assumed it was the rattling of windowpanes from the storm still raging and rumbling. But I sat straight up in bed when I heard it again—the light tinkling of piano keys.

Could it be Tzazi? No, that would be silly. Could it be the murderer? I shook my head. That was even sillier.

I swung my legs down from the bed and grabbed a silver candlestick holder from the mantel. With so many doors, it wasn't out of the question to think someone could have broken into the house. But to play the piano?

I tiptoed into the study and then peeked into the music room, where the grand piano sat in a corner. I saw nothing.

Bewildered, I stepped into the middle of the room. Maybe I imagined it. Tzazi and I had drunk a whole pitcher of sangria last night, and yesterday was definitely one for the books. Perhaps my imagination had gone into overdrive.

I passed through the doorway leading to the front entry and made sure the door was locked. As I entered back into the music room, I stopped. A woman sat at the bench before the piano, bone white fingers poised above the piano keys. Her silver, chin-length bob blew in a nonexistent breeze, which also ruffled her long white gown.

As she turned to me, a chill ran down my spine. A low, familiar meow drew my attention to the piano itself. Pyewacket? He rested next to the piano's music stand; tiny tail curled around his feet. He meowed again.

The woman looked at me and smiled. A string of white, glistening pearls hung around her neck.

She ran a finger down the keys of the piano. "I love this house. Your great-great-great-grandfather built it, you know."

"Grandmother?" I stammered. "Am I dreaming?"

"You're not dreaming, dear," she answered in a silky Southern voice. "Come sit."

She patted next to herself on the bench, but I eased into the chintz cushioned chair against the wall instead and held the candleholder in my lap.

"I see you have wasted no time making a splash in our little town," my grandmother said with a laugh.

"That's not funny," I protested, but couldn't help chuckling myself. "At least I met Chase because of it."

"Chase is a good man. And he does a fantastic caviar facial. You must make an appointment. Tell him I sent you."

Um. No. He'd think I was mad.

"You are gathering a worthy group of friends here, Windsor. I was proud of your life in the city and I know I will be proud of you here on Darkly Island."

I hung my head. "But it's all so overwhelming. I'm so afraid that anything good that happens to me is going to be snatched away, no matter what I do."

"Don't let what happened at your last job scare you, Windy." My grandmother rose and drifted around the room. "Honey, you can do anything you set your mind to do. You know why? Number 1—" she stuck a finger up in the air "—you are an Ebonwood. Number 2—" a second finger flew up "—you are a

Southern girl. And Number 3—" she raised a single finger on her other hand and shrugged "—you're a witch."

"What an awful thing to say!"

"No, no, Windsor. Goodness gracious! I'm talking about magic, darling. You come from a family of powerful witches and warlocks going back centuries."

My mouth gaped open.

"Now I know this is a dream." I mumbled, walking back into my bedroom and placing the candleholder on the mantel. Pye trailed along behind me as I curled up under the comforter once again.

My grandmother drifted into the room and sat down on the edge of the bed. The comforter dimpled under her ghostly weight. "Do you really believe this is a dream?" she asked.

I hesitantly reached out my hand and touched her face. My hand passed right through her filmy skin, but instead of feeling nothing, I felt a cold, misty air flow around my fingers.

"No," I whispered.

"Good. Now, let's talk about the bookshop."

Grandmother moved over to a nearby chair and crossed her legs after she sat. I wondered if she had been this prim and proper in real life. Probably.

"The MET is not a normal bookshop," she began.

I sat up and wrinkled my brow. "The MET?"

"Magically Enchanted Transportation," Grandmother explained. "All portal shops in the Charming Isles are METs. Ours is the Darkly MET. I've always liked the sound of that. I guess in mundane terms, METs would be travel agencies."

I laughed until I saw her face. "Oh, you're serious."

"Absolutely," she continued. "These books can not only be read, but they can be used as portals to the Charming Isles as well."

"The Charming Isles?" I thought back over my college geography course. "I've never heard of it."

"Of course not, darling. The Charming Isles are of another

world than the one you grew up in. As is Darkly Island, as a matter of fact.

"Don't look so dumbstruck. It's quite simple. When you ventured through the Elysian Swamp with Char, you passed through a portal to the Charming Isles, of which Darkly Island is just one region. Now, not just anyone can find the Charming Isles. One of its trusted residents must give you permission. When I died and provided for you in my will, that gesture gave you preferred residential privileges. Visitors, such as those who are arriving in Darkly for the portals, are only given touring privileges."

"But what about the airboat operator?" I asked. "Couldn't anyone hire a boat like I did and come to Darkly?"

Grandmother shook her head, her bob flying back and forth. "Your finding Char wasn't random. He is the ferryman to the Darkly region of the Charming Isles. He knows who is allowed and who is not. As docile as he may appear, he protects the Isles with a ferocity one doesn't want to witness. Not to mention, his demon form is horrifying."

Grandmother shrugged when I squeaked.

"So how does the MET work?" I asked, not wanting to think further on Char, the demon ferryman.

"The books bewitch themselves through a self-fulfilling spell crafted eons ago by one of the original Ebonwood witches. When a book needs attention, it appears in your lab rather than reshelving itself. Every time you make a repair, you reinforce the magic within the book. Just maintain repairs and be sure the enchantments are working properly. Which they always do," she added.

"To order supplies for the lab, just say aloud the names of the items you need and they will appear in the storage cabinets. But be very precise in your descriptions. Once I ended up with a 250lb. roll of Washi paper instead of two 50-lb. rolls.

"Eventually, you and the MET will bond, allowing you to work in concert with the portals to allow admittance and provide

TOLLING BELLS & DARK SPELLS

recommendations. Many believe MET owners can see into the soul. But I believe it's more a case of paying attention to people and understanding what they need."

"But how are the portals used for travel?"

"Most people journeying through the Charming Isles know exactly where they want to go," she explained, "so they know which book they need. Others want to go on a surprise vacation and will choose a particular book knowing it will send them to a location based on the title, theme, plot, or setting of the chosen portal.

"For example, *Jane Eyre* or *Gone with the Wind* takes the traveler to the Aerie Mountains. *To the Lighthouse* naturally takes one to the windswept shores of Menai. My absolute favorite, however, is *The Expedition of Humphrey Clinker*, which takes you to Queen Ermione's bathroom in Charming Castle." She laughed. "Wouldn't that be a great surprise to Her Royal Majesty?"

"Where would *Dracula* send someone?" I asked, truly curious.

Grandmother shuddered. "Perhaps Kvikov Ruins or the Wandering Deads."

"Wait a minute. Did you just say there's a queen of Charming?"

I preferred to not think about any wandering deads.

"Oh yes, dear. Also, a prince consort, a prince, and two princesses. All very charming, of course."

She chuckled at her joke as I sat back against the cushioned headboard.

This was nuts. Wasn't it?

"And Mom?" I asked, pulling Pye into my arms. "Was she a witch too?"

I looked at Grandmother and was surprised to see the startled look on her face.

"Yes, dear. Your mother was a witch. Sadly, her magic was her downfall."

She opened her mouth as if to say more but instead pushed

herself up from the bed, picked up Pye, and glided to the French doors.

"Let's not speak of your mother, dear. I don't know how much longer I can maintain my appearance here tonight, and I have some very important things to say."

More important than what I just heard? I wasn't sure I wanted to hear more.

"The creature that chased you through the swamp wasn't a dog, Windy. It was a werewolf."

"No," I exclaimed, jumping up from the bed. "There's no such thing."

"You didn't think witches were the only supernaturals here, did you, dear? Darkly Island is home to many magical creatures. There are a variety of witches, many kinds of elves and fairies, vampires, sirens." She waved a hand nonchalantly. "Let's see. The florist, Dianthe, is a sprite. The innkeeper is an air wizard. Mr. Bosada, who you've met, is a brujo. The bartender at the Gator is a goblin."

"Goddesses? Leprechauns? Dragons?"

"Yes, yes, and yes."

"What about succubi or sorcerers?"

"Yes. Oh wait. I mean, no. Darkly no longer has a succubus in residence. Many of the wives protested her visiting their husbands at night, so the Mayor asked her to move back to the Isles. Naturally, I didn't agree. I thought the issue lay with the husbands, but I was in the minority on that one. The woman was absolutely smashing at galas and fundraisers. Yes, to the sorcerer."

"What is Keir? He must be a god."

Grandmother laughed. "Yes, you would think so, wouldn't you? But I'll let your friends tell you about themselves."

"Grandmother, why didn't I know about you? About magic?" I tugged the blanket up under my chin, afraid to hear the answer. "Did Dad know?"

She sighed. "He knew, dear. He knew about the magic, and he

feared it. After what happened to your mother, I can't say I blame him."

I looked out the doors leading to the courtyard and the swamps below. The rain still pelted the glass, but it no longer brought comfort.

"What happened to her?" I whispered.

"She's gone, Windsor. She's gone, and there was nothing I could do about it."

The harshness in her voice drew my attention from the storm.

"But—"

"You are in Darkly now, and I thank the goddess for that," she said, drawing in a breath. "Here, your magic will thrive and grow. You will be a powerful witch one day, Win. After all, you are now the Ebonwood imperative."

"The imperative?"

"The witch who carries on the traditions and protects the MET and its portals."

I furrowed my brows. "You say I can do magic, yet never in my life have I ever done anything remotely magical."

"Haven't you?" Grandmother's eyes sparkled as her lips quirked up in a cheeky grin.

"Never," I said firmly. "No shrinking sweaters. No apparating up to rooftops. Nothing."

Grandmother rolled her eyes. "I can't decide whether those *Harry Potter* books are a boon or a blight on the magical community," she mumbled.

Crossing her thin ghostly arms on her chest, she cocked her head. "What about books?"

"Books?" My voice trailed off.

Come to think of it, my ability to diagnose and repair books was uncommon, and well-known around the world. Many renowned institutions entrusted me—and only me—to protect and mend their most delicate and valuable items.

I stared at Grandmother in amazement, the realization sinking in.

"And with time and a lot of practice, you will learn other kinds of magic. Like this." She cupped her hand and a kaleidoscope of yellow and blue butterflies flurried up from her palm, swirling and fluttering about the room. With a flick of her wrist, they disappeared.

"Amazing!" I breathed.

"Just a lovely parlor trick," Grandmother said. "You, however, must focus on learning crucial magic, such as defense, healing, and protection."

"When do we start?" I felt a flush of excitement spread across my face.

"We? I can't be your magical mentor, Win, as much as I would like to be."

My face fell at her words.

"But Grandmother, how can I practice if you can't teach me?" I laughed weakly. "Is there a *Witchcraft for Dummies* book?"

"Probably. But you won't need it. Life on Darkly Island will provide all the training you need. When you're ready, opportunities will appear. But remember, it's only an opportunity. You must put in the time and hard work yourself. Innate talent will only take you so far."

I nodded and bit my lip. "I understand. But can you at least teach me that butterfly trick?"

Grandmother laughed. "Always so impatient."

Her face turned serious as she gazed out on the swamp, absentmindedly running a ghostly hand through Pyewacket's fur. "I really don't like this Dorian business. Darkly has always had its secrets, but I'm afraid their coming to light will unleash even more tragic consequences. Like everyone else, I detested the man, but murder is not the solution. A tragic death creates a nasty ripple in the continuum of life, and I doubt Dorian's murder will be the last.

"Stand by Jessamin," Grandmother continued as she turned to look at me. "She will need the support and friendship of you and

Tzazi. Stay close to each other and, through your strengths, you will be protected.

"Lastly and most importantly, Windsor, you must beware of the swamp. Until your powers are stronger, you are vulnerable to the beings that dwell there. Trust me, Windy. Creatures far worse than werewolves are hiding in the Darkly Swamp. When you visit Mizizi again, stay on the white stone path and you will be safe. It wasn't by chance that you found his cabin yesterday."

Grandmother drifted back to my bedside and lay Pye in my arms.

"I am glad you are in Darkly now, and know of your legacy," she said, caressing my cheek. Again, I felt a cool, moist touch of air. "Trust Pyewacket and Hildegard, dear Windy. Pye is the Ebonwood familiar and has been with us for ages. His advice is always sound, and his presence will heighten your powers. Hildegard may be unbearable at times" —I would have sworn Pye snorted— "but she is fiercely loyal and honest. You couldn't have a more skilled and dedicated person on your side."

As she began to fade, she whispered, "Never forget. Even if you can't see me, I am always with you. I love you, Windsor."

My heart broke as my grandmother's apparition dwindled into a small ball of white light.

"I love you too," I whispered, the white light fading even further until it disappeared.

CHAPTER 10

The next morning, Tzazi had gone home before I awoke, leaving me a handwritten thank you note and a bouquet of gardenias from the garden. The heavenly scent filled the house, and I appreciated that she had gone to the trouble, but I was disappointed she was gone. I wanted to talk to her about everything I had learned last night. Plus, I was dying to know if she and Jessamin were witches also.

However, it also bothered me that Tzazi knew about my magic, yet said nothing. What if I had slept through Grandmother's appearance last night? Would I have only found out when I—I don't know—accidentally turned someone into a bullfrog? I had so many questions, and no idea who could answer them for me.

I dressed and hurried to the kitchen, eager to see whether I would meet nice Hilde or not-so-nice Hilde this morning. She was standing at the entrance to the dining room with a frown on her face.

"So. Finally decided to wake up."

Definitely not-so-nice Hilde.

"I had a rough night of sleep, or lack thereof," I said, sighing and pushing a stray lock of brown hair out of my face.

Hilde's face softened. "Sit, and I'll bring out breakfast."

I hadn't realized how hungry I was until Hilde placed a tall stack of blueberry pancakes in front of me. Hilde sat, drizzling warm maple syrup on a huge mound of bacon. She passed me the container.

"Now tell me what happened. Did you and Tzazi quarrel?"

"No, no. Nothing like that…" I hesitated. "What if I told you I talked to my grandmother last night? That she came to see me?"

"Did she now?" Hilde looked up from her plate. "Well, took her dad-blasted time, didn't she? That woman knows I'm not good at keeping secrets!"

"You knew I was a witch?"

"Well, of course I did, honey." She puffed out her ample chest a fraction farther. "I myself am a shifter."

"A what?" I asked through a mouth crammed with pancake.

"Hun, don't talk with your mouth full. A shifter. A bear-shifter, to be precise. I can change into my animal form whenever I feel like it. Let me show you."

Hilde stood, and before I could say Grizzly Adams, a large brown bear stood before me. The bear raised its arms above its head and growled menacingly.

"What the!" I screamed, as the bear shrunk to human size and Hilde sat back down at the table. "Hilde, that was amazing!"

"Why, thank you, hun." Hilde smiled and dug back into her breakfast.

"But why did you growl at me? I thought you were going to attack."

"I was neither growling at you nor attacking. I was asking how my hair looked. I can't help it if I speak bear when I'm in bearform. When shifters are in their animal forms, we can understand you perfectly. Unfortunately, you can't understand us."

"Are there a lot of shifters in Darkly?"

"Quite a few," Hilde said. "We can be a rowdy bunch, especially the wolf shifters. But Keir Bain keeps them in line."

"Keir?" I put my fork down. "He's a shifter?"

"Oh, that's right. You've met our Keir. That sure didn't take long. Keir is the alpha of the wolf pack. Those boys can get wild, but Keir doesn't put up with their shenanigans. Especially not from that little weasel, Dorian Wilde. Always causing trouble and challenging Keir for pack leader. I'm sure Keir's not sad to see him gone. One less claw in his side."

A sudden rap at the back door drew our attention. "Oh! There's the butcher with my steaks."

I sat back in my chair as Hilde cleared the table and hurried to meet the butcher. As much as I hated the thought, Keir had good reasons to want Dorian out of the way. Plus, they were both wolf shifters. I suddenly gasped as I realized. A wolf shifter is a werewolf! A werewolf chased me through the swamp and then Keir suddenly showed up! Could it have been Keir all along?

I needed to go to my lab, where I could work and think. And I had a lot to think about.

"Hilde," I called. "I'm going into town. I want to get some work done today."

"Okay," she grunted back, but then poked her head around the door. "Don't stay out past dark, Win. Not with a killer prowling around. It's just common sense."

Back in my bedroom, I pulled on a silk blouse, jeans, and a pair of high-heeled sandals. I reached in the closet and grabbed my Italian leather equipment case, which housed my conservation tools. It had cost me a pretty penny when I bought it, but I was so glad I splurged. The case kept my expensive tools safe and in pristine condition.

I opened the door, yelled, "Pyewacket, let's go!" and he darted past me into the front yard. The path through the garden was littered with leaves and petals from the storm last night, but other than that, nothing seemed amiss. A woodpecker bounced down the trunk of the magnolia, pounding his beak into the tree with each hop. We stopped to watch him for a few minutes and then set off down the lane that led to Darkly.

TOLLING BELLS & DARK SPELLS

AS WE ENTERED THE TOWN, I couldn't help but view the townspeople through fresh eyes. Could the woman with the long thin nose and legs to match be a harpy? What about the child with the larger-than-normal ears? Possibly a changeling or an elf? The experience was unnerving, but the people themselves smiled and carried on as usual.

By the time we reached The Magic Cup, the news of Jessamin's release had spread through Darkly like fireflies through a swamp. Tzazi and I weren't the only ones who believed Boddy arrested the wrong person, and I had yet to hear any whispered words of sympathy for the man who died.

As I stood in line for my morning chai, I ran into Tzazi, who was leaving for a day of court in Rosewood, another town on the island. We chatted for a few moments, then Pye and I headed to the MET.

I stuck the key into the lock and then hesitated. I was a witch, right? Then shouldn't I be able to open this door with my powers? Withdrawing the key, I glanced around to make sure no one was watching and took a few steps back. Giving the door, most particularly the lock, my full concentration, I chanted "Open. Open. Open."

Nothing.

TV witches wrinkled their noses or snapped their fingers to use their magic. I figured, let's try that. I checked around again and wrinkled my nose up and down a few times. Then once more.

Again, nothing.

Concentrating hard, I repositioned myself in front of the door and snapped my fingers.

Wait! Did the doorknob just jiggle?

Perhaps not.

Frustrated, I threw out my hands and said, "Abracadabra!"

"That's not how it works," said a rich, cultured voice next to me.

I jumped, throwing my hands to my sides, and spun around. No one was there. Well, only ... Pyewacket?

He paused from licking his paw and peered at me with his one eye. "You can't be surprised at this turn of events, bébé. I am your familiar after all."

I yelped, scooped him up, and quickly entered the shop, slamming the door behind us.

I held him up under his front legs, so we were face to face. "You can talk?"

I would swear he shrugged. "Actually, it's more that you can understand me. Everyone else? They hear meows."

I set him down on the counter, grabbed my tool case from outside, and flipped on the lights. The fluorescents lit up with a buzz.

"But why can I just now understand you?" I asked.

"Simple," he said. "Before last night, you didn't believe it was possible for cats to talk."

"Wow." I shook my head. "Every time I think life can't get any stranger."

"Indeed," Pyewacket said as he stuck his nose up, lifted a leg, and licked his nether regions.

"Yuck!" I wrinkled up my nose. "Do you have to do that here?"

His yellow eye popped up, bright against his ebony fur.

"Sooo—" I averted my eyes, not quite sure whether it was appropriate to look. "How long have you been the Ebonwood familiar?"

Pyewacket raised his head. "I have protected and worked alongside the Ebonwood witches since the 2000s—"

I laughed. "So recent. I assumed—"

"—BCE," Pye finished with a hint of disdain.

"You've got to be kidding me!"

"I don't kid." He deadpanned.

That's for sure.

Pye straightened and pinned me with his eye. "The magic you hold is powerful and ancient. A fact you'd do well to remember."

No wonder Grandmother and Pyewacket were so tight. He'd been in her life since the day she was born, supporting her, loving her, assisting her.

I stood up straight and pumped my fist in the air. "You know what this means, right?"

"That it's nap time? Because this conversation is literally putting me to sleep."

"No. You can teach me magic!"

"Not possible." He stood up and turned his rump into my face. "And now I'm going for a lie down."

With that, Pye jumped from the counter and wandered into the stacks.

CHAPTER 11

*A*s much as I wanted to follow Pye and ask him a million questions, it was more important I start getting the MET ready for its upcoming re-opening. Still, Pyewacket had given me a lot to think about.

Once the shop was ready to go, I could turn my full attention to finding the lock opened by the golden key. Truthfully, I was a little afraid of what might happen once I found it and chided myself for not asking Grandmother about it when I had my chance.

Unlocking the lab door, I headed to the equipment stored on the back countertop. I'd remembered that a few of the projectors and splicers back there were wrapped in old newspaper. As I uncovered them one-by-one, arranging them on the counter, I noticed all the newspapers were one called the *Daily Shade*, published here in Darkly.

Unwrapping the final projector, a headline along the top of the newspaper caught my attention:

DARKLY ELDER CORRUPT TO THE CORE?
A Tell-All by the Beautiful Beatrice Snarkle

Well, Miss Snarkle, aren't you a bit full of yourself?

My eyes darted to a picture of Dorian Wilde, who smiled and shot his middle finger at the camera as he strode past the Gator.

This was interesting. It seems Dorian got himself in a bit of trouble a few years ago. Pulling a polyester sleeve from a storage shelf, I slipped the article inside to read at home.

Now, to see what I had in my lab. Opening my tool case, I removed the leather-bound journal where I kept all my handwritten records of conservation projects. Starting to the right of the door, I meticulously examined and noted the name of each item, its quantity, and its expiration date, if applicable.

At some point, Pye joined me in the lab, spreading out lazily in a ray of sunshine striking the center of the table. He pawed at the dust fairies floating through the air. For such an ancient cat, he sure could be cute.

When I finished, it shocked me to see it was almost one in the afternoon. I had found no expired ingredients and was pleased with the quality of all the items. I politely ordered a few products that I preferred to work with (I didn't know if politeness made a difference, but it surely couldn't hurt), and when I checked in the cabinets, the items were there, unwrapped, tucked away, and ready for use.

Before I left the lab, I picked up a piece of cardstock and created a simple, but creative, sign stating the shop would reopen on Monday. Happy with my morning's work, I stuck the sign on the glass of the front door and retreated behind the counter.

There, I located several drawers and cabinets. Rummaging through them, I found various office supplies—pencils, pens, a pink sponge of some sort—and a bag of cat kibble, but no portal inventory list. On the top of the counter were two small saucers along with a crystal globe on a wooden stand, but strangely, no cash register. How did customers pay? I doubted Grandmother used Venmo.

Pyewacket! He would know. Just as I was about to yell his

name, the bell above the door jingled and a jolly face with a tuft of bright red, frizzy hair appeared.

"I know you're not open yet," Mayor Mayór said, his whiskers swishing back and forth, "but are you allowing well-wishers?"

I thought about what Tzazi said last night, but I couldn't exactly say no, could I?

"Um. Of course. Come in, Mayor."

The door swung shut behind him as he strolled in, thumbs crooked behind black and white polka dotted suspenders supporting a pair of mustard-colored pants.

"It's looking great in here," he said, swiveling his head around. "You'll have the place up and running in no time. No time at all."

Standing in front of the counter, the top of the Mayor's head barely reached to the bottom of the trim (and that was including the three inches of puffy hair on top). His mustache continued to swish back and forth. I wondered if he was doing it on purpose.

"Th-thank you, sir." He made me nervous, but I couldn't help staring at that fascinating mustache.

"No thanks necessary, dear girl. You have the complete endorsement of Mayor Mayór, you do." He smiled up at me, looking very proud of himself. Was he this happy because he had finally gotten rid of his competition, like Tzazi surmised?

"Are you going to change the name?" Oh my, he was still talking. "Some METs change the name when a new witch takes over, which is their right, of course. But as I always say, why change it if it ain't broke! Am I right? Anyway, glad to see everything's going well. We'll all be glad to see the Darkly MET in business again. Brings a lot of tourism dollars to our splendid town, it does."

"Me too, sir. I'm looking forward to it. And I have no plans to change the name."

"Ah. Good. Good." He stepped toward the door and then turned around. "By the way, I'm awfully sorry about your finding... um... the body the way you did. Sad business there. Sad indeed."

Was that a crook of a smile I detected?

The Mayor continued, "I hope it hasn't turned you against Darkly and its fair citizenry."

"Not at all. I am quite entranced by Darkly and everyone I've met," I said.

"Good. Good," he said. "Oh! Before I forget, these are for you from my wife, Lilith."

With a flourish, he pulled out a dozen red roses in a vase from behind his back and held them up above his head.

"Oh!" I exclaimed as I set them on the counter. "That was quite remarkable, Mayor! How did you do that?"

Real magic was going to take some getting used to!

The Mayor beamed, obviously flattered by my words.

"Every mayor needs to have a few tricks up his sleeve. Or behind his back, as in my case," he laughed.

"Please thank Lilith for me. What perfect roses, and they smell heavenly!"

"She has a way with flowers, she does," he said with a tight smile.

The door jingled again and a tiny round woman with a poof of white hair surrounding her head stood in the doorway.

The Mayor waved his fingers at me and, with a bow to the woman, left the shop.

"Bye, Mayor," she chirped and then turned to me. "He is such an interesting man."

"Hi there," I called. "What can I do for you?"

"My name is Constance Verity, dear, and I was—I am—Minta's best friend."

Her gloved hand fluttered primly in the air as she toddled up to me at the counter. A white leather handbag hung in the crook of her arm.

Plop a crown on her head and I'd believe Queen Elizabeth just walked into my shop!

"Ms. Verity, it's so nice to meet you." I hurried around the counter and clasped her outstretched hand.

"Please call me Conny, dear."

"Conny then," I said with a smile. "Can I help you with something? The MET doesn't reopen until next Monday."

"No, no, dear. I just brought by my prize-winning chess pie to welcome you to our island."

A large pie box suddenly appeared in her hands, and she placed it on the counter.

"You didn't need to do that," I stammered.

"Oh, but I did. We're all just pleased as punch you're here."

"Thank you so much, Conny. You are very sweet."

I led her to a cushioned seat pushed up next to the stained-glass windows. "Please. Have a seat."

"Thank you, but I can only stay for a moment," Conny said sweetly, settling next to me on the bench.

"How are you liking Fernwood?" she asked. "It's such a beautiful old house."

"It is," I said, "but I can't help feeling I don't deserve it. That I don't deserve this." I raised my hands, indicating the shop.

Conny cocked her head and smiled. "You've spoken to her, haven't you?"

"Last night," I said with a sigh.

"Well then, you know she loved you very much."

"Conny, I appreciate everything she has done for me but, honestly, she didn't even know me."

"But she did. Minta knew everything about you. She knew when you graduated from Stanford, when you received your doctorate from Harvard, and when you landed your first job at the museum. She even knew when you got engaged to that 'poser,' as she called him. What was his name? Lewis, Lenny?"

"Lucas," I offered.

"That's the one!"

"Huh. You know all about me," I said in wonder.

"How could I not, dear? If you were friends with Minta, you

knew all about her granddaughter Windsor." She glanced at a large gold watch strapped to her wrist. "Oops, I'm going to be late for my yoga class. You be sure and let me know if I can do anything for you, dear. I am thrilled you've returned to Darkly."

With a smile, the old woman sashayed back onto the street.

I was dumbstruck. Grandmother followed my life—every single twist and turn—and she was proud of me. I wasn't angry at Dad for not telling me. I knew he thought he was doing the right thing but, at the same time, he should have told me about Grandmother and Darkly.

I wiped a stray tear from my cheek. This week was turning out to be a big ol' jumbled-up box of surprises.

After a day of constant—yet amusing—interruptions, I discovered exactly what it meant to move to a small Southern town. As I turned the sign to "CLOSED," sitting on my counter were: thirteen jars of pickled, preserved, whisked, or stewed fruits and jams; one lemon pound cake; two chess pies; four devil's food cakes and one angel food cake; chocolate chip, sugar, and snickerdoodle cookies; along with one extravagantly designed mud pie from little Bettina Starles. How was I ever going to get all these desserts home?

I pulled out my phone to give Tzazi a ring, hoping she'd have time to lend me a hand, when the door jingled, and Jessamin Wilde scurried into the store. She hovered by the door, her face strained and flushed as her eyes darted fearfully around the shop.

"Hi Jessamin," I said cheerily. "How are —"

At the sound of my voice, she darted back out the door.

Oh, my gosh! What had I done to spook her?

I heaved myself over the counter for a better view of the sidewalk outside the door. Shadows of passersby flowed behind her, but Jessamin stood motionless outside the shop, still as stone.

I waited a moment to see if she would come back in, but when she didn't, I pushed myself back to the floor and tidied up the front counter.

The door jingled once more, and I looked up to see Jessamin

again. She made her way towards me with slow, cautious steps, as if she wasn't sure if she was going to run again.

"I didn't do it," she said in a whisper.

I dipped my head closer to hers. "Pardon?"

"I didn't kill Dorian," she said in a louder voice.

At that very moment, Boddy Grim passed in front of the windows of the shop. He paused and peered through the multicolored glass. Seeing Jessamin, his look turned to one of distaste. I felt a rush of anger. That bully was really pissing me off!

Jessamin gasped and took a step to run from the bookshop again.

Recalling Grandmother's words last night, I reached over and clutched Jessamin's wrist. "I know you didn't," I said.

Her wide eyes met mine. "Really?"

I nodded and patted the stool next to mine. "Absolutely."

Her face lit up. "That's what I was hoping you'd say."

"Do you have any idea who may have killed Dorian?"

She shook her head, fiddling with a plastic fork next to a jar of boysenberry jam. "Not really. Everyone disliked him, so it could have been just about anyone."

"Hmm," I said. "That doesn't make it very easy then, does it?"

She looked up curiously. "Make what easy?"

"Figuring out who killed Dorian, so we can get Mr. Grumpity-Grim off your back." I said, hooking a thumb toward the window where Boddy had passed by.

"Do you think we could?"

"Of course," I said. "Tell you what. Why don't we get together tonight and come up with a plan?"

Her face fell. "I have to work tonight. What about tomorrow?"

"Perfect," I said, handing Jessamin a sugar cookie, while I took a bite of one myself. "We can meet at your house, if that would be easiest."

As soon as the words were out of my mouth, Jessamin's face crumpled, and I remembered what Tzazi had told me last night.

"Or actually," I added quickly, "we should meet at Fernwood, since I have all these goodies." I spread my hands over the haul on the counter. "Wouldn't want all this to go to waste. That is, if I can figure out how to get it all home."

"I can help you there," Jessamin said, pulling a set of keys from her pocket and jangling them in my face. "My car's out front. It's the least I can do."

After I finished closing the shop, I picked up as many jam jars as I could carry and stepped outside. My jaw dropped when I saw the black convertible Bentley parked at the curb. What on earth was Jessamin doing driving a Bentley? And a new one at that?

I quashed my look of amazement and tilted my head toward the open backseat. "Back here?" I squeaked. Yeah, that sounded natural.

"That's fine," Jessamin said, ducking back inside to grab more welcoming gifts.

We filled the back seat with the remaining items, and I yelled for Pyewacket, who was sleeping in a cat bed on top of a bookcase. Piling into the car, we drove to Fernwood.

Jessamin passed the front driveway and turned onto a narrow lane leading straight back to the kitchen area.

"How did you know about this driveway?" I asked.

"Anyone Minta considered a friend was told to use it," Jessamin said. "In fact, she called it her Friends' Entrance."

"Why didn't Tzazi use it? Does she not know about it?"

"Oh, she knows about it. I'm sure she just wanted you to see Fernwood the way it was meant to be seen."

As we began unloading the desserts, Hilde hurried down from her apartment to see what was going on and, of course, stayed to help. By the time we finished, desserts covered the entire center island of the kitchen.

"Well, my, my," Hilde said, hands on hips, as she surveyed the bounty on the counter. "Seems you've made quite the impression on Darkly."

She looked at me warmly over her glasses, and I grinned like an elementary school student with straight A's.

"I best be going. But tomorrow night, right?" Jessamin chewed on her bottom lip, gazing at me. I knew she was afraid I'd changed my mind.

"Definitely. And I'll supply all the desserts you can eat," I said.

With an excited grin, Jessamin ran to her car and hopped inside.

I waved until the brake lights disappeared. When I turned to head back into the house, I found Hilde staring at me from the back porch.

"What?" I asked.

"Minta was right," she said quietly. "Damned if that woman still isn't always right."

CHAPTER 12

After dinner, Hilde excused herself to her apartment to catch up on her "stories." Apparently, "stories night" consisted of binge-watching all the episodes of *EastEnders* from the previous week, while sipping scotch and eating whole, unsalted walnuts.

Left to ourselves, Pye and I sat on the kitchen counter as I tossed strawberries, blueberries, and chunks of melon into a bowl in preparation to watch a movie.

"More melon," he directed, swishing his tail back and forth, knocking over a vase full of wildflowers Hilde had placed on the counter.

"You know, you're turning into a little dictator," I said, catching the vase before it crashed to the floor. Still, as ordered by his majesty, I cut up a few more pieces of melon and tossed them into the bowl.

"How's that, your royal highness?" I quipped.

I cleaned up the kitchen, grabbed a bottle of water from the ice box, and we headed to the sitting room with our snack.

I pulled the newspaper article I had found in the conservation lab out of my bag and curled up on the sofa. Now, what was this about?

DARKLY ELDER CORRUPT TO THE CORE?
A Tell-All by the Beautiful Beatrice Snarkle

The construction of Dorian Wilde's posh new hotel, Dorian Interworldly Hotel, on Alligator Point, Darkly Island, has hit a snag. Investors accuse the businessman of misappropriation of funds and self-dealing. According to sources in the Magical Enforcement Agency, construction on the multi-million-dollar luxury hotel is halted until a thorough criminal investigation has reached its conclusion. Wilde, Beta of the Silverfang Clan, owns businesses across the Charming Isles and in New Orleans, Louisiana.

"Well, well, well, Dorian. Why am I not surprised?"

I tossed the paper onto the coffee table and relaxed back into the sofa with my water.

As the theme song to *The Cat Returns* wafted from the speakers, Pye leaped onto the coffee table and rolled his eye.

"Oh great," he deadpanned. "A talking cat movie."

"Stop it," I said. "I love this movie."

I waved off his negative vibe and wrapped the blanket around me.

Pye dipped his head into the bowl, emerging with a bright red berry clutched in his mouth. Dropping it on the table, he hunched down and gently nibbled the strawberry.

Oh, my gosh! So adorable! But I wasn't about to tell him that.

"By the way, has anyone ever told you that you sound like Tom Hardy?" I asked, popping a blueberry in my mouth and curling back into the sofa.

Pye turned his eye to me as he continued to chew.

"Or maybe a bit like Rob Pattinson."

Chewing an excessive number of times, he finally swallowed and then cleaned his face with his paw.

"I've been told Laurence Olivier and Sir John Gielgud many times. But Tom Hardy is a first. Who's Rob Pattinson?"

I rolled my eyes. "Don't worry. They're both dreamboats."

Pye snorted. "Naturally." Hopping to a spot next to me on the couch, he spread out on his side, head facing the tv, and batted a paw at me.

"You know, you're awfully snarky for a magical cat," I said as I rubbed his full belly.

"If you could understand other cats, you'd find we're all snarky," he purred.

"What do you think about getting a dog?"

He batted my hand away. "Bugger off. I'm trying to watch the movie."

Chuckling, I scratched his ears instead.

Suddenly, he jumped up, muscles taut, ears rigid.

"Pye?"

"Shhh!" he hissed.

My pulse quickened, and I paused the movie, moving to the edge of the sofa.

Suddenly, I heard it: a light scratching sound, like fingernails on a window screen, and then farther away, a steady slapping of the water.

Pye leaped to the floor and dashed toward the kitchen, hissing, "Stay here!" in a voice that rumbled like thunder.

The voice threw me for a moment, but I shook it off and sprinted out the door behind him.

Stumbling through the dark, I rounded the back of the kitchen and stood next to a short wooden dock. A boat, tied to one of the pilings, bobbed gently on the water.

As my eyes adjusted, I scanned the nearby area for Pye. The silence was unnerving, and he was nowhere to be seen.

As I turned back toward the house, in the still air, my footsteps crunching through the grass seemed as loud as firecrackers.

Across the driveway, a stone shed caught my attention. Its brown door stood ajar, and from within came the curious scratching sound I heard earlier.

I hurried to the shed and flung open the wood door.

"Pye!" I exclaimed as he pushed past my feet and darted from the shed, a brown bundle in his mouth.

He raced past the dock, and I heard a slap as something hit the water, followed by a much more resounding splash. The water around the dock rippled wildly.

When he returned, his one eye blinked at me. "What part of 'stay here' did you not understand?"

"Pye, what just happened? What did you throw in the water?"

"Vermin. Now go back into the house!" he replied angrily.

"Pyewacket! What's going on?" I said, following him into the shed. When I pulled the chain of an overhead bulb, darkness gave way to light, and I found him filling in a hole that had been dug in the corner.

"You aren't telling me anything. What are you doing?"

"Tidying up."

I gave a deep sigh, shaking my head. I doubted he had raced out of the house as if his life depended on it just to catch a rat. But I gave up trying to get any information from him, instead gazing around the walls of the shed. Paint cans, tools, and gardening supplies filled the shelves.

My eyes settled on a wicker basket toward the back. Investigating, I discovered it was strapped to a mint green bicycle.

Rolling it out of the shed, I looked at Pye, who was sitting on the railing of the back porch staring toward the swamp.

"Why didn't you tell me Grandmother had a bike?"

He shrugged. "You didn't ask."

"Oh, quit being mad at me," I said, sliding onto the seat. I pedaled to the road and back, then stopped in front of him.

"This is great!" I said. "No more walking for us!"

"I'll alert the media," he drawled. "Can we now finish the movie? I am dying to know if Prince Lune marries Haru."

"I knew it!" I teased, rolling the bike onto the porch and leaning it against the house. "You like talking cat movies!"

After we returned to the house, Pye stayed closer to me than usual. He watched as I locked the deadbolts, then followed me back into the sitting room.

"Want a blueberry?" I asked, unpausing the movie.

Pye stuck his tongue out at me. I wasn't sure whether that meant yes or no, so I slid one over to him, quickly pulling my hand away, so he couldn't stab me with a claw, or five. Hey, I'm not stupid!

I glanced over at him as he nibbled and played with the blueberry. His actions tonight confused me. Something spooked him, and I couldn't shake the feeling that whatever happened back there had more to do with me than some rat hiding out in the shed. I knew he wouldn't talk to me about it, at least not now —but why?

Pye saw me looking and leaped over to the couch to curl up next to me. I guess we were okay.

We finished the movie, and no matter what Pye might say otherwise, he loved it!

After I'd checked all the locks again, I scooped him up and headed to the bedroom. I gulped down the last of the elixir from Ileana and marveled at my healed and pain-free ankle, rotating my foot from side to side.

I climbed into bed and leaned against the headboard. The light in the swamp was already casting its glow across the water. With a sigh of contentment, I slid under the sheets and fell fast asleep.

THE NEXT MORNING, I straddled my new bike and pleaded with Pye as he parked himself on the back porch, refusing to budge.

"It's going to be fine. I promise. How about if I give you extra treats tonight?"

His eye narrowed. "I'd prefer a scoop of Cherry Garcia."

"Done," I said, patting the basket.

Pye took a step. "Two scoops."

"Fine. Two."

"Three."

"Pye!"

"Okay! You don't have to yell!" he snarled and jumped into the basket.

By the time we reached the bookshop, Darkly was abuzz with a turn of events concerning Dorian's murder. Overnight there had been another arrest, but from the fragmented sidewalk chatter, I couldn't discern who exactly had been arrested.

In the MET, Pye hopped up on the counter as I tossed my bag beneath it.

"I'll be glad when you learn how to use your magic. I think I'm going to be carsick," he complained, sticking out his tongue and pretending to gag.

"You are such a terrible actor," I said. "I'm going to Azalea's. Want anything?"

"Naturally. Can you get me a large, steamed almond milk with a pump of cinnamon dolce syrup?" he said, swishing his tail back and forth. "Oh, and make sure they hold the dolce sprinkles. Last time she added them, I was sneezing out little colored candies from my nose for a week."

I laughed and shook my head. I would never get used to a talking cat, especially one as demanding as this one.

When I stepped into The Magic Cup, the chatter was far louder and more excited than usual. Keir stood by the display case, holding a large cup, talking to Solara, as she smiled and fluttered her long eyelashes. My heart plummeted, but I took my place in line, trying to not look in his direction.

He glanced toward the exit, and our eyes met. His face brightened and—to my amazement—he said a few more quick words to Solara and strolled to where I stood in line. I didn't have the courage to look in her direction. But I did wonder what magical powers she held, and whether I was in mortal danger at that moment. She wouldn't dare in such a crowded room, would she? Tzazi did say she was crazy.

"Morning, Win," Keir said.

"Hi." I replied, shifting uncomfortably. Why did this man make me as nervous as a crushing schoolgirl?

"Did Boddy Grim really arrest Dorian's murderer?"

Keir frowned. "I dinnae know that he's arrested the murderer, but he has made another arrest. Fernando Mayór. Grim took him in this morning."

"Really?" I stood dumbfounded.

Tzazi elbowed her way in next to us. I guess being the owner's daughter had its privileges.

"Did you hear?" she asked.

"Ladies, I need to get going," Keir said abruptly. "Win, good to talk to you. Tzazi."

He looked at me for a second longer, then pushed his way out the door, greeting everyone he passed.

I tore my eyes away and turned to Tzazi. "I did. Tzazi, Mayor Mayór came to my shop for a few minutes yesterday. Could he really be the murderer?"

I thought back to everything the Mayor and I had discussed. He seemed so normal. Well, as normal as anyone in Darkly could be. Wouldn't a murderer seem more murderer-y?

"A witness saw the Mayor running from the scene," Tzazi said.

I frowned. "I was right there, and I didn't see or hear anyone."

Tzazi shrugged. "Depending on the witness, that's pretty good evidence, Win."

"Maybe you're right," I conceded, but deep down, I didn't think so. "That reminds me. What's the deal with the bells? I went into the tower after I found Dorian. No one was there."

"The bells tolled because Dorian died. It's an old spell. The bells only toll when something dark happens. That's how the town got its name."

"Can't someone remove it? Or replace it with a spell that causes the bells to toll when something good happens?"

Tzazi shook her head. "Many have tried. Minta even tried. No one's succeeded."

When we finally made it to the front of the line, I placed my orders, half expecting a laugh from the barista for Pye's goofy drink request. As she prepared them, Tzazi and I continued to chat. I wished I had thought to ask Jessamin if we should invite Tzazi. I didn't want to do so without talking to Jessamin first, but I thought it'd be a good idea to have an attorney on-hand to help with any legal issues. Plus, to be honest, I really liked Tzazi.

Drinks in hand, Tzazi and I said goodbye, and I walked back into the bookshop. I poured Pye's drink into the saucer on the counter and watched for a minute as he lapped it up.

"Boddy Grim arrested Fernando Mayór for Dorian's murder. A witness saw him running away from the murder scene," I said, sitting down on one of the nearby stools.

Pye raised his head. "Now that's interesting."

"Do you think he did it?" I asked, rummaging around in the drawer for a hand towel. Pye may have been prissy, but that didn't prevent him from also being messy.

"Not a chance," he answered, cleaning his whiskers with a paw. "Fernando might have wanted to kill Dorian, but he wouldn't have."

He stuck his nose back in the saucer, and I readied my towel.

"How can you be so sure?" I asked him.

"Because he won Lilith back. And what fun is a win if you can't rub it in the loser's face?"

"That's a good point, Pye."

"Naturally," he purred as I scratched him lightly behind the ears.

CHAPTER 13

*L*ater that afternoon, I'd just created a new inventory sheet and hopped off the front desk stool when the door opened and Lilith Mayór swept into the shop in a flowing floral skirt and red wrap top tied at the waist.

"Lilith!" I exclaimed in surprise.

"Hello, Win," she said, approaching the counter. "I know we don't know each other well, but I need to ask you for a favor." She gripped the strap of her straw summer handbag between clenched fists and looked around the shop before turning back to me. "I hope you don't mind."

I'd never noticed her light accent before—husky and alluring —and as she advanced closer to me, I felt mysteriously drawn to her, almost as if I had developed a sudden fascination or obsession with the woman.

I shook it off, letting the inventory sheet fall to the counter. Patting the seat next to me, I invited Lilith to sit. No doubt this had something to do with Fernando's imprisonment, but I had no idea what she thought I could possibly do about it.

"I've heard you are helping Boddy solve the murders."

Laughing, I said, "Well, I wouldn't say that. I don't believe Boddy is happy with my interference."

She nodded and tossed her long hair back behind her shoulder, throwing one long leg over the other. Long, black stiletto heels graced her tiny feet.

"In any case, I know you are looking into it. Windsor, Fernando didn't kill Dorian. It's not in him to commit such horrors. In fact, I can vouch for him. I was with my husband at the time someone killed that awful man. In Oakspider Park. Fer was dedicating a statue to himself!"

I cringed at the park name—I had a complete and total fear of spiders—but the distress in her voice was clear. However, why hadn't I heard anything about a town statue dedication? Wouldn't that have drawn quite a few townspeople?

Suddenly, I realized what she had just said and scrunched up my brows. "To himself?"

"Yes." She shrugged her shoulders.

"This is the first I've heard of this. Were there many people there?"

"Unfortunately not. Fer dedicates so many statues to himself, no one bothers to attend anymore. Except me, and sometimes Jaime."

I bit my lip and thought. "Was Jaime there for this one?"

She nodded emphatically. "Yes, he was. Fernando persuaded him. Fer was very proud of this statue. It was for 'Best Dressed Mayor.' He wanted his son to be there for the honor."

"And he really awarded it to himself?" I asked, suppressing a laugh.

"Of course," she said, smiling sadly at me and sighed. "All I ask is that you prove who killed Dorian. Fernando had nothing to do with his death."

"I promise I'll do what I can, Lilith."

She nodded, moved to the door, and turned to face me once more.

"Fernando may be a silly man, Windsor, but he's no killer," she said. Her floral skirt billowed from the breeze outside and then the door closed firmly behind her.

TOLLING BELLS & DARK SPELLS

I picked up the blank inventory sheet again. Almost no one believed Mayor Mayór killed Dorian—but, if the alibi held, here was actual proof he hadn't committed the murder. I put my investigation thoughts on hold, concentrating on the tasks at hand. I had loads to do today and needed to get started.

After climbing the stairs up to the second-floor gallery, I examined each volume for tears, mold, or infestation. Grandmother had assured me the books needing repair would show up in the lab on their own, but what if the spell didn't work? What if my presence caused the spells to go as wacky as my own magic seemed to be? I wasn't taking any chances.

Thankfully, I found I had no reason to worry, as each leather-bound book I examined was in pristine condition, especially considering the ages of these books. Nevertheless, I couldn't resist continuing my inspection. Getting back to doing what I loved was calming and gave me a chance to see what books the shop held. How exciting to know each one held an adventure, not only within its pages, but also in real life!

By lunch, I was starving, so I decided to head over to the Green Gator for a quick sandwich. When I couldn't find Pye, I guessed he was asleep in the stacks somewhere, so I poured kibble into his saucer, locked the front door, and sauntered down to the tavern.

Across from the Gator, a large blue wand puffing out the name of Chase's and Lorenzo's salon, Spells & Gels, caught my attention. I had a change of thought. Even though my stomach was rumbling, I wanted to see how soon Chase could work me into his schedule. My hair needed a trim and my mahogany highlights were looking dreadfully dull, no doubt from their swamp water encounter.

As I pushed open the door, the smell of perm chemicals, dye, and shampoo tickled my nose. The salon bustled with customers and boisterous chitchat. Now this is my kind of place, I thought, until I glanced at the shampoo station—where Solara sat; her long, glorious mane tipped back into a shampoo bowl.

I quickly stepped up to the bright reception desk where a young woman with lavender braids sat. She gave me a big smile and closed the magazine she was reading.

"Hi, there. Can I help you?"

"Does Chase have any openings soon for a trim and highlights refresh?"

"Sure. Let me see."

"Windsor Ebonwood!" I turned to find the owner himself, who clasped my hands and gave me a kiss on either cheek. "What a delightful surprise, ma chéri! Come to take me to lunch?"

I laughed. "Maybe. But what I need first is an appointment. These highlights need some pepping up."

Chase turned to the desk. "Ariel, put Windsor Ebonwood down during my lunch break tomorrow." He turned to me. "Does that work?"

"Oh no, Chase! Don't do that." I looked at Ariel. "Just give me next available."

Chase patted my arm. "My next available is in two months. Those highlights can't wait that long. Besides, it's my pleasure. Give us some time to get to know each other better."

"Okay then. I'd love that. And thank you, Chase."

He smiled and slipped his arm in mine. "Now about lunch."

BEFORE WE'D EVEN OPENED the door of the Green Gator, we could hear the loud chatter inside.

Phenny Guthrie gave us our menus and a table in the corner, a perfect spot for people watching.

"Chase," I began carefully. "I saw Solara Nova in your salon. Is she a regular customer?"

"Ugh," he said, banging his head on the table. "Solara Nova is the bane of my being. Nothing is ever right. Nothing is ever good enough." He raised his head. "You have made the acquaintance of Ms. Nova, I take it?"

"No," I admitted. "However, she was giving me plenty of dirty looks the other night when we were here."

"Ah, yes. The woman is ridiculously jealous of anyone she believes Keir is interested in. But she brought it all on herself. Keir Bain's the perfect man—intelligent, handsome, and sexy as all get-out."

I laughed at Chase but definitely agreed.

"Too bad he plays for the wrong team," Chase said with a melodramatic sigh.

A sudden raucous shriek filled the room, and we turned to see Maenad Grog alone at the end of the bar, clutching a pint to her chest. She stared transfixed at a soccer game playing out on the large flat screen on the wall above her.

Chase followed my gaze.

"You know, she's not like people say," he said. "She may not have the best of manners, but Mae always means well. In fact, I meet her here often. We're both big soccer fans."

Maenad jumped up, spilling her drink down the front of her blouse as she pumped her fist in the air, shouting and whooping in excitement. She grabbed a bar towel and absentmindedly dabbed it against her chest, while the soccer fans in the seats next to her covered their ears.

"She's something of a fanatic," Chase grinned.

"That's an understatement." I rolled my eyes. "Hey, why don't you invite her to eat lunch with us?"

"You sure?" Chase asked hesitantly. "You don't need to do that."

"I want to. I'd love to meet her."

Chase trotted to the bar, where Mae still celebrated her team's win by punching the guy next to her. The man smiled at her ruefully, massaging his arm.

After listening to Chase for a minute, Mae nodded her head enthusiastically and followed him back to our table.

Chase introduced us and Mae took a seat at the table just as Phenny Guthrie arrived to take our lunch orders. I ordered a

Cajun turkey sandwich and sweet tea, then relaxed in my seat as Chase and Mae placed their orders.

Mae turned to me. "You like soccer?"

"I do, but I really don't understand the rules very well."

"I can help you with that," she said. "You should join me and Chase for the next match. Right, Chase?"

Chase gave her a thumbs up, just as Phenny set our drinks and a large platter of thick, crispy fried yellow disks in front of us. Mae accepted her pint and immediately took a large gulp.

"What in the world?" I said, pointing at the platter. Chase picked up a disk with his fingers and took a big bite.

"Plantains. Kind of like bananas, but better," he mumbled. "Thank you, Phenny."

"My pleasure, Chase. I know they're your favorite," she said before moving on to the table next to us.

Chase pushed the platter in my direction and nodded his encouragement.

Following his lead, I picked up one of the caramelized disks and tentatively took a tiny bite along the edge. The taste was smooth and savory, its crispy texture, sweet as sugar.

"Mmmmm," I moaned. "Mae, wouldn't you like one?"

She raised her pint. "No, thank you. I'm quite good."

Chase looked at me with a sad twist of his mouth.

"Did y'all hear I caught the murderer?" Mae asked, a wide grin spread across her ruddy face.

Chase and I both choked on our plantains.

He recovered first and asked, "Mae, what do you mean?"

She waved her arms in the air. "I remembered I saw the Mayor running away after he killed Dorian."

I whispered to Dorian, "So that's why he was arrested."

"But see here." Mae swallowed another large gulp of her pint. "The mistake the murderer made was dropping the evidence. I picked it right up. After I heard about Dorian, I put two and two together and went straight to ol' Boddy with my evidence."

"You found evidence?" Chase asked, his eyes wide.

"I found evidence," Mae nodded smugly.

I couldn't stand the suspense any longer. "What did you find?"

"Dorian's sunglasses, dripping with blood," she said triumphantly.

"Huh," I said, tapping my finger on my lip. "That's interesting."

Something didn't seem right with Mae's story, but what?

"Carter says I'm a hero," Mae said, lifting her head high. "I don't think I've ever been called a hero before. And these are free for life," she added, lifting her mug into the air.

"Well, congratulations, Mae," I said, and I meant it sincerely. The old dear deserved this bit of luck. "We'll all sleep better tonight knowing Dorian's murderer is off the streets." Mae's eyes shined with pride.

"You're a regular Nancy Drew," Chase added.

Mae's eyes grew wide. "Who?"

WE FINISHED our meal in quiet conversation and by the time we parted, I realized I liked Maenad Grog a lot.

But I couldn't fight the feeling that something didn't ring true about her story. What had she said that was rubbing me the wrong way?

Chase insisted that for all her obvious faults, the one thing Maenad was not was a liar. I could see that. Maenad was a very what-you-see-is-what-you-get kind of person. I didn't believe she'd lie about seeing the Mayor with the evidence if she hadn't.

But I also couldn't see Mayor Mayór climbing up the bell tower and pushing Dorian off the edge. Even if Dorian had been caught off guard, wouldn't he have had the upper hand against the Mayor? The only person we knew for sure was up on that bell tower terrace was Dorian Wilde. And what was he doing up there anyway?

There was one other aspect of the murder that had me utterly perplexed. When the body fell, when I climbed the tower, and when I ran to the road, I saw no one. And yet, obviously, somebody was there.

∽

I SPENT the rest of the day sweeping and mopping the hardwood floors in the shop. Once they were gleaming, I packed up my bag and locked up.

I slid onto the seat of Grandmother's bicycle as Pye hopped into the wicker basket fastened to the handlebars. He hunkered down and glared at me with his yellow eye. "Do you think you could try to miss a few bumps this time?" he complained.

"Do you want to walk or ride, cat?" I asked him, pushing the bike onto the cobbled street.

"Wait! Wait!" I heard behind me and was surprised to see Phenny Guthrie rushing up with a large brown bag dangling from her hand.

"I'm glad I caught you," she said, panting heavily. "Hilde called and asked me to bring you this." Whatever it was smelled delicious.

"Thank you, Phenny," I called to her retreating back. Every time I saw the woman, she was rushing somewhere. I wondered if the woman ever took some time to relax as I placed the bag next to Pye before finally pushing off on my bike.

I breathed in the thick, sweet scent of the island's flowers as I pedaled home. I hoped the ride would clear my mind. Instead, I puzzled over Dorian's murder—in particular, Mae's role in it all.

According to her, she saw the mayor running away from the scene, clutching Dorian's sunglasses. But didn't that seem ludicrous? Why steal the glasses and make himself the obvious suspect? It wasn't like they were expensive or held sentimental value to Mayor Mayór, not that I knew of.

I didn't believe Mae was lying, but I also didn't believe her story was true. But how could both statements be fact?

CHAPTER 14

I was still puzzling over the contradictions as Pye and I rolled up to Fernwood. He leapt out of the basket and scampered up onto the back porch. Grabbing my satchel along with the Green Gator bag, I followed him to the back door and into the kitchen.

"Thank you, dear," Hilde grumbled, when I placed the bag on a cleared space among the desserts. "Do you want to eat early or wait until Jessamin gets here?"

"Definitely wait," I said, retreating to my bedroom. "I'm going to get cleaned up."

After a quick shower, I changed into sweatpants, plus a large comfy top, and plopped down on one of the sofas in the sitting room. I flipped on the TV but ignored it to gaze out the windows overlooking the swamp. Dark, threatening clouds crept over the bald cypress lining the pond on the far side.

Hilde entered, placing a tray with two large wine glasses and a pitcher of sangria on the coffee table. I gestured to the windows. "Looks like we have another storm coming in."

"Well, we are in hurricane season," she growled. "I better go round back and make sure the boat's tacked down. Wouldn't want to find it on the other side of the swamp tomorrow."

I sat up straighter. "The small boat docked behind the kitchen?"

"That's the one. Minta didn't use it often, but when she did, she'd go out into that swamp for hours. Come back with all kinds of herbs and plants for her spells. I'll only be a minute."

After Hilde disappeared out the back door, I wandered around the room, plumping up pillows while I sipped a glass of sangria. Remembering Grandmother's phonograph, I carried it from the music room and placed it on a wooden bureau next to the fireplace. I flipped it on, set the needle on the vinyl, and soon the sweet voice of Édith Piaf floated through the room.

After a few minutes, Hilde stomped back in and waved a tray of appetizers under my nose. Before she could stop me, I plucked a triangular wedge off the tray and popped it into my mouth.

"Mmmmm. What is this?" I asked with a full mouth as I reached for another.

Hilde swatted my hand away. "These are mini empanadas. Wait for your guest."

A sudden rap at the door startled me. I hopped up to answer it, but Hilde beat me to it. She looked through the curtain and then flung the door open.

Jessamin stood on the front porch, wearing an adorable pink sundress, a mischievous grin on her face.

"Look who I found!" she exclaimed

Tzazi popped out from behind her. "Me! I hope you don't mind."

"Of course not. Get in here you two."

Hilde closed the door, and I watched as she fastened all the deadbolts and latches. Why was Hilde suddenly being so cautious? Had she seen something at the dock?

"Looks like Fernwood is the place to be tonight," Hilde harrumphed. "Glad I made extra."

She left the room, returning shortly with another wine glass. "I'm going up and leaving you girls to it." She glanced at the clock. "My show starts in five minutes."

She took a step toward the kitchen, but then turned back to face us.

I set down my glass. "What is it, Hilde?"

"You know I don't like to get in anybody's business," she said. "However, you three need to be careful. I don't know what you're up to, but I do know there's some tricky business going on in Darkly right now. Dangerous business. You three need to stay out of it!"

"You don't have to worry about that, Hilde," I said, sighing with relief. For a moment, I had been afraid she was going to quit.

"Alright," she said, tipping her head at us. "Have fun. I'll see y'all in the morning."

"Thank you, Hilde! Goodnight!" we all called, then Tzazi pointed at the phonograph. "You found Minta's records."

"There are more? The Èdith album was already on the turntable. I guess it was the last record she listened to. I enjoy playing it. Makes me feel close to her. I, um, get the idea she loved music."

"She adored music," Jessamin said.

"And she could play the piano?" I asked.

Tzazi looked at me suspiciously. "Like a concert pianist. Why?"

I hesitated a moment. "What would you guys say if I told you I spoke to my grandmother last night, and she told me I was a witch?" I said hesitantly, taking a large gulp of sangria to hide my discomfort.

What if they thought I was crazy? What if I *was* crazy?

The room was silent for a moment. and I was just about to tell them I was joking when—

"Oh, thank goodness!" Jessamin burst out. "I almost let it slip a few times."

She threw an arm around my neck and gave me a hug.

"You both know?" I asked, relief flooding my body.

"Welcome to the club," Tzazi smiled, relaxing into the couch and popping an empanada into her mouth.

"You're witches too?"

"No, no," Jessamin said. "I'm a fairy—a hearth fairy, to be exact." Orange iridescent wings slipped from her back and unfolded before me.

"Your wings are beautiful," I whispered.

"Tzazi's talents are a little more exotic," Jessamin said with a grin.

Tzazi shrugged. "I'm a vampire."

I heard a crash and realized I had popped up from the sofa and dropped my glass—drenching myself, the floor, and the sofa in red wine, shards of glass, and fruit. The sound sent Pye flying onto the sofa from the library and Hilde running back down the stairs.

"Ah," she said, surveying the scene. "You told her."

Tzazi grinned. "She found out I was a vampire, and her drink exploded."

Hilde turned to me. "You sit, and I'll bring another glass. Jessamin, would you be a dear please and clean up that mess?"

Jessamin spread her arms as if directing a symphony, and I felt a sudden wash of warmth flow over me. When I looked down, the sparkling clean floors had returned, and the sofa and I were clean and dry. Not a speck of broken glass was to be seen.

"All done," Jessamin said, as Hilde returned with a new wine glass. She filled it and placed it in my hand. With a nod, she retired back up the stairs.

Jessamin sat me down on the couch and knelt beside me.

"You okay?" she asked, a worried look on her face.

I patted the spot on the sofa next to Pyewacket. "I'm fine. That was just ... unexpected. You seem so normal."

Jessamin giggled, as I gave Tzazi a huge grin to show her I was teasing. She rolled her eyes and then laughed herself.

"Seriously though," I said, "Is there any danger with all these supernaturals—people who, until a day ago, I never even thought existed—living together? What's stopping a werewolf from going on a rampage and killing everyone walking down the streets of Darkly?"

"What's stopping a human from gunning down innocent people at an outdoor concert?" Tzazi countered.

"Evil isn't in the species," Jessamin said. "It's in the individual, for both humans and supernaturals alike."

She took a sip of sangria and raised an eyebrow. "Although you have to admit, you hear about more vampires and werewolves going to the dark side than fairies or elves."

"I do not admit that!" Tzazi retorted. "Remember the Leanhaum-Shee who showed up on the Isle of Man a few years ago and killed about a dozen men? Fairy!"

"Oh, my stars!" I exclaimed.

Jess shook her head. "My point is—and thank you, Tzazi, for helping me make it—the only thing that matters is what's on the inside, whether or not you're magical."

"And I prefer being magical," Tzazi said and raised her glass in the air. "To magic!"

"To magic!" Jessamin and I repeated.

"Now let's catch a killer! But first, more sangria!"

As I waited for the pitcher to make its way around to me, I suddenly remembered today's event. "But the Mayor," I reminded them as I stroked Pyewacket's soft fur. "Boddy arrested the killer."

"Mayor Mayór didn't do it," Pye said.

"Fernando didn't kill Dorian any more than I did," Jessamin said. "Did Pyewacket just agree with me?"

I nodded.

"I don't know about that, Jess," Tzazi said. "Remember the affair? Fernando had to have been crazy angry. I can't believe he took Lilith back after all that. Plus, the Mayor is a fairy, with access to unlimited gold." She turned to me for a second. "He's a leprechaun."

I giggled. A leprechaun? Why was that not a surprise?

"And we all know the greediness that was Dorian Wilde. The

mayor could have lured him to the top of the clock tower and then, when Dorian was busy counting his gold, plowed into him and pushed him off the side."

"Pushed off the clock tower by a leprechaun. Yeah, that's plausible," I mumbled.

"Except that leprechauns are terrified of heights," Jessamin countered. "There's no way Fernando would ever go to the top of the clock tower."

"That is true," Tzazi conceded. "But Jess, someone saw him leaving the scene of the crime with the murder weapon."

"I wonder if he found it and picked it up after the fact," Jessamin said.

"But why do that?" I asked.

Jessamin shrugged.

"You know, I haven't heard yet who witnessed him running away from the scene," Tzazi said.

"Me neither."

"Oh, it was Maenad," I said, glad to offer some useful information.

"What?" Tzazi exclaimed.

"Oh no," Jessamin said with a grimace.

"Why 'Oh no?'" I asked.

"Maenad wouldn't lie about something like that. But I'm telling you. The mayor didn't do it." She shook her head. "None of this makes sense."

I had to agree with her.

"Then who do you think killed him, Jess?" Tzazi asked.

"I don't think. I know."

"What?" I sat up. "Who?"

"Solara Nova."

"Keir's ex-girlfriend?" I asked.

"That's the one." Tzazi poured herself another drink, then topped off our glasses.

"She-devil," Jessamin growled.

Jessamin crossed her legs on the couch and leaned forward.

"Listen. Keir and Dorian never got along, you know. Dorian saw Keir as a threat and always challenged everything he did as pack alpha. Oops. You're aware Keir is a shifter?"

"Yep," I said. "And I know Hilde's a werebear. She let the bear out of the bag last night."

"Huh?" Jessamin looked perplexed, while Tzazi chuckled and rolled her eyes. Pye quietly sniggered while pretending to sleep.

"Anyway," Jessamin continued. "A guy like Dorian can make someone's life hell if they choose to. I should know." She took a sip of her sangria. "When Keir and Solara were together, everyone knew she was cheating with a guy from Strawbridge."

"But no one had the heart to tell Keir," Tzazi added.

"One thing you have to understand about Dorian, he did nothing unless it benefitted him or hurt someone else," Jess said.

I nodded. "Hilde told me he was a troublemaker—always challenging Keir for pack leader."

"When none of the werewolves even wanted Dorian for their leader," Tzazi added. "They love Keir. He's a good alpha."

"Rather than being there for Keir, he used Solara's infidelity to humiliate and embarrass him," Jessamin continued. "Dorian planned a night out with Keir and all the guys and made sure they ended up at the same bar where Solara always met the Strawbridge guy. And guess what?"

"Oh, no! Poor Keir! They broke up after that?"

Jessamin nodded. "Right then and there. Ever since then, she hasn't stopped trying to get him back. By getting rid of Dorian, she kills two frogs with one stone—"

"Frogs?"

"—revenge on Dorian for breaking up her and Keir, along with brownie points for being the one to make Keir's life better."

"Hmm. Maybe," I said. "But wouldn't she have to tell Keir she killed Dorian to get the brownie points?"

Jessamin ran her finger around the top of her glass. "Perhaps she wouldn't be able to tell him she did it, but she could reap the benefits of Keir not having to deal with him anymore. Maybe she thinks if Keir's happier, then he'll be more receptive to taking her back? I haven't got it all worked out, but I'm telling you, she's the one."

Some of what Jessamin said made sense. People often killed for revenge over lost love. But if this were true, it also meant I needed to stay far, far away from Keir Bain, if I didn't want to end up next on Solara's list.

"So why does Boddy keep arresting people willy-nilly?" I asked. "It doesn't even seem as if he's conducting any type of investigation."

"Willy-nilly?" Tzazi asked.

"Be quiet," Jessamin chided her. "I like that word."

Tzazi laughed and said, "For centuries, Boddy was the grim reaper."

I gasped. "The grim reaper?"

"The grim reaper," Jessamin said.

I nodded. "I can see it."

"He's used to dealing in absolutes. When it's your time, it's your time. There's no such thing as a gray area. With Boddy, it's either black or it's white. He knows no other way to deal with the job," Tzazi said.

"The fact that everyone in town hated Dorian gives pretty much everyone a reason to want him gone," Jessamin said, her voice quivering. "Including me."

"We know you didn't do it," Tzazi and I said together, and then the three of us burst out laughing.

"What do you think about Keir being a werewolf?" Jessamin asked, once we had finally quieted down.

"Hmmm," I said. "Honestly, I'm not sure how I feel about it. Fairy? No problem. Vampire? Um, ok?" Tzazi raised an eyebrow. "But werewolf? I don't know. Especially a werewolf who may have killed one of his own pack members."

I refilled my glass and noticed the pitcher was still completely full, even though Jessamin and Tzazi had arrived here hours ago. Undoubtedly enchanted. I was going to enjoy this magic thing.

Tzazi threw a leg over the sofa arm. "One of his reckless and out-of-control pack members," she reminded me. "The Vampyr Assembly would never have stood for someone like Dorian's nonsense all these years."

"Is that like the Volturi in *Twilight*?" I asked.

Tzazi grinned and snapped her fangs into place. "Yes, but the real ones are much scarier," she said as she and Jessamin burst into laughter. Pye lifted his head and displayed his fangs.

"Stop that," I complained, but couldn't help but laugh. With her platinum pixie cut and beautiful features, Tzazi didn't look remotely scary, even with her fangs in place. Cool, yes. Scary, no. And Pye? The epitome of cuteness.

"Even my grandpa couldn't stand Dorian," Tzazi said with a light sigh. "And Papi likes everyone."

"Your grandpa lives here?" I asked.

"Of course. You've met him."

"I have?"

"The old man in the swamp. Mizizi," Tzazi said fondly.

"Mizizi's a vampire?"

Tzazi laughed. "Still worried about vampires? No, Papi's a voodoo priest."

"One of the most powerful in the Charming Isles," Jessamin added. "Most of the protections around Darkly were crafted by Mizizi. Including the ones on your shop."

"What would Mizizi have against Dorian?"

"You mean besides Dorian's natural horribleness?" Tzazi asked.

"Besides that." I grinned.

"When Dorian was in wolf form, he liked to harass and kill Papi's chickens. Dorian enjoyed prowling the swamps, looking for someone to chase. He thought anyone was fair game."

"That means Dorian could have been the creature chasing me in the swamp," I said slowly.

Jessamin nodded. "I was pretty sure it was him when Tzazi told me about it."

"There's also Keir," I said. "He could have killed Dorian for all the same reasons as Solara."

"Keir? Never! Hun, he wouldn't hurt a fly. Plus he's got that fantastic accent."

"You realize you just said a werewolf leader wouldn't hurt a fly," I said.

"You don't know Keir," Tzazi said. "Well, not yet anyway." She winked at me. "Keir comes from were-royalty. It's just not in his nature. Solara, however? As much as I hate to agree with Jess, I wouldn't put it past her. But Keir? Personally, I think you're just trying to find a reason to not like him."

"What kind of supernatural is Solara?" I asked, steering the conversation back into safe territory.

"Goddess," Jessamin said.

"Half-goddess," Tzazi interjected.

"Doesn't that just figure?" I grumbled.

"Do y'all know how Dorian was killed?" Tzazi suddenly asked.

"I'm guessing it was the chunk of pointy granite impaled through his chest," I said.

Jessamin paled.

"Oh, Jessamin," I grabbed her hand. "I'm so sorry. I wasn't thinking."

"It's fine," she said. "It's just all so surreal. Dorian wasn't a nice person, but he was Brychen's brother. I'm sad in that regard. But it's true. We don't know for sure how he died, do we?"

"We need to get Grim's death report," Tzazi said.

"How, though? He'd never give it to us," I said.

Jessamin and Tzazi both grinned at me.

"What?" I asked.

"Do you know what one of the coolest talents of a vampire is?" Jessamin asked.

I shook my head. "Draining all the local cows of blood?" Jessamin snorted, but Tzazi pointedly ignored my comment.

"A vampire can make others do what she wants them to do,"

she said. "It's a powerful talent. One I rarely use, of course. But in this circumstance, I think it's warranted."

"When we were around ten years old," Jessamin said, "I encouraged Tzazi to mesmer Mr. Sugarloaf so he'd give us an extra scoop on our ice cream cones, but she wouldn't. I was mad at her for days."

Tzazi laughed. "And that is an example of when it was not warranted."

"Seriously though," Jessamin said, "we need to do it soon."

"Tomorrow morning then," Tzazi said. "Anyone want to go with?"

"Can't," Jessamin said. "Working double shifts again tomorrow."

"I can," I said.

"Cool," Tzazi grinned.

"We can meet back here tomorrow evening to tell you what we found, Jess," I said.

"Sounds good!"

That settled, I held up the pitcher. "Another drink anyone?"

"Last one," Jessamin said and held out her glass. "Then I really have to go. I'm opening the Gator tomorrow, even though Carter hasn't paid me in over a week."

"What?"

Jess shrugged. "He said there was a mixup at the bank. I'm sure it'll get sorted soon."

"You know, Jessamin, you're welcome to stay at Fernwood whenever you like," I said as I refilled her glass. "Both of you are," I added quickly.

I moved to the settee to freshen Tzazi's drink.

"I know," Jessamin said. "And I appreciate it. But it really works out just fine with me staying at the Gator right now. As soon as a room opens at White Hart Inn, I'll move in there."

"As long as you're sure," Tzazi said. "Maman and I have room as well."

"I'm sure," Jessamin said. "But thank you for caring."

When I walked my friends to their cars an hour later, the rain had abated to a drizzle, drawing out the nighttime calls of bullfrogs and crickets. I watched as the taillights disappeared in the distance, then withdrew into the house, bolting and locking the door the way Hilde had done earlier.

Rinsing our dishes and placing them in the sink, I wondered again at Hilde's urgency in bolting so many locks. She seemed almost... not scared but... concerned. Had she seen something while checking the boat earlier?

CHAPTER 15

The next morning at the MET, I was evaluating the medieval manuscripts in the first-floor gallery when the now-familiar jangle of the bells sounded. Preparing to scold Tzazi roundly for her early arrival before our lunchtime adventure, I rolled out from the stacks on my library stool and met a choking mouthful of rippling, iridescent fabric.

Astonished, I spat the material out of my mouth, as a nasally voice said, "I thought I'd check on your progress. You know, with all of this being so new to you."

Before me stood Solara Nova, standing as though she were posing for the cover of Vogue. One hand curled primly in the air, the other gripped a melting triple-scoop ice cream cone. Her eyes roamed around the shop, then stopped on me.

Good grief! What a drama queen!

As I stifled a laugh and stood, the door opened again and Jaime Mayór strode in behind her. He waved a feeble hand at me.

Pasting on my brightest smile, I said, "Nice of you both to drop in, but do you think you could take that cone outside?" I waved up to the portals lining the bookshelves. "These are books, after all."

Solara ignored me. Cocking her head, she smiled. I had to admit the woman was drop dead gorgeous.

"I'm Solara Nova," she said.

"Hi. I'm —"

"I know who you are," she said, stepping farther into the shop. "Here, Jaime. Take my bag."

To my surprise, Jaime stepped forward, allowing Solara to hang a tiny sparkling wristlet on his finger. I gazed at him curiously, but his eyes remained fixed on the half-goddess as she glided over to the counter where Pye's saucers sat. She ran a finger down its gleaming surface, curling her lip when it came back clean.

"Can I help you with something?" I was trying to be cordial, but this woman was seriously weirding me out.

Solara turned and narrowed her eyes, drips from the cone now running down the back of her hand and splatting onto the thick Persian rugs.

"I just couldn't understand why everyone was making such a fuss about you. Quite frankly, now that I've met you, I still can't."

Okay, so this was the game we were playing. I headed back toward the closet, where I kept cleaning supplies. Solara trailed along behind me.

"I have work to do. Thanks for stopping by, Jaime," I said, giving him a nod.

"Now, Sol," Jaime began, the wristlet swinging on his finger, "let's just—"

"Don't!" She continued to face me, but sharply pointed a finger in his direction. Jaime shook his head and turned to the front glass.

"You were the one who supposedly found Dorian's body, weren't you?" Solara sniffed.

I raised an eyebrow. "There was no 'supposedly,' Solara."

She waved my words away. "It would have happened eventually. Everyone hated him."

Now she had my attention. I stopped my retreat and turned to face her.

"Even you?" I blurted out.

Solara stared at me for a few seconds.

"Especially me," she answered. "But you already knew that, didn't you?" A sly grin spread across her face as she circled around me. "You think I killed Dorian." She laughed. It was a dry, unfriendly cackle. "No one would ever believe you."

Oh, I knew a few who would.

Tossing the rest of her cone in a waste can by the counter, she moved back around to face me.

"For your information, Shitlock, I have an airtight alibi. I was shopping with Zelda Merryman in Strawbridge the day of the murder." She looked me up and down. "Something you might want to try."

Clothes again? I rolled my eyes.

"In my opinion," she continued, "you're the one Boddy needs to be looking at for Dorian's murder. You come to town and a day later, a man's murdered, and you were right there when it happened. What are you? A psycho? I have a feeling you're not as innocent as some people want to believe.

"With a little persuasion, I'm sure Boddy Grim would come around to my way of thinking. Here's some good advice. Stay out of my way, Windsor Ebonwood, if you know what's good for you."

With a flash of light, she disappeared, leaving poor Jaime to sputter his apologies and rush out of the shop, Solara's sparkly wristlet still swinging on his finger.

Tzazi charged into the bookshop around 11 a.m., nearly knocking the bell off the door and startling Pye into a frenzied leap straight up into the air.

I motioned to the book in my hand. "Look at this," I said,

placing it on the counter. "This is a 1623 compilation of William Shakespeare's plays. It's worth a fortune."

She shrugged and thumbed through the book. "Not surprised. Remember—the METs were created centuries ago. I'm sure most of the books are worth a lot."

"But what's stopping anyone from stealing these treasures?" I closed the book and lightly ran a gloved finger down the cover. "I'm going to have to lock this one up in a safe and add a security system. I can't believe Grandmother never did."

Tzazi laughed. "The MET is plenty secure."

"It is?" I looked around. "But I haven't seen a security alarm box."

"And you won't. No one in their right mind would ever steal from a portal shop. It's protected by enchantments that deliver an existence worse than death—enchantments layered on by every Ebonwood witch who ever lived. Not to mention a shadowman or two from Papi. You have nothing to worry about, Win. The MET is the safest place in all of Darkly."

The thought of shadowmen lurking around in the bookshop didn't make me feel better, but at least the portals were safe.

Closing the book, I removed my gloves and grabbed my jacket, bag, and coffee. "You ready?"

"Have coffee. Will travel," Tzazi said, tipping her cup in my direction.

I looked for Pye and found him curled back up in a basket. "You coming?"

He cocked his eye open, yawned, and then covered his face with his tail.

"I'll take that as a no."

BODDY GRIM'S office was in City Hall, a cluster of one-story brick buildings close to the docks. The sultry heat of the past few days had not yet emerged, and Tzazi and I enjoyed our stroll through downtown.

We stopped for a few minutes to peer into the windows of Giselle's, the local boutique where I gazed longingly at a formal gown created from iridescent pearls.

"It's lovely," I said, sighing.

"Hmm," Tzazi agreed. "But it reminds me of Solara's hair."

Ugh. Speaking of.

As I tore myself away and we continued our short walk to City Hall, I linked my arm through hers.

"Guess who I met early this morning?" I asked.

She released a dramatic sigh. "Keir's parents. You're getting married," she quipped.

"Close," I said. "Solara."

"Really?"

"Yep. She came by the MET."

"Oh, no," Tzazi said.

"It wasn't too bad. She only threatened me once."

"To stay away from Keir?"

"No, to stay away from her." I laughed. "When have I ever been around her by choice?"

Tzazi shook her head. "She's just flexing. Solara's so predictable. You'd think with a goddess for a mother, she'd have more confidence than to pull stunts like that."

"Maybe it's because of her mother that she acts the way she does," I considered. "Jaime Mayór came into the shop with her. He didn't seem too impressed with her behavior though."

"Jaime's too decent and intelligent for her. That won't last long," Tzazi said.

"You can tell Jess there's no way Solara killed Dorian, by the way. She was shopping in Strawbridge with someone named Zelda when he was killed."

"Was she now?" Tzazi grinned wickedly. "Don't tell Jess until I've had a chance to make a bet with her."

"You wouldn't do that." I laughed.

"Oh, I would," she said, throwing her head back and laughing. "I would."

When we reached the juncture veering off to the City Hall buildings, my nerves were frazzled. Looking over at Tzazi, I was pretty sure she felt the same. She fidgeted with her fingers, twisting and rubbing them as we walked.

"I have to go into full-on vamp mode," Tzazi explained as we drew closer. "You aren't going to freak again, are you?"

"I might," I answered truthfully. "Are you going to bite him?"

I pasted a look of exaggerated terror on my face.

Tzazi rolled her eyes and pushed me through the open door into the office.

A life-size portrait of a woman with ash-blonde curls—arranged dramatically around a heavily jeweled crown—graced the entire back wall of the room. The woman's emerald dress flowed in an invisible wind, and when she saw me staring, she gave me a wink.

In front of the portrait sat a brown desk where a light-haired woman plunked away, one finger at a time, at a typewriter. She looked up at us and frowned. Not a good start at all.

Tzazi drew in a breath. "Oh no," she mumbled.

I put on my brightest smile. "Hi! We're here to see Boddy Grim."

"Do you have an appointment?" Bulbous eyes glared at me over black-rimmed glasses.

"Um. No, ma'am. Is he available?"

"Not if you don't have an appointment." She turned back to her typing.

"But we'll only be—"

"Not if you don't have an appointment."

"Oh, for crying out loud, Delilah," Tzazi said. "It'll only take a minute."

"Not if you don't have an appointment."

"Okay. Thank you," I said, grabbing Tzazi's arm and pulling her outside.

"When did Delilah Ragefire start working for Boddy Grim? Last I knew, she was in the Mayor's Office!" Tzazi exploded once the door closed behind us.

"What was that about? Why didn't you mesmer her?"

"Delilah is part dragon. If you have a drop of dragon blood in you, you can't be mesmered. Dragonkind developed immunity after centuries of being exploited for their hides and wing bones."

I gasped. "That's horrid."

"It is," Tzazi said. "Which is why you rarely see a dragon in their winged form. I've heard talk of a peak in the Aerie Mountains of the Isles where dragons fly freely, but I've never been there. That doesn't really help us today though, does it?"

"Well, great. What are we going to do now?" I asked, as we stepped under an enormous, shady oak.

Tzazi thought for a moment. "This way."

I followed her back to a grassy, park-like area running behind the buildings along the edge of the swamp. Benches ran alongside the water, and in the center were several long picnic tables shaded by large oaks.

We took a seat at a bench with a direct view of the road.

"This is Oakspider Park. From here, we can see the road back to Tataille," Tzazi explained.

I shuddered, glancing around for any sight of the little buggers dangling from tree branches.

"Delilah takes her lunch break every day at the same time to meet Clobber Mudkipp," Tzazi added with a mischievous grin.

"The bartender?"

She nodded. "When she leaves, we'll duck back in and talk to Boddy."

"How do you know so precisely when she leaves for lunch? Is that also a vampire thing?"

"Nah. Her soon to be ex-husband is one of our clients. In fact, we have a PI watching her right now." She waved up at the tree branches above us and a small green hand popped out of the leaves and waved back.

I didn't want to know.

We only had to wait a short time before the door flew open and Delilah, quilted tote in hand, stepped out of the building and headed toward downtown.

Tzazi and I hurried back to the Sheriff's Office and stepped inside. I followed Tzazi through a narrow hallway with multiple doors opening off it. Boddy's office sat at the end.

As we entered, Boddy looked up in surprise, and then his eyes narrowed to slits.

"No, Tzazi. I'm not telling you anything. Out!" he said in his gravelly voice while avoiding looking at her face.

"You don't even know why we're here," she said.

"I don't need to know. Out!"

Tzazi brought up her hands, palms up, catching Boddy's attention. "Boddy, c'mon. We're only here to give you some information we came across."

He looked up with cautious interest. In an instant, his demeanor changed. His face went slack, and his arms fell to his sides.

I glanced at Tzazi and drew back at the transformation. Her normally brown skin was pale, almost white, with a blue tinge. Her fangs were long and razor sharp, unlike the innocent incisors she snapped at me at the house. Most startling of all, though, were her eyes, which glowed blood red. I pulled myself away when I started to feel the lure that had captured Boddy.

"Boddy. I need to know what happened to Dorian Wilde in the cemetery last Monday," she said in a loud whisper.

He stood stock still for a few seconds as he fought her control. I was afraid he wouldn't speak.

"Dorian was killed by magic on Monday morning at 11:37 a.m.," he finally muttered.

"By magic? What do you mean?"

"His body was rife with it."

"What are you saying? Did the magic kill him? How?"

I could hear the frustration in Tzazi's voice. Was Boddy not telling the truth?

"He was already dead before his body was impaled on the grave marker belonging to his brother, Brychen Wilde. Massive internal injuries. Broken bones."

"Hmm…" Tzazi considered for a moment. "Boddy, we need you to make us a copy of your report."

Like a goldfish in an aquarium, his mouth opened and closed a few times. Then he walked to the file cabinet, rummaged around, and withdrew some papers. Setting them on the copy machine's document feed, Boddy stood silently, arms hanging limp at his sides. I sidled over, pushed the Copy button, and glanced at Tzazi, who gave me a wink.

After the copier spit out a freshly stapled duplicate, I handed it to Tzazi, who slid it into her bag. With heavy, slogging steps, Boddy returned to his desk and collapsed into the chair behind it.

"Before we head out, I have to know something, Boddy," Tzazi said.

The former reaper looked up at her with no sense of recognition or interest in his blank stare.

"Do you know who killed Dorian Wilde?" she asked him.

Again, he seemed to hesitate, his mouth opening and closing a few times. "Negatory," he finally said.

"What about suspects? Do you have anyone good for the murder?"

"Affirmative!" Boddy exclaimed, startling me with the force of his word. Until this moment, his tone had been calm, low, and rather reticent.

Tzazi looked startled as well. "Really? Who do you suspect?"

"Fernando Mayòr, Jessamine Wilde, and …Windsor Ebonwood!" A smirk creased his lips.

I sucked in my breath as Tzazi shook her head and whispered

to me. "Don't worry. We're going to find out who really killed him."

With Boddy's words, I suddenly realized how much trouble I was in. If this man decided to do so, he could haul me off at any moment and throw me in jail—just like he did to Jess and the mayor!

"Well, I guess we're done here," Tzazi said to Boddy, carefully maintaining eye contact with the lawman. "Let me apologize ahead of time for the massive headache you're going to have. It's been a pleasure doing business with you," she said upon snapping her fingers, her features returning to normal.

Boddy regained control of his mind. He slammed his hands down on the desk in front of him. I glanced at Tzazi, who displayed such an angelic look on her face you'd have thought she'd just helped an old lady cross Tataille Street, rather than spent the past ten minutes bamboozling the town lawman. I edged toward the door, anticipating an explosion of temper.

Boddy didn't disappoint.

"I'm not playing games with you two!" he yelled in that terrifyingly deep voice. "Say what you came to say and then get out of my office!"

"Well, Boddy, we thought you should know…" —Tzazi's voice tapered off, and she looked at me—

"…that Solara couldn't have killed Dorian because she was shopping in Strawbridge," I finished lamely, tilting my head and opening my eyes wide in an attempt to demonstrate my innocence. I'm pretty sure I looked quite maniacal and only confirmed his suspicions.

"Solara? I never thought Solara killed Dorian!" he blared. "And what's wrong with your eyes?"

Tzazi opened her mouth in fake-shock, put her hands on her hips, and drew in a deep breath. "We take time out of our busy day to come all the way down here to help, and that's how you want to act?" She let out the air with a loud harrumph. "This is the last time we provide you with any tips, I promise you that, Bodderick Grim! Come on, Win!"

She linked her arm through mine, and we rushed into the hallway.

"Your mesmers don't work on me anyway, Tzazi Strangeland," he crowed triumphantly.

"Keep thinking that," she mumbled as we walked out the door, Dorian's death report safely tucked away.

"THAT WAS AMAZING, BUT TERRIFYING," I gushed once we had stepped back onto the sidewalk.

"Thanks. Being a vampire does have its benefits." She handed me the report. "You keep this. I've got to get back to work. Just make sure no one knows we have that."

I dropped the report into my bag as a small, towheaded woman with a quilted tote caught my eye. Here came Delilah, swinging her hips back and forth and humming, a faraway look in her eyes.

"Hi, Delilah," Tzazi sang. "You look like you had a wonderful lunch break."

Delilah glared, as she pushed in between us and continued on her way.

Once she was a good bit down the sidewalk, we both burst out laughing.

Tzazi and I parted ways in front of her law office, and I walked the rest of the way to the bookshop alone.

CHAPTER 16

"Sangria Squad reporting for duty!" Tzazi called out, as she and Jessamin rushed into the kitchen. They slammed the door shut, a strong wind blowing in behind them.

"Bad storm's coming in. Those winds nearly blew us into the swamp," Jessamin said, shrugging off her jacket and tossing it onto a coat rack on the wall.

As a clap of thunder rocked the house, I picked up the tray of sangria Hilde prepared for us and we retreated to the cozy sitting room.

Jessamin leaned forward in her seat. "I've been very patient so far. Now tell me about the mission…"

"It wasn't a mission," I said pointedly.

"…and leave nothing out," Jessamin finished.

"It was kind of a mission," Tzazi shrugged.

Jessamin nodded. "It was definitely a mission. Now tell me." She pulled her legs under her, sitting crisscross on the sofa and leaning forward expectantly.

Tzazi and I took turns telling Jessamin about our encounters with Delilah and Boddy at City Hall.

"Let's see the autopsy report!" Jessamin said excitedly.

"I haven't looked at it myself," I said, handing her the document.

Jessamin read for a few minutes. "Hmm. This says Dorian was beaten before being thrown from the bell tower," she said.

"Let's see," Tzazi said, reaching for the report.

"Who could do that to a grown man?" I asked. "Dorian wasn't small."

"Lots of people here in Darkly," Jessamin said.

"Look at this!" Tzazi exclaimed, pointing at the report. "Dorian was in the middle of a change when he died."

"Now how would Boddy have determined that? Werewolves turn back into their human form when they die, don't they?" I asked.

Jessamin and Tzazi looked at me like I had grown three heads —although in Darkly I fear that may be more the norm than one would think.

"Don't tell me," Tzazi said with a huge grin on her face. "*American Werewolf in London,* right? Look, being a werewolf isn't a curse or a spell. Werewolves are a species, just like a witch or a wyvern—"

What the heck was a wyvern?

"When they die," she continued, "werewolves stay in whatever form they are in when the body stops living."

"Actually, it was *Fright Night,* but thank you for the clarification."

"Glad I could help," Tzazi quipped, handing the document back to Jessamin.

I chuckled and topped off our glasses.

"What does that tell us?" Jessamin asked, sitting back with the report.

"Well, for one, it means Dorian didn't believe he was in danger until it was too late," I said. "When Hilde changed in front of me, it only took seconds. She would have had plenty of time to defend herself if she needed to."

"Hilde changed with you in the room?" Tzazi asked.

"Yeah, I think she just wanted me to realize this was all real. It worked."

Jessamin and Tzazi nodded. "No denying a big furry bear suddenly standing in your house."

"That means Dorian trusted the person," Jessamin said.

"Or wasn't afraid of them," Tzazi countered. She turned to me. "That lets Keir off the hook. If it were Keir on the bell tower, Dorian would have for sure been ready for a smackdown."

I shrugged. "Maybe."

"Oh!" Jessamin suddenly exclaimed, startling both Tzazi and me.

"Second-degree burns covered 60% of his body," she said.

"That's interesting."

"What injuries do you have with second degree?" I asked.

"Blisters and hardening skin," Tzazi said. "Extremely painful."

"Okay," I said, tapping my lower lip with my finger. "Dorian was badly beaten, enough to rupture internal organs and break bones. He was thrown or made to jump from the bell tower to the ground below. And he had second-degree burns over most of his body. Who could do all that damage?"

"Maybe it wasn't just one person," Jessamin said. "What if it was a gang of people?"

"Like in *Murder on the Orient Express*," Tzazi said.

"Exactly," Jessamin agreed.

I shook my head. "There's no way. It's true he was disliked by just about everybody. But if there had been multiple people on the bell tower, I would have heard something. But other than the sound of the high winds that day, I didn't hear a thing."

"Maybe you couldn't hear the fight over the wind," Jess offered.

"Maybe, but I definitely would have seen them leaving the tower."

"I guess that's true," Jess admitted.

"Okay, let's think about this," Tzazi said. "Mayor Mayór is a leprechaun. He has superhuman strength, but he's also terrified of heights." She turned to me. "Won't even sit on the dunk cauldron at the All Hallows' Eve Festival every year, and it's only six feet off the ground." She shrugged.

"Superhuman strength? Wow," I said. "What about Solara?"

"She could easily knock him off the tower with her energy," Jessamin said. "Her mother is Eos, the goddess of dawn and light. She could also hit him with fire if she transformed into her divine form."

"But that would incinerate him completely, Jess," Tzazi said.

"True," Jessamin conceded.

I almost laughed at the disappointment on her face.

"Who else could cause those burns on him?" I asked. "Is there a fire wizard on Darkly Island?"

"Not here," Jessamin said. "A phoenix used to live on the island."

"But Blaise moved away long ago," Tzazi said. "However, she did hate Dorian more than most and blamed him for the death of her husband…" Tzazi's voice trailed off.

"She's not the only one," Jessamin said quietly.

"What do you mean?" I asked.

Jessamin sighed. "I believe Dorian killed Brychen. In fact, that's why Boddy was so quick to point the finger at me."

"Oh, Jessamin. I'm so sorry." I hurriedly topped off her glass again, then Tzazi's and mine.

"Brychen was such a good man. Nothing like his younger brother," Tzazi said.

"Thanks for saying that, Tzazi," Jessamin smiled sadly. "We always did what we could to help Dorian, but nothing was ever enough."

Jessamin turned to me.

"See, Brychen was the oldest son. His parents left him the family home, Greywolf, when they moved on. Just like Fernwood, Greywolf's been passed down to the firstborns of the family for generations. It was large for just us, but we always planned on filling it up with as many children as we could." Jessamin wrapped her arms around herself. "One night, Brychen was called out by Dorian to help capture a feral werewolf that was terrorizing the town."

"Scary times," Tzazi added.

I shivered at the thought.

"According to Dorian, he and Brychen entered the forest north of Silverfang Cairns, the were settlement. They hunted the feral for hours until they finally cornered him close to the falls. The feral knocked Dorian unconscious. Brychen and the feral engaged in a terrible fight. Dorian says when he regained consciousness, he discovered Brychen, his body pierced through with a jagged oak branch. He was so upset at seeing his brother, he fell into a rage and killed the feral instantly. However, when the rest of the pack reentered the forest to retrieve Bry, they never found the body of the feral. But there was also never another feral attack."

"You don't believe he killed the feral?" I asked.

"I don't believe there was a feral werewolf terrorizing Darkly Island. It was Dorian all along, setting up his brother," Jess said sadly.

"This may be a stupid question, but couldn't the pack have smelled the killer wolf on Brychen?" I asked.

"Usually," Tzazi explained. "However, really old werewolves can hide their scent. Both Brychen and Dorian were ancient and powerful. There's no way a feral could have beaten Brychen in a fight. The only way Dorian could overpower him was by surprise. Brychen never expected it."

Jess nodded and continued. "The very next day, Dorian showed up at Greywolf insisting that the manor and everything else we owned belonged to him. That was the moment I knew for sure he'd killed Brychen. He said I could continue to stay in the home and carry on the duties of the lady of the manor. I knew exactly what he meant."

Her lips curled in disgust.

"I took off in my car—the only thing I still have of Bry's—and never looked back. Dorian punished me monthly by giving me a small allowance but only if I came to the manor and begged for it. He loved seeing my humiliation. I was sleeping in a closet in the tavern when Phenny found out and set me up in a spare room next to the pub office, since none of the tavern's few rooms were available."

She stopped speaking, her eyebrows knitting together.

"Jessamin, what is it?" I asked, concerned at her sudden reaction.

"The Saturday before Dorian was killed, I was at Greywolf to pick up my allowance. When I arrived, Dorian was subdued. Usually, he would taunt me or say something terrible about Brychen, just to be cruel. This time, though, I could tell something troubled him. After he opened the safe and gave me my money, he waved me off without giving me another look. But before I left the room, I saw him pick up a thick envelope lying on his desk and put it in the safe."

She looked up at us. "We need to see what's in that envelope."

"How would we get into the safe?" I asked.

Tzazi and Jessamin both gave me quizzical looks.

"You forget," Jessamin said, "Greywolf used to be my home, and I would bet Dorian never figured out how to change the code."

I nodded excitedly. "Let's go tonight."

"Another mission!" Jessamin squealed. "And this time, I get to be a part of it!"

"It's not a mission!" I said, emphasizing each word.

"Oh, it's a mission alright," Tzazi said.

CHAPTER 17

As the grandfather clock chimed midnight, I found myself in head-to-toe black clothing. Tzazi and Jessamin borrowed some black warmups, hoodies, and tees, and we all climbed into Jess's black Bentley. We were the epitome of stealth.

I gasped when we slowed down in front of the sprawling Tudor-style mansion I had noticed during my tour of Darkly.

"This is Greywolf Manor?" I asked.

"Yes," Jessamin said proudly. "Home of the Wildes."

Although the house was just as beautiful as I remembered, no light shone from it, nor from the grounds, and the somber darkness left me with an eerie, foreboding feeling.

"Is it too late to back out?" I asked.

"Yes!" Jess and Tzazi exclaimed together.

Jessamin flipped the car lights off. We coasted to a stop next to a short stone wall surrounding the property. Enormous oleander bushes hid the car from anyone who might drive down the street.

Jessamin handed out flashlights, while the sky broke open again, rain thundering down around us. We covered our heads with our hoodies and followed Jess through a metal gate, down a path leading to the side of the house.

The moon—hidden behind storm clouds—provided little help

in the cloying darkness; I could barely see Jessamin and Tzazi, though they were just a few steps in front of me.

As we crept to the side door, thunder rumbled around us, and I couldn't help but think we couldn't have asked for more appropriate weather for breaking into a creepy old mansion.

What Jessamin called a side door turned out to be an enormous pair of scrolled wooden doors, opening onto a small patio. Next to the doors perched a colossal stone statue—a screaming gargoyle, posed in mid-flight.

To my amazement, Jessamin tickled its underbelly, and the gargoyle lifted its back paw to reveal a key. The gargoyle purred, rubbed its giant head against Jess's hand, and with a quick flick of its tongue, stretched its neck for more cuddles.

"Wow," I said quietly, releasing my breath.

"Yeah. Gargoyles are the best. This is Mongo," Jessamin whispered, running her hands along his scaly forehead, right before he pushed off into the air.

Jessamin unlocked one side of the double doors and we slipped in.

"Brychen's study," she whispered.

Once inside, I flipped on my flashlight and looked around the room. Paintings of landscapes and hunting scenes hung on walnut stained walls, between plant stands and plump leather chairs. An ornately carved wooden desk, in front of a trio of floor to ceiling windows, dominated the room.

Jessamin darted to a large oil painting, on the left of the desk, partially shrouded behind a large ficus tree. The entire painting swung to the side, revealing a concealed safe hidden below the canvas.

Jessamin tapped a set of numbers into the keypad. The safe beeped twice and a green light lit up above the keypad. As we squeezed in next to her, she turned the knob and the safe door popped open.

Tzazi suddenly grabbed my arm and put a finger to her lips.

She pointed to the door leading to the interior.

"Someone's in the house," she hissed.

Jessamin, Tzazi, and I held still as statues and listened. I heard the soft creak of a footstep on the wooden floor in the next room.

In a flash, Jessamin withdrew everything in the safe, stuffing it into a leather satchel. She quietly shut the safe door and swung the painting closed.

"What do we do?" Jessamin whispered.

"We can't make it to the door," Tzazi hissed, her fangs snapping into place.

I pointed to the desk. "Under there."

We scrambled underneath, pulling in the chair just as the door slowly creaked open.

I gripped Jessamin's hands, doing my best to keep her calm. I was afraid she was going to pass out—or, worse, start crying. Tzazi looked like she was about to launch herself out of our hiding spot, so I gave her hand a squeeze too, and she retracted her fangs.

The desk had a raised opening of a few inches along the bottom where I could see about a foot along the floor. Able to do little else, I hoped whoever was in the house didn't decide to peek under the desk.

The intruder carefully entered Dorian's study. For the longest time, they stood perfectly still. Jessamin was trembling, and I tried to wrap my arms around her the best I could. I wanted to comfort her—but to be honest, I was also afraid her trembling knee would hit the desk and give us away. Hopefully, the rain pounding the windows would provide cover for any small sounds we made.

A flashlight clicked on, briefly panning across the red oriental rug in front of me. Moments later, the room erupted in crashes and bangs, as books and knickknacks flew off the shelves, slamming against the walls and floor. I pulled Tzazi and Jessamin closer.

"Any idea who that is?" I whispered.

Jessamin shook her head, eyes wide.

"No, but I'm taking care of them," Tzazi hissed as she moved out from under the desk.

I pulled her back. "Wait! Let's see what he's up to." Tzazi grumbled and eased back into our hiding spot.

The intruder, most definitely a man, circled around the room, continuing to swipe books from shelves, pulling open cabinet doors and drawers.

He cursed under his breath and took a step toward the desk. When he did, a pungent smell hit my nose. Strong and familiar, yet I couldn't identify it.

I heard the soft click of Tzazi's fangs as they snapped into place again. Jessamin tucked her face into her knees, and I gave her a soft pat.

Suddenly, the safe gave off three sharp beeps, relocking itself. The three of us jumped, while the intruder gave a small cry, followed by a mumbled expletive. The intruder raced toward the sound, tearing paintings from the wall until he arrived at the hunting scene. He ripped down the frame, and upon seeing the exposed safe, cackled victoriously. We heard the metallic clink of the handle as he attempted to open it.

He swore and stomped into the middle of the room.

By now, Jessamin was quaking.

"Make us invisible," Tzazi whispered.

"Me?" I pointed at my chest.

Tzazi frowned. "Of course, you."

Now I panicked. "Tzazi, you know I can't do magic. I've tried. I could seriously harm you and Jess if I screw it up."

"I trust you," she hissed. "You can do it. It's in your blood."

Nothing like a vampire in full on vamp-mode mentioning blood to provide motivation.

Jessamin smiled at me and nodded.

As the man continued to rage, stomping around the room, I

concentrated and then quietly chanted, "Invisibility spell. Invisibility spell. Invis—"

Tzazi nudged me. "What are you doing?"

"A spell?"

Jessamin stifled a laugh. Glad I could help lower her anxiety level, at least.

"Think of your magic as flowing through your body and then out into the world," she whispered. "Envelop us in your magic and show it, in your mind, what you want it to do."

I did as Jessamin suggested, picturing my magic as a soft blue mist, soothing me, filling my body. It spread throughout my limbs and down my fingers. As I watched in awe, my magic flowed from my fingertips and shrouded all three of us, replacing my anxiety with feelings of warmth, calm, and power.

Suddenly, the chair flew out from under the desk. Tan trousers and a pair of muddy brown boots stood in front of us. I closed my eyes, focusing my entire being on keeping the blue mist flowing, even as a slight ache and a feeling of lightheadedness, spread across my brain.

Cautiously, I opened one eye, half expecting to see a pair of rough hands reaching for me. Instead, I saw—nothing. Tzazi and Jessamin were gone! Where they had crouched moments before, I now saw hazy outlines, like heat coming off pavement.

The man stood to the side of the desk, opening drawers and slamming them shut. In the middle of the ruckus, a sudden loud crash resounded from elsewhere in the house, startling us all. Jessamin and Tzazi blinked into solidity, just as the man dashed from the room.

"C'mon." I grabbed Jessamin's arm, pulling her out from under the desk. Tzazi was already at the double doors. She flung them open, and we rushed out into the rain and darkness.

I stumbled across the front lawn, trying desperately to set a course for the oleander bush hiding the car. In the dark, it was nearly impossible to see. I ran blindly until I smashed into a thornbush, sharp jabs stinging my arm. Rolling a few feet, I felt an arm on my shoulder and tensed.

"This way," Tzazi hissed, her red glowing eyes piercing the darkness.

Latching onto her arm, I let her guide the way, until I felt the brush of soft foliage against my face. The gate creaked open and Tzazi pushed me through.

The car!

Jessamin hovered in the air on the other side. She gave a thumbs up, quickly lowering to the ground and climbing into the backseat.

I leaped into the passenger seat, a wet streak of fur jumping in after me. "Pyewacket! What are you doing here?"

"You can thank me with an extra saucer of cream tonight!" he exclaimed.

Tzazi started the car and gunned it into the middle of the road. "The envelope!" I screeched. "Did we forget it?"

"I've got it!" Jessamin squeaked, raising it up above the headrest.

"Now that would have been unfortunate," Pyewacket grumbled.

CHAPTER 18

"Goodness!" Jessamin exclaimed when we settled around the sitting room with hot chocolate and dry clothes. Pye was enjoying his second saucer of cream.

"I should have taken care of that murdering little—" Tzazi said.

"We don't know for sure that was the murderer," I cautioned. "Are you both positive you didn't pick up on anything that could identify him for us? His voice? His smell?"

"I didn't," Jess said. "To be honest, I was so terrified, all I heard was his screaming and cussing. I could barely make out what he was saying. Wasn't his voice deep?"

Tzazi shook her head. "I distinctly remember his cursing being high-pitched."

As those two battled it out, I recalled the aroma that had drifted under the desk when he stood next to it. I still couldn't place the scent, but I knew I had smelled it recently.

"I wonder what he was after. Do you think it was the envelope?" I asked.

"Possibly." Jessamin opened it, turning it upside down. Two thin leather-bound books, along with a few additional items, fell into her lap.

She gave me the first book and tossed the other to Tzazi.

"Looks like ledger sheets for a company of some sort," I said, flipping through the pages.

"This one also," Tzazi said.

"Why are there two?" Jessamin asked. "What's the difference between them?"

"Let's see." I placed both books on the table and compared them, page by page. "They're very similar. Just a few differences here and there. Like this one dated March 4: $1,326 in this book, and $1,513 in the other. The vendor is Mystic Foods. Does Dorian own a restaurant?"

"Not that I know of," Jessamin said. "But he purchased a hotel in Alligator Point a few years ago. I seem to remember him getting into a lot of legal trouble over it."

I nodded. That jived with the article I found at the MET.

"Two ledger books with different amounts for the same business transactions? Sounds like our friend Dorian was cooking the books," Tzazi said. "That gives someone a superb reason to want to get rid of him."

I threw a blanket over my shoulders, cradled my mug between my hands, and curled back onto the sofa. Pye sprawled out, belly up, in the space next to me. He purred softly as I rubbed his stomach.

"Keir has pants and boots like that," I finally said.

"So do half the men in town, hun, just like Tzazi said," Jessamin said. "You need to stop trying to find reasons to not like Keir. He's a good guy."

"Maybe the envelope isn't what the murderer was after," Tzazi said.

"Hmm. Jessamin, can I see everything you grabbed from the safe?" I said.

"Sure." She handed me a hodgepodge of random items and papers.

As Jessamin and Tzazi chatted, I browsed through the items and found receipts for three Michalopoulos paintings, Brychen's birth certificate, four Juicy Fruit wrappers, a wine list for someone's birthday party, and then a document caught my eye.

Separating it from the rest of the items, I scanned it briefly.

"I think this is a DNA test."

"What?"

"Let me see!"

"Hold on." I read further and then fell back onto the couch. The air left my lungs. I stared blankly at the fireplace in front of me, letting the sheet of paper fall to the floor. Pyewacket immediately walked up onto my chest and stroked my cheek with his paw.

"What is it, Win?" he asked softly.

Tzazi and Jessamin pounced on the paper and huddled together on the rug, reading it.

"Oh, Win," Jessamin said quietly as Tzazi moved to the bar cart in the corner.

"That paper says I have a sister," I whispered.

"Here. Drink this." Tzazi handed me a glass.

I downed the brandy and thrust the glass back out for a refill.

"Your color's coming back, hun." Jessamin gently stroked my back.

"You okay?" Tzazi sat down on the other side of me and handed me a newly filled glass.

I took a deep breath to steady myself. "Yeah," I said. "Just shocked. Did either of you ever hear anything about my mother and Dorian Wilde having a child?"

"Never," Jessamin said.

"No way."

"Well, then. Any idea who this woman could be now? She'd be —" I picked up the report again "—twenty-six years old now. Five years younger than me? Wait. This makes no sense. Mom died when I was three."

"Oh, my goodness!" Jessamin said. "Do you know what that means, Win? If this is true, your mother could still be alive."

Could it be true? The room spun before my eyes.

"Maybe the report's wrong, or fake," Tzazi said, trying to sound hopeful.

"Maybe," I agreed. "But I have a feeling this is for real."

I sighed. I'd watched too many *Maury* episodes to believe otherwise.

"Do you guys mind if we call it a night? I feel exhausted suddenly."

"Oh hun. Of course. We understand," Jessamin said.

"You sure you don't need us to stay?" Tzazi asked.

"Hilde's here. Plus, I've got Pye. I'll be fine."

I walked Jessamin and Tzazi to the back door. Pyewacket padded along next to me so closely I could feel his soft fur caressing my ankle. The rain had lessened to a light patter, and I watched as the car eased down the driveway and disappeared into the darkness.

I checked to make sure all the doors and windows were locked, before I shuffled to my bedroom, washed my face, and put on my coziest pajamas.

As I climbed into bed, Pye curled up on the pillow next to mine. I ran my fingers through his soft fur, then flipped off the light on my nightstand.

"Are you okay, bébé?" he asked in a hoarse purr.

I let out a large sigh and flopped my head back onto the headboard. Both my stomach and heart ached. "Is my mother alive, Pyewacket? I know you know." He unfurled his body and sat down in front of me.

"Windsor. Genevieve is gone. She died when you were but a child."

I heard the heartache in his voice but pressed on. I had to know.

"But how? Grandmother said magic killed her. Whose magic? Her magic? What does that mean?"

He opened and closed his mouth a few times, as if having trouble forming the words. I don't know if it was the time he was taking or his inability to articulate the words that caused a terrible dread to rise in my chest.

"Your mother was murdered, Win. By a dark magic, fouler and more ancient than any I've ever encountered."

"What?" I sat up, grasping my quilt in clenched fists.

"I like to believe your mother fought the darkness, but her magic wasn't enough."

His voice cracked. I knew I was asking a lot from him.

"Who? Who killed her?"

"Win—"

"Who, Pye?" I demanded, my voice rising.

"A sorceress. A dark sorceress," Pye said, hanging his head. "Using blood magic and dark spells."

I pushed him off my chest and stood.

"Pyewacket! I'm not a child! Who killed my mother?" I screamed.

"Malicent! The dark sorceress Malicent!"

We stared at each other for a few seconds, then I climbed back into the bed, my rage spent. I fell back against the cushion.

"I'm sorry, Pye," I whispered.

He climbed back up on my chest and swiped gently at a tear rolling down my face.

"It's not something I like to think on," he said. "However, I admit you have a right to know"

I scratched his neck, grateful he had forgiven my outburst. For all his uppity ways, I already couldn't imagine my life without him.

I frowned. "The name Malicent is familiar."

"Perhaps the evil fairy in Sleeping Beauty?"

I laughed halfheartedly. "That's Maleficent. But I'm sure I know of someone with the name Malicent."

Pye's eye widened. "I highly doubt that, Windsor."

"It's such an unusual name," I insisted. "I've heard it somewhere. Where is this sorceress now?

"No one knows."

"Pye, tell me."

"I just said I don't know!" he turned his head away.

"If you knew, would you tell me?"

"Absolutely not," he exclaimed, turning back to pierce me with his one bright eye. "But I don't. Please don't ask me about Malicent again. Some things are best left in the past."

I'd rattled him with my questions, unnerving his usually cool demeanor. I hadn't seen him this upset before—the closest being the night he found something in the gardener's shed. I felt bad for my questioning, when it obviously brought up some terrible memories; still, like he said, I had a right to know. I let it go that night, but I knew it wouldn't be the last time I brought up the sorceress, Malicent.

"What do you know about this child my mother supposedly had with Dorian Wilde?"

My lips curled in disgust at the thought.

"The dead can't have children. Good night, Win," Pye said, settling in next to me, our conversation at an end.

I plumped the pillow behind me, easing back down into the blankets myself and staring at the ceiling.

Nothing made sense.

Why hadn't Grandmother told me the truth about Mom's death when she had the opportunity? Did Grandmother not know? And what about Dad? Had he known? Where was this sorceress and why did her name ring a bell? What about the DNA test?

The rain had stopped. Moonbeams now pushed through the clouds, immersing the pond in a warm glow. A lump—probably Greta Garbo—glided through the dark water like one of the golden ships on the Nile.

I sat up for hours, staring at the marshy pond. Around three in the morning, the familiar golden glow blinked on deep within the swamp.

Instead of its usual comforting presence, I felt a stab of annoyance. I was growing tired of being surrounded by unknowns. Unknowns from my past, raising their dark heads in my present. As the small disk pulsed and radiated, I pulled Pye to my chest, turned away from the window, and fell fast asleep.

CHAPTER 19

The next morning, before heading into the MET, I met Tzazi and Jessamin at Azalea's. I was in a funk, and looked it, dressed in baggy sweats and a hoodie. Nevertheless, I ordered my usual chai, plus a to-go milk for Pye, and slid into a seat next to the counter. Jaime Mayór stood in line with some friends. He gave me a nod and smiled.

Seriously?

I turned away from him, as Tzazi and Jessamin joined me, hot coffees in hand, bringing a bag of raspberry scones to share.

"How are you this morning, hun?" Jessamin asked.

I could see the concern in their eyes and felt a sudden rush of anger—the last thing I needed was anyone's pity.

"How do you think I am, Jessamin?" I snapped.

Jess's eyes widened. She cupped her hands over her mouth and let out a little squeak. My heart dropped. Beside her, Tzazi recoiled.

"Oh geez, Jess," I said, dropping my head and squeezing my eyes tight. Hot tears welled up behind my lids. "I didn't mean that."

"I know, hun." Jess slid over to my side of the table and put an arm around me. Her chin rested on my shoulder. "You know we're here for you, right?"

Tzazi reached over and patted my arm. The simple gesture broke my reserve. Tears rolled down my cheeks like drops from a summer storm on a glass pane.

After a few minutes of my blubbering, Tzazi reached into her bag and withdrew a tissue.

"Here, love," she said, handing it to me, causing me to cry even harder.

My eyes were red, my face was splotchy, and my nose was stuffy from all my crying. I dabbed at my eyes and then blew hard into the tissue. To my horror, the sound of a trumpeting bull elephant blasted through the coffee shop. I quickly crammed the used tissue into my bag, then looked up to see Tzazi staring at me.

"Well, that was impressive," she said, grinning.

Jess giggled next to me. I shook my head, laughing along with them, feeling a little better. I should try crying in a coffee shop more often.

"I'm truly sorry, guys," I said. "I shouldn't have lashed out at you. I'm feeling overwhelmed."

"And you should," Jess said, handing me a scone and biting into one herself. "However, I'm telling you, Win. That DNA test isn't real."

"I don't know," Tzazi said. "It looked legitimate to me."

I set down my scone, looking back and forth at the two.

"That's not all."

That got their attention.

"Pyewacket told me more about my mother last night. And it's not good."

I took a deep breath to steady my nerves.

"Not only is my mother dead, but she was murdered. By a dark sorceress named Malicent." My voice cracked as I stumbled on that horrible name.

"Oh, Win," Jess said.

I looked at Tzazi, whose eyes were narrowed as she stared at me. She bit down on her bottom lip.

"You're not going to vamp out on me, are you?" I joked, nervously.

Tzazi shook her head and smiled. "Sorry."

"I know that name somehow," I said. "But I can't place it. Malicent."

Jess cocked her head to the side. "What an odd name."

"Villain in Sleeping Beauty," Tzazi said, grabbing a scone. "Has to be."

"Maybe," I conceded. "But that's Maleficent, not Malicent. One thing's for sure. The DNA test we found can't be real. Mom was already dead when that child was conceived."

"Ooh, that's true," Jess agreed.

I nodded. "It's not much, but it's more than I knew a day ago."

"Maybe the fake DNA test has something to do with Dorian's murder. Maybe that's why someone killed him," Jessamin suggested.

Tzazi nodded. "It's a strange coincidence, if not."

"I hadn't thought of that," I said. "To be honest, until my talk with Pyewacket last night, I was assuming the test was legit."

"Not me," Jessamin said. "I've never heard rumors about Dorian and your mother being in any relationship, and you've seen how this town talks."

"Maman talks about your mother," Tzazi said thoughtfully, "but only about how much she misses her. They were close friends, you know."

That caused me to perk up. I looked over at Azalea, hustling around behind the counter. She saw me staring and gave me a smile and a wave. I needed to talk to her. Maybe she could shed some light on what happened to my mother.

Jess turned to me and took my hand. "I've got to get going, hun, but you know we're here for you, right? No matter what you need, you let us know."

"We should do a sangria sleepover soon," Tzazi said.

I felt my emotions rise again and stifled a sob as I attempted a weak smile at my two friends.

As we stood to exit, a warm gust of wind blew in from the entrance. Keir stepped inside, accompanied by a man I recognized from his pack.

"No, no, no," I hissed, ducking behind Tzazi. "I don't want to see him right now."

Jess followed my gaze, grinning as the men strode to the counter and took up an empty spot near our table. "Hun, don't worry about it. You look lovely."

Tzazi grabbed my chin in her hand, examining my face. "No, she doesn't," she said. "Her face is covered in bright red splotches, and her eyes look like she's been on a three-day bender."

"Tzazi!" Jess gave Tzazi a soft punch in the arm.

"No, it's true," I said. "Let's just get me out of here before I cry again."

Jess harrumphed. "I still think you look lovely."

I squeezed her hand gratefully, then tossed my hoodie over my head. My heart lurched as I glanced in Keir's direction. Everything about him caused my breath to catch in my throat; from his long brown hair, curling loosely to his shoulders, to the blue chambray shirt with rolled sleeves exposing his tattoos, tight jeans, and … I exhaled quickly… brown leather work boots dusted in a layer of mud.

I stared at the boots. There was no mistaking it. They were exactly like the ones worn by the mysterious intruder from last night. As I regained my composure, attempting to skirt around the two men, Keir suddenly reached for his back pocket. The crook of his elbow jutted into the walkway, grazing my chest, halting me in my tracks.

"Oh! Sorry," he began, then looked down at my face. "Win?"

I felt his eyes narrow on me. With a sigh, I lifted my hoodie.

"Hi, Keir. I didn't see you there."

His smile widened, then turned into a frown. "Are you okay?"

Jess softly touched my arm and waved a few fingers at me. "I'll see you in a bit, alright?"

I nodded to her and Tzazi.

"Rein, I'll be right back," Keir said to his friend, his eyes never leaving mine. "I'll walk you to the MET, if that's okay."

"Um. Sure."

We worked our way through the tables and then out of the coffee shop, onto the sidewalk. Townspeople rushed around us—late to school, early to work, everyone going about their daily routines—while I seemed to be stuck in an outtake from an Alfred Hitchcock movie. I gave Keir a sideways glance. On the one hand, I couldn't deny the attraction I felt for him. The feelings were like nothing I'd ever experienced, even with Lucas—who at one time I thought was the love of my life.

Yet I couldn't ignore the fact that Keir had good reasons for wanting Dorian dead. As an alpha, Keir could easily have inflicted most of the injuries found on Dorian's body. And then there were the boots.

But was I just making up a reason to not like him, like Tzazi and Jess believed, because I was afraid of being hurt again?

"Anything I can help you with?" he finally asked, after we had walked a few minutes in silence.

I shook my head. "I'm fine." Looking up into his warm brown eyes, I shivered. Could this man really be capable of murder?

"Just family stuff." I forced a smile. "And a crazy night with Jess and Tzazi."

He laughed. "Now that I understand. My night was a little crazy as well."

"Really? What did you do last night?" I asked, assuming a singsong voice, one that I hoped sounded much more normal to him than it did to me. Would he even tell me if he had been at the manor?

We reached the doors to the portal shop, and he turned to face me with a slight grin on his face.

"Why, Ms. Ebonwood," he said. "Are you asking if I was on a date last night?"

"No," I said, a bit too forcefully, as I pushed past him to unlock the door. "What makes you think I care if you were on a date last night?"

He shrugged and turned to head back to the café. "Anyway. I'm glad you're alright."

I fumbled with my keys, watching as he took a few steps down the sidewalk, then spun around.

"By the way, the answer is no," he said, his mouth quirking in that obnoxious grin again, as he took a few steps backward.

I looked up.

"The answer to what is no?"

"Whether I was on a date last night. Feel better?" And with that, he spun around and sauntered back down the sidewalk.

Arrrgh. That man got on my every last nerve.

I finally shoved the key in the lock and threw open the door. Pye launched himself out of my bag, landing hard on the floor as I slammed it shut.

"What was all that about?" he screeched, leaping up onto the counter. "You can't tell me you weren't curious whether he was out with someone last night."

"That has nothing to do with this situation! Jess and Tzazi refuse to believe Keir had anything to do with Dorian's murder, but all the evidence is there, Pye." I set my bag down on the counter next to him.

He rolled his eye and jabbed a claw toward his saucer. "You're barking up the wrong tree with this." He deadpanned.

"Ha ha. Just listen." I poured his morning milk into his bowl and sat down at the stool behind the counter to watch. "Everyone knows Keir and Dorian didn't get along. Keir had plenty of opportunity. For goodness' sake, he was right there when the murder occurred! Plus, not even Jess can say Dorian's death doesn't make Keir's life much easier."

I thought for a moment. "You know what? I need to prove my suspicions once and for all or put all this Keir stuff to bed."

Pye stopped lapping up his milk long enough to quip, "Not literally, I'm guessing?"

I ignored him. "I need to know, Pye. Did Keir kill Dorian Wilde?"

CHAPTER 20

The morning rushed by in a blur. Before I knew it, the clock was coming up on 10:00 a.m. Work improved my mood, and I pulled my hair up into a messy bun and slapped on some lipstick, wishing I hadn't thrown on a hoodie and warmups that morning. Looking in the restroom mirror, I smiled, liking what I saw, then moved back out into the main gallery.

Only three more days until the MET reopened, and it still felt like I had so much to do. I was rethinking my commitments for the day—hair appointment with Chase, lunch with Jess. The whole town was looking forward to the MET being in business again, and the last thing I wanted was to disappoint everyone.

I was so deep in my own thoughts I didn't realize someone had entered the bookshop until a cheerful voice in front of me said, "Hello, Ms. Ebonwood."

I looked up to find a young man with floppy blond hair, grinning.

"Aren't you Evon?" I asked. "You came out to my house a few days ago when Tzazi was there."

"That's me," he said with a shy smile. "Evon Frick. My parents own the White Hart Inn. I was wondering when you expect the

TAM LUMIÈRE

MET to be in service again. My girlfriend Tanqueray lives in the Emerald Lagoons of the Charming Isles, and I haven't seen her in weeks."

"The MET will reopen Monday," I assured him.

"Perfect!" Evon exclaimed. "Her birthday is in two weeks, and I was hoping to portal out to see her. Thank you so much, Ms. Ebonwood!"

"Glad I could help, Evon."

As the door slowly closed behind him, my eyes drifted across the street, where I spotted Keir and Solara deep in conversation. Solara gestured wildly, her hands drawn into fists, before she unclenched them and reached forward to adjust the collar on his camo jacket.

I meandered to the front window, just as Keir pried Solara's hands from his jacket and they broke apart, each heading in the opposite direction.

Here was my chance!

Grabbing my bag and locking up, I hurried across the street, tripping over Pye as he circled my feet.

"Hold up, pet," he said. "You can't think you're going without me, eh?"

I picked him up and eased him into the tote. "For such a small cat, you sure are heavy."

I barely missed a sharp claw as he swiped at my hand.

Keir continued along the sidewalk next to the cemetery, then entered through one of the side gates.

Hah! Don't they say criminals always go back to the scene of the crime? Maybe he's retrieving evidence Boddy missed. The blue plastic bristles—could that be it?

I stepped into the coolness of the cemetery. Keir was nowhere to be seen, until a flash of movement sent me toward the bell tower. Cautiously, I weaved through the tombstones, staying far enough back that I wouldn't be detected, but close enough to not lose him.

After a few minutes, I realized we were heading away from the crime scene, not towards it. Baffled, I watched as Keir took a step and disappeared.

As I drew closer, the exit closest to City Hall loomed in front of me.

Peeking around the stone wall, my forehead suddenly bumped against something hard and warm. I looked up to find Keir, leaning casually against the stones, hands in his pockets, examining the shops across the cobbled street.

"Well, hello, Windsor. Care to explain why you're following me?" He turned to me with a cocky grin. "Just couldn't stay away, could you?" he added, removing his sunglasses.

He was so close I was sure he could hear the butterflies duking it out in my stomach.

I flushed. "Well, I just… I mean…"

A lock of his long brown hair fell into his face, smile growing wider, and my heart melted.

"I get the distinct impression you believe I could be the person who killed Dorian," Keir said, his expression turning serious.

I flushed. "It's not that, Keir," and then I sighed. "Oh, I don't know."

"Win, I understand why you might think that. It's no secret Dorian and I dinnae get along," he said, voice tinged with a hint of sadness. "But I wouldn't kill him."

He gazed across the street for another moment and turned back to me. "Why not have dinner with me tonight? Just so we can discuss it, of course."

That was unexpected. I dropped my bag on the ground and stared at him.

"Ow!" Pye howled.

"Seriously?" was the first word out of my mouth.

Keir stepped away from the wall. His grin disappeared, and his eyes darted between me and my bag, where Pye's angry face peered up at him.

"I don't mean it like that," I said quickly. "I'm just surprised."

"Surprised in a good way, or surprised in a bad way?" He leaned against the wall once more, giving off that cool guy vibe again.

"Good way," I said and smiled. "I'd love to have dinner with you. Although I should warn you, I have a lot of questions."

"Aye, I would expect no less. Pick you up at seven?"

"Sounds good."

As he waved goodbye, I couldn't help but notice his boots again, brown and caked with mud. What had I gotten myself into?

Running late after my hair appointment with Chase, I dashed across the street to the Gator, where Jessamin already sat in a booth next to the window. Clobber stood next to her, staring down at Jess like a love-sick puppy. Poor Delilah!

As I made my way over to the table, Jessamin's eyes grew wide. "Win! Your hair! Those highlights are fabulous! Chase's work?"

"None other," I said, tossing my bag on the seat next to me.

"He's fantastic."

Clobber stared at my hair. "I don't see a difference."

Jessamin laughed. "You wouldn't."

After Clobber took our orders and moved back to the bar, I couldn't hold my secret any longer.

"Guess what?" I said with a huge smile on my face.

Jess's eyes grew wide. "What?"

I laughed. I could always count on Jess to show an overabundance of excitement.

"Keir asked me out. We're going to dinner tonight."

"Aww. I knew he was interested in you. Are you excited? I'm excited!" Her face glowed with happiness for me.

"I'm super excited, but also nervous," I admitted.

"Don't be. You're going to have a wonderful time," she said. "I wish I could be the one to tell that murdering Solara."

"Solara has an alibi, Jess," I said. "She's not the killer."

I was tired of arguing with her, so I wasn't going to mention Keir's lack of an alibi.

"She's lying," Jessamin insisted. "I know she is."

I shrugged. "Maybe, but we have no proof."

Jessamin twirled a fork between her fingers, deep in thought.

"Jess, did something happen between you and Solara? I know she's annoying, and pretentious, but your dislike seems to run deeper," I said, attempting to tread carefully around the topic.

"Something happened alright," she said. "When Solara and I were young, our families were close. After spending so much time together, we couldn't help but become good friends—in fact, best friends. We were so close we'd complete each other's spells.

"Back then, Solara was beautiful, but not the otherworldly beauty she has today. And she was sweet," Jessamin said, with a sad smile. "I wouldn't imagine you'd know the history of the Charming Isles?"

She raised a brow, and I shook my head "no" in response.

"About a century ago, King Pilston and Queen Vermier ruled the Isles, which includes Darkly Island, of course. They were the parents of Queen Ermione, the current queen."

Jess quieted as Clobber arrived with our plates.

"On second thought, Clobber, can I get a glass of white wine?" I asked.

Jess nodded and smiled brightly at the man. "Same here."

"Of course," he said. "I'll be right back."

"What kind of supernatural being is Clobber?" I asked once he was gone.

"A goblin," Jessamin said. "A descendent of the imperial family. That's why he's so—" she hunched her shoulders like a bear "— huge."

That's crazy. I shook my head, waving at her to continue.

"My father's family—the Darkmoons—were the Royal

Sorcerers to the House of Charming. The Darkmoons were granted rare and unconditional access to the palace and, of course, the Royal Family. Unfortunately, that meant my aunt Chartres started spending a lot of one-on-one time with King Pilston."

"You don't mean an affair?"

Clobber arrived and set down our wine glasses. I grabbed it and took a good, long sip.

"I do mean. One day, King Pilston and Aunt Chartres were gone. My aunt left only a note to my poor Uncle Tobius, apologizing for falling in love with the King. My cousins, Theodora and Aurelia, were only toddlers."

"What did the queen do?"

"She was furious. Banned all remaining Darkmoons from ever setting foot in the palace again and—ironically—hired a wizard to attach wards along the palace walls, preventing magic from being performed anywhere on the grounds. She was positive Aunt Chartres had enchanted the king into falling out of love with the queen and in love with her."

"What a sad story," I said. "I don't understand though. What does this have to do with Solara?"

"In the fallout after the scandal, all the courtiers chose sides. Mother and Father, of course, sided with my uncle, who was unfairly punished. Solara's family sided with the Queen, sacrificing friendship for their place in society," Jessamin shrugged, as if it were no big deal.

"Solara never spoke to me again. So, believe me, I know better than most how cold and self-serving the Novas are. Familiar with the Malfoys in *Harry Potter*? Throw in a tad of Bellatrix and that's the Novas through and through."

Jessamin spoke of disliking Solara, but what I saw was hurt and grief on her face when she talked about her. Reaching across the table, I patted her hand.

"And that's why I know Solara's lying. I just need to prove it." She looked toward the entrance and suddenly perked up. "And here's my chance."

I followed her gaze to a pretty blonde woman, who was standing just inside the front doors.

"Zelda! Zelda!" Jess called, waving a hand in the air. "Just follow along," she whispered to me out the side of her mouth.

The blonde approached our table and hugged Jessamin.

"How are you, hun? I haven't seen you in ages."

The woman's perkiness and bright smile reminded me of Jessamin.

"I'm good, sweetie," Jessamin replied. "I'd like you to meet Windsor. She just moved here."

"Why, of course. Miss Minta's granddaughter. Pleasure to meet you."

"Nice to meet you too," I replied.

"I'm about to take Win shopping. You see how she dresses," Jessamin added quietly, as if I couldn't hear, and fluttered her hand in my direction.

The woman wrinkled her nose and nodded. "Rather dull for Darkly."

My face flushed with embarrassment. I wanted to yell, "I don't usually wear hoodies and warmups!" but I kept quiet.

"Exactly," Jessamin continued. "I was thinking Strawbridge, but I haven't been shopping in so long, I thought it best to ask an expert."

Zelda stared blankly for a second, but then her eyes lit up. "Oh! You mean me!"

I nodded eagerly, playing along through my pain. "Who else? I love your outfit." She did look really cute.

"Why thank you, hun. That's sweet of you. But I haven't been to Strawbridge in ages. At least two years. You should try Rage though, a new shop that recently opened here in town. They have the sweetest dresses and rompers. Perfect for our hot summers."

I was about to thank Zelda when she slid out a chair and plopped into it. "Did you ladies hear about the mayor being arrested for Dorian Wilde's murder?"

We both nodded.

"Sad, isn't it?" Jess said. "I, for one, don't believe he did it."

"Well, of course not, silly!" Zelda exclaimed. "He was dedicating a statue in Oakspider Park that morning, and you know how long his dedications can run."

I sat up. "You were there, Zelda?"

Her faced turned bright red. She leaned in and whispered, "Well, I was. But no one is supposed to know."

Jess and I both instinctively leaned in with her.

"Why not?" Jess whispered.

Zelda looked over her shoulder a few times. "Because I was there with Clobber."

"Clobber?" Jess exclaimed.

"Shhh," Zelda hissed. "My boyfriend would explode if he knew. But I saw the mayor there, along with his wife and son, giving a speech as if the whole town was there watching. He's such a funny man. Oh, there's my table."

She promised to stop by Rage and put in a good word for me with Borda, the owner, then hurried to her table.

"My, that goblin sure gets around," I said, once Zelda was out of earshot. "I guess that gives Mayor Mayór a strong alibi."

"And Solara a weak one," Jessamin said with a smile.

I grinned. "That look of smugness on your face is not at all attractive."

She stuck her tongue out at me, then finished her lunch with glee.

As Pye and I biked home, my mind twisted and turned around everything that had happened the past few days. To find out I came from a family of witches and had witchy powers myself was big enough, but then to also come across a dead body, become fast friends with a vampire and a fairy, and now have a date with an alpha werewolf was just—wow!

But most unbelievable and disturbing was the discovery that

my mother was murdered. No doubt there was a story there. What could Mother have possibly done to enrage this Malicent to the point that she would kill her? And where were Dad and I when the murder occurred? I had so many questions, but no one to answer them. I needed to know, and I resolved to find out.

CHAPTER 21

That evening, I stood in front of the mirror peering at my backside. This floral wrap dress was the fifth outfit I'd tried on.

I posed before Pye.

"What do you think?"

He cocked his head from side-to-side a few times. Finally, he nodded. "Love it. Very Darkly, but also very you."

A thumbs up!

I gave him an affectionate scratch on the neck, then slipped into a pair of sandals.

Long, loose curls cascaded down my back. I ran my fingers through the dark brown waves one more time and added a little shine spray. Done.

I glanced at the clock on my nightstand. Ack! Keir should be here any minute. I quickly swiped a coat of mascara across my lashes, glossed my lips, and then tossed it and a compact into my handbag.

I was pouring myself a glass of wine, hoping to calm my ragged nerves, when a blood-curdling scream pierced the air—a wailing so mournful and torturous I was certain someone was being murdered on my front porch.

I felt a rush of adrenaline and bolted out the door, running smack into a broad chest smelling of pine trees and warm spices. I breathed a sigh of relief when I looked up. Keir.

"Whatever is that?" I exclaimed, my breath rushing out in a panicked burst.

He looked at me with a sad smile. "It's Clíodhna. Nothing to fear from her."

Keir followed me into the house, while the horrible keening continued.

I pointed to my glass and mouthed, "Would you like a drink?" Keir gave me a thumbs up.

The wailing went on and on, as I poured wine into a glass for Keir. I almost set down the bottle and clamped my hands over my ears.

"Who's Clíodhna?" I asked during a moment of silence.

"Clío's a banshee. She—"

I whipped around. "Someone's going to die?"

Keir shook his head. "Someone's already died. She's crying for her family."

I handed Keir his glass. "What happened?" I asked.

He joined me on the sofa, flinging an arm on the backrest and relaxing into the cushion. He sipped his wine.

"About a hundred years ago—"

"Wait. A hundred years? She's been around that long?"

He shrugged. "Aye. Most supernaturals live long lives; a hundred years is just a drop in the bucket."

"Even witches?"

He shrugged. "Not as long as were's but yeah."

"Good to know. So how old are you?" I had to ask.

"One-hundred-seven. I'm a wee one."

My wine glass slipped from my hand (no, I wasn't nervous at all) and, in a flash, Keir grabbed it out of the air before it hit the floor.

When he handed the wineglass back, his fingers slipped around mine and lingered there for a few seconds.

"We also happen to be pretty good with our hands," he said with a cocky smile.

I drew in a breath, heat pulsating through my body.

Blushing, I nodded for him to continue.

"About a hundred years ago, a feral gang of werewolves terrorized the mainland of the Isles," he said.

"Like when Brychen died?" I asked.

Keir's mouth fell open. "Jess told you?"

I nodded.

"Yeah. Almost exactly like Brychen," he said, shaking his head as if warding off terrible memories.

"The wolf packs banded together to find the rogues and take care of the problem. I badly wanted to go, but Father forbade it. I was too young. Many innocent people died before the packs discovered the lair of the rogues and destroyed them. I lost a few distant relatives. Clíodhna lost her entire family. She moved to Darkly to get as far away from her past as she could," he said.

"That poor woman. How sad," I said.

"It is," Keir said. "Her youngest was only two."

My heart broke for Clíodhna, and I resolved to befriend her if I ever got the chance.

A thought suddenly occurred to me.

"Maybe that's her I've seen at night. A glowing light in the swamp that suddenly disappears," I said.

His eyes narrowed. "You've seen someone in the swamp?"

"A light," I clarified. "Many times. Sometimes it's there for hours. Other times, just minutes."

"I doubt that's Clío," Keir said slowly. "In fact, I'm surprised she's wandered this far from the Gnarl, the forest surrounding Wulver Cairns, the were settlement. You are staying out of the swamp at night, right?"

"Yes," I said with a smirk, deciding to take the high road on that topic. "I don't want to be Greta Garbo's dinner."

The look of relief on his face touched me and I was glad I

hadn't gotten offended at his question. Maybe I was judging him too harshly.

He glanced at his watch and stood.

"You ready? Don't want to miss our reservation."

"Yes, I'm starving," I said, taking his outstretched hand. As we walked out the door, Keir leaned down and whispered in my ear,

"You look beautiful, by the way. That dress is amazing."

My heart fluttered helplessly in my chest as my fears finally vanished from my mind. There's no way this man could have killed anyone.

I CLIMBED into Keir's classic Land Rover and ran my hands along the leather seat. "Wow! Where did you ever find this?"

"It was my dad's," he explained. "It passed to me when I became alpha."

"Wow. That's some perk."

"Yeah," he said with a grin, closing the car door for me.

"Where are we going?" I asked as he slid in on the other side.

"Since you haven't seen any of the other villages on the island yet, I want to take you to one of my favorites, Cradlerock. Do you like seafood?"

"Love it."

As he drove, Keir explained how Darkly Island was comprised of several distinct communities—each with its own unique personality and style, such as Wychwood, with its towering black trees and fog, Strawbridge, known for its nightlife and trendy boutiques, and Rosewood, a glamorous vacation spot for the rich and famous.

His descriptions of the island gave me a chance to look him over without having to be sneaky. That evening, his hair was loose, hanging around his shoulders. He wore a diamond stud in each ear and multiple leather necklaces around his neck. Tattoos peeked out of the cuffs of his long-sleeved, striped button-down.

TAM LUMIÈRE

The man was gorgeous, and I don't think he even tried.

After about thirty minutes of pitch-black landscape, a warm glow of lights appeared on the horizon. Soon I was marveling at the small town nestled against the rocky shore. Tiny white homes climbed pale stone streets and tall palms rose above the blue roofed dwellings.

"This is amazing," I gushed. "Is every town on the island as enchanting as Darkly and Cradlerock?" I stared at a clear fountain, where a bevy of dolphins danced and leaped through cascading sheets of water.

"No, unfortunately not," he said. "The Dead Forest of Wychwood is an evil place. I wouldn't advise going there at night. Actually, I wouldn't advise going there ever. But there are plenty of good people in the town. You just have to know who is who."

Keir drove the Rover through a circular driveway and parked in front of an extravagantly carved doorway built into a gigantic grey rock. Waves crashed on the beach, not fifty feet behind the monolith. Two liveried valets appeared from the sides of the rock. One of them was quick to open my door, graciously extending his hand as I stepped from the Rover.

I turned to Keir, confused, but he simply took my arm as the valets swung the mighty doors open. The warm glow of wall sconces guided me down a narrow, cut-stone staircase. I ran my hand along the wall, where slivered veins of turquoise peeked through, sparkling under the light.

The steps continued to curve down into the earth, until I finally stepped out onto a smooth rock floor. A jolly round man—with a curling mustache and shiny black hair combed back over his crown—took Keir in a tight and friendly hug.

"Keir Bain! It is so good to see you, mio buon amico! It has been too long! And who is this bella signorina?" he said, turning to me with a bright smile.

"Giuseppe, this is Windsor Ebonwood. Windsor, Giuseppe Maurice, the owner of Grotto."

Giuseppe bowed deeply, and upon rising, kissed my hand

dramatically. As Keir and Giuseppe spoke for a few moments, I looked around in awe. The decor of the restaurant was subdued, but elegant. Delicately carved wood tables were spaced discreetly, ensuring privacy for diners; some placed in alcoves or on ledges. Tapered candles and single white roses topped the tables. A soft breeze ruffled my hair, and I looked up to find a gap in the rock, where thousands of tiny stars blinked in the midnight blue sky.

"This way please," Giuseppe's booming voice caught my attention. "When I was told you were coming tonight, I prepared my best table!"

We followed him down another set of winding stone steps to a small private dining area. I gasped when I looked around.

"Il profondo mare blu!" Giuseppe beamed.

All I could do was stare, because there before me was the magnificent blue-green ocean, with the dark sky above and the expansive depths below. The view was so clear, so real that the urge to reach out and grasp the swaying seagrass was overwhelming. As I stood transfixed, a red octopus with large, intelligent eyes glided over the reef and squeezed between the cracks in a rock formation.

"Thank you, Giuseppe," Keir said, the man quietly retreating from the room.

"It's breathtaking."

Keir pulled out my chair and waited until I finally drew back from the ever-changing scene before me.

The sommelier approached our table, and Keir ordered a fine vintage Bordeaux.

"Our server will choose our meals," Keir explained, as the sommelier backed into the shadows.

"Seriously?" I asked.

"They're highly trained. I guarantee you'll love what he chooses for you."

Our server arrived with a flourish, introducing himself as Geoffrey. As the sommelier returned and poured our wine, Geoffrey turned to me. He asked a few questions (having nothing to do with food or flavors), then tapped his brow, and excused himself.

"That's it?" I asked.

"You worried?" Keir grinned.

"A little." I laughed.

I sipped from my glass, relaxing into the plush seat as a shoal of yellow and purple tangs skimmed over the tops of the undulating seagrass in the ocean before me.

"What do you think?"

I snapped back to reality. "Uhhh."

He laughed, a powerful yet comforting sound.

"What do you think of Darkly?"

I chuckled. "It's too hot and rains quite a bit. But it's also beautiful and the people are incredible. I've already made some good friends."

"Jessamin and Tzazi are the best," he said. "I'm glad Jess has you and Tzazi to stand by her. The lass's been through a lot these past few years."

"Jessamin wouldn't kill Dorian. Although I don't know if I'd be the same in her position."

"And I wouldn't blame you. I'll admit. Dorian lived a despicable life. My father and I both tried to make him see how destructive he had become. He didn't care. To be honest, I believe he enjoyed hurting people."

"Like how he hurt Jessamin." I took a sip of my wine. "Keir, why didn't you help her?"

"Believe me, Win, I tried and I'm trying now." His brows furrowed as he spoke. "But even an alpha who goes against pack law risks being exiled. Our laws are based on the goodness and integrity of our pack members. I honestly dinnae know Dorian was treating her the way he was. He told me she was living at Greywolf, and I saw the amount supposedly coming out of the estate for her each month. The sum was very generous."

I thought about the two ledger books we found last night.

"It's obvious I failed her." He sat quietly for a moment. "I only kept Dorian around because he was my dad's beta."

"Your dad made you alpha after him?"

"Aye," he said. "That's how it works. Pack leadership is handed down to first-borns. I'm an only-born, so leadership went straight to me."

Keir looked up as Geoffrey returned with our food. He placed a plate of tilapia caprese with thick slices of mozzarella and a side of polenta in front of me.

"Do you approve, my lady?" he asked.

"Good gracious, yes," I exclaimed.

Before Keir, he set a platter with the largest porterhouse steak I'd ever seen, covered with a mound of fried shrimp.

"You'll never finish that," I teased him.

He grinned. "Wanna bet?"

Geoffrey bowed low before Keir. "Do you approve, Your—"

"Yes. Thank you, Geoffrey," he said quickly.

Geoffrey bowed once more and withdrew from the room.

I dug into my tilapia and stared out at the sea, chatting with Keir in between bites. The silver dollar moon sat low in the sky, casting a metallic sheen that pierced the surface and rippled down through the water below. The sea life was abundant, colorful, and active. A lionfish paraded across the glass and I was overwhelmed with the magnificence of it all.

Suddenly, a motion in the distance caught my eye—a bright flare, like the reflection of the sun in a mirror.

"Keir, look!" I pointed out the window.

"Ah. They're here," he said.

Hundreds of fins and tails of various colors and sizes rippled along the surface, like a flight of jewel-toned dragonflies. They drew closer and closer. Then with a sudden splash, which sent droplets of water cascading onto the glass above us, the silverscaled body of a man broke through the surface and flipped in the air, an iridescent fish tail crashing through the waves and then spiraling down into the depths of the ocean below.

"Mermaids!" I exclaimed. "And men."

"And sirens," Keir said. "That's Oannes, ruler of the Merj'ir. And a bit of a showoff, as you can see." He chuckled and sipped his glass of wine.

For the next hour, we watched the Merfolk frolic and play in the ocean. They swirled and chased each other through the spiny coral, rocketing upward where they somersaulted in the air, better than any gymnast I'd ever seen.

We finished our meals, and I followed Keir up the stone steps to the main floor of the Grotto. He signaled to Giuseppe, who gave a sweeping bow and unlocked a side door for us, throwing it open with a flourish.

"You come back and visit anytime, signorina," Giuseppe said, leaning forward and kissing both my cheeks. "Always welcome."

The pleasant chatter of other guests followed me as I thanked our host and stepped through the doorway.

With an open palm, Keir motioned to the entryway of a rickety wooden bridge, the only visible path outside the restaurant. Faint illuminations ran along the ground, leading to its entrance.

"After you."

I looked at him quizzically.

"Trust me."

He took my hand as I stepped onto the bridge. A thousand tiny lights lit up along both sides of the narrow walkway. To my delight, as I made my way along the rambling structure, more lights lit up with each footstep. Finally, the bridge took us through a pile of black boulders, where we landed on a sandy white beach, stretching to the horizon on either side.

With an excited yip, I shook off my shoes and wiggled my toes into the sand, still warm from the sun. Out past the waves, where the ocean grew calm, an array of sparkling fins still danced and spun like fireworks on the surface of the sea.

As we strolled along the glittering shore, the salty breeze filled my lungs. Keir's arm bumped against mine a few times, sending chills throughout my body, and then he casually intertwined his fingers with mine.

"Cradlerock is home to the Merfolk," he explained. "Deep under the sea is their city, Merj'ir."

"No," I said, without thinking.

"Aye," he laughed.

I stopped and turned to him. "Have you ever seen it?"

"I've been there once. Magnificent is the best way to describe Merj'ir."

I looked up to the sky, where a million stars twinkled above us. The salt-tinged breeze ruffled my hair and for the first time in a long time—I was happy!

I laughed, threw my arms out to the sides, and spun. The sparkling stars and fins created an amazing kaleidoscope of jeweled colors, which whirled as I spun, until my foot suddenly danced into a dip in the sand and I careened off balance. Keir instantly grabbed my waist and pulled me to him. I gazed into his chocolate brown eyes.

"That was close," I whispered.

"I wouldn't let you fall."

Our bodies fit together perfectly, and I could feel the beat of his heart as he slowly dipped his head, brushing his lips against mine. His soft lips were sweet as wine and twice as intoxicating. Another thrill passed through my body—only this time, less sharp and more tender, filling my body with warmth. Like Ileana's elixir, when I injured my ankle. He kissed me lightly once more, when a rumble of thunder echoed in the distance.

"Looks like another storm's coming in," he whispered. "You're ready to head back?"

Nope. Not at all. "Sure."

We cut across the sand to the front of the restaurant, where Keir's Land Rover already waited.

After helping me into the Rover, Keir pushed an errant curl behind my ear. I sighed, resisting the urge to reach out and run my fingers through his thick waves of hair. How did I ever believe this man could be capable of murder?

As if he could read my mind, he laughed softly and closed the door.

We drove back to Darkly, listening to the strains of soft guitar playing in the background. I casually rested my hand on the center console, hoping Keir would take notice. After a few minutes, he intertwined his fingers with mine again, and I felt that familiar flutter.

The dark countryside gradually made way for warmly lit small homes. When the bell tower rose in the distance, I reluctantly realized we were almost back in Darkly.

As we came upon Greywolf Manor, I was debating with myself whether to ask Keir in for a nightcap, when a small motion in the front yard of the manor caught my attention. I pointed.

"Keir! A light!"

"What is it with you and lights?" he said, playfully.

"I'm serious. Look."

A softly glowing light jogged across the side yard of the house, closely along the path Jessamin, Tzazi, and I had taken last night. The light passed up Dorian's study, disappearing behind the manor.

"That can't be good," Keir growled.

CHAPTER 22

*K*eir slowed the Land Rover, pulling up next to the oleanders growing against the stone wall. "Stay here," he said.

"Not on your life."

I heard him sigh in the dark.

Quickly, I exited the car and joined him next to the hedge.

"There's a gate. Over there," I said.

Keir gave me a quizzical look and followed.

We crept into the yard toward the back of the house where the bobbing light appeared to be headed.

Peering around the corner, I sucked in my breath. I'd never seen such a beautiful garden. There were towering oaks with twirling wisteria. Clusters of large white flowers the size of dinner plates. The entire garden shone under the moonlight, as if silver beamed glow sticks were planted in the ground. The crackling lightning along the horizon created a moment that would have been enchanting if not for the air of melancholy the mansion exuded.

Keir stepped in front of me, and I heard a slight whoosh sound —much like when Tzazi's fangs slid into place, but without the final click.

Keir put up a hand to stop me from going farther into the yard. I flinched slightly at the extended sharp claws in front of my face. He quickly put his hand down and sniffed the air.

The silence was disarming, unnatural. Whereas my yard was full of the sounds of bullfrogs, crickets, and the occasional hoot of an owl, this garden was completely and eerily silent.

Out of the silence, we heard a thump, followed by a quick gasp. Keir took off at a speed I couldn't keep up with, especially in sandals. I flipped them off my feet, trailing behind his white shirt in the moonlight until he vanished.

I tripped, almost falling, when my feet met something soft on the ground. Puzzled, I looked down.

Maenad Grog lay at my feet, next to a stone bench, bleeding profusely from her head.

"Oh, Mae." I knelt in the grass next to her, taking her hand in mine. "It's me, Windsor. I'm here with you." Her eyes fluttered, then opened wide.

"Win," she said.

"I'm here, Mae."

"I saw him," she said, smiling.

I pushed back the hair around her face. "Saw who, dear?"

"Cristiano, of course."

"Cristiano?" I wracked my brain, trying to think of someone with that name. "Who are you talking about, Mae?"

Her brows suddenly furrowed, as if she were trying to hold on to a memory or puzzle out a brain teaser.

"But that means I was wrong. He couldn't have done it. Silly Mae. He couldn't have." She whispered some more, but her voice had grown so faint, I couldn't make out what she was saying.

"Who did this to you, Mae?" I said. "Please tell me."

Mae's eyes opened again. I bent down, putting my ear close to her lips.

"Kuh—" she whispered, followed by a warm exhale against my ear. When I looked back at her, her eyes were dull and lifeless. I knew she was gone.

Tears fell from my eyes as the horrible tolling of the Darkly bells began. Mae was a kindly old soul, who hurt no one. Why would someone kill her? Did it have something to do with the mayor? With Dorian's death? Why was Maenad at Greywolf in the middle of the night? What in the world was going on in Darkly?

Keir ran back to me. I felt the familiar but uncomfortable feeling that all the air was being sucked from my lungs, and Boddy Grim appeared.

Not exactly my favorite person at the moment, I moved off to the side as he and Keir talked. Stepping a few feet away from the body, I kicked something hard. It rolled a bit, and I bent to pick it up, but then dropped it immediately. A flashlight.

"Keir!"

He was at my side immediately, along with Boddy. I pointed. "Could it be the murder weapon?"

Keir shook his head. "No blood on it." He sniffed. "But it's Mae's. She must have brought it with her."

Boddy looked at me and narrowed his eyes. "And I suppose you just happened on the body. Again."

"I—"

"Grim! Dude, stop it!" Keir interrupted. "Win was with me this evening. We saw a light and stopped to investigate."

I looked at Keir gratefully, then glared at Boddy, who looked rightfully shamed.

"I think it's time you called in the MEA, don't you?" Keir said, putting an arm around me and steering me toward the front of the house. "I'm taking Win home now."

"What's the MEA?" I asked, once we were a safe distance from the reaper.

"The Magical Enforcement Agency. Royal inquisitors of Charming. Now, I'm thinking this is probably enough excitement for tonight. What do you think?"

KEIR WALKED me into the house. While I changed into warmups, he ran upstairs to rouse Hilde in the guesthouse. When I returned to the sitting room, he was waiting with a large, fluffy blanket.

Pye sat in the middle of the room, yellow eye narrowed to a slit, tail twitching violently back and forth.

"What happened?" he growled.

"I'm fine, Pye." I curled up on the sofa and he sprang onto it next to me. The fur on his back stuck straight up, and I stroked his soft fur to calm him. "I'll tell you everything later."

"I shouldn't have stopped," Keir said as he wrapped me in the blanket. "I'm sorry I put you in danger, Win."

Pye turned his piercing eye in Keir's direction. His muscles tensed under my hand, and I grabbed onto his thin back to keep him from pouncing.

Before I could reply, Hilde pushed open the door and lumbered into the room, grumbling the whole while.

She wrapped me in her arms. "I told y'all not to go messing around. Now look what's happened. You've found another dead body."

"Another dead body!" Pye exclaimed. His gaze darted between Keir and me.

Hilde stood, moved to the bar cart, and returned with a large snifter full of brandy. "Good for the nerves, Miss Minta always said. Keir?"

"If you don't mind, Ms. Orso."

"None of that," Hilde grumbled. "I've known you since you were in diapers. I'm Hilde. Plain and simple."

She poured him a drink, then sat down next to me.

"Thanks, Hilde," I said, as she awkwardly patted my arm.

"Want me to call Tzazi or Jessamin?" Keir asked. "I'm sure they'd come over tonight."

"Don't you think you've done enough?" Pye growled. He glared at Keir.

"Pyewacket!" I hissed.

"No need," Hilde interrupted, her eyes shifting between Pye and me. "I'll stay in the main house tonight."

"There you go," I said. "I'm fine, Keir. Really. Nothing a bit of brandy won't cure."

I suddenly felt myself choking up again, the picture of Mae lying in the grass flashing into my mind. "Mae really liked brandy."

Keir and Hilde both nodded solemnly.

"Something happened to Mae?" Pye shuddered as the realization hit him. "Mae's dead?"

I nodded sadly.

"She was a good duck in my book," Hilde said, standing and stomping toward the kitchen. "Excuse me. Tragic events always make me hungry."

Keir sat down next to me, pushing back a tress of hair that had fallen into my face. "You sure you're okay?"

"Of course."

Keir nodded. "Now that you're safe at home with Hilde and Pye, I'm going back to Greywolf to help Boddy."

"Be careful, Keir."

"I always am," he said. The cocky grin was back. "I'll be by to check on you tomorrow."

"That won't be necessary," Pye muttered.

I gave Pye a "nip it" look and stood to walk Keir to the front door, but he put up a hand. "Good to see you picking up some of our Southern habits. But you sit. I'll show myself out."

He strode across the sitting room and turned in the arched doorway. He gave me one last smile, then disappeared, the door clicking shut behind him. I snuggled farther under the blanket and was about to stream an episode of *Midsomer Murder*s when Pye's tail suddenly whipped into my face!

"Hey! What was that for?" I exclaimed.

He pounced onto my chest.

"Let me get this straight," Pye said, his words crisp and staccato with anger. "A murderer is loose in Darkly. Yet he allows you to go running around at night—chasing someone or something—and then Mae ends up dead. Keir's right. He shouldn't have stopped."

"Pye, it wasn't like that," I said. "I saw the light, and it was me who wanted to stop."

"But he was the one who did."

Pye paced up and down the blanket, from my chest to my feet, his sharp little claws pricking my skin as he turned around at each end.

"Ow! Look. You have no reason to blame Keir. I—"

"Oh, I don't only blame Keir," Pye said. "You should know better."

"What does that mean?"

"It means we don't know who is killing the people of Darkly, or why. It could be anybody, so you need to stop taking chances. You are the Ebonwood imperative. If you won't do it for yourself, then do it for the legacy."

I started to defend Keir once more but stopped. He was standing next to me when I heard the thump, wasn't he? Or had he run ahead? Come to think of it—why didn't he stop and help Mae when I did? Could he have run ahead to an accomplice? Did he purposely let the murderer escape?

I felt a chill run up my spine, remembering Mae's answer when I asked who had hurt her. My head fell back against the sofa cushions, and I let out a trembling breath. How could I have been so stupid? I was so enthralled by his pretty face I let myself forget he might have something to do with all this. If I hadn't gotten carried away, maybe Mae would still be alive.

"I know what you're doing," Hilde groused, stomping back into the sitting room, a large yellow serving bowl full of berries in her hands. "And you need to stop."

I leaned over and plucked out a blueberry. "What are you talking about?"

"Blaming yourself for what happened to Mae," she said between mouthfuls.

I shook my head. "If I had found her just a few minutes earlier, Hilde. If I had been faster. If…"

"How would that have changed a thing? Other than mayhap you and Keir meeting your maker too."

Hilde sighed and set the bowl on the coffee table, as Pye leaped up to help himself to the leftovers. "I've worked for the Ebonwoods a long time and, believe me, I've loved every second. But Ebonwoods, bless their hearts, believe they must take on the weight of the world. Now, that's not necessarily a bad way to think, Win, but is it realistic? No one can save the world from all injustice. They couldn't and you can't."

"That doesn't mean I shouldn't try, Hilde."

"Listen to me," she continued. "Of course you should try. But you also must realize that bad things are going to happen no matter what you do. Bottom line? Mae's death isn't your fault, hun."

Hilde reached over and patted my face, a rare show of affection, which moved me, and then she stood.

"What I can't figure out for the life of me is, what did the killer say or do to get Mae to the manor house," she said, her brow wrinkling with concern. "She wouldn't have gone out there of her own accord. No, no. It wasn't a random accident. The murderer lured Mae to her death."

Hilde picked up the empty bowl. "I'm sleeping down here tonight. No buts!" she added, quickly raising a finger as I opened my mouth to protest.

She plodded out to the kitchen. "You get to bed. You're going to need plenty of rest after the goings-on tonight."

She was right. Besides, an episode of *Midsomer Murders* no longer appealed to me. Go figure. As I turned off the TV and padded into the bedroom, it surprised me to see Pye scampering alongside. He hopped up onto the dresser against the windows and peered out at the incoming storm and the dark swamp below. As the winds moaned around the eaves of the house, I was especially grateful for his company.

After shrugging off my sweats and slipping into a pair of PJs, I flipped off the light, climbed into bed, and peered out into the night. No matter what Hilde might have said, Mae's death lay heavy on my conscience, and I knew what I needed to do.

Mae treasured three things above all else: her friendships, her ale, and her soccer. Not necessarily in that order, I reminded myself, laughing sadly. As far as Mae was concerned, the best place for all three was the Green Gator.

Pye jumped onto the bed and padded up to the pillow. He spread out next to me and rolled onto his back, bumping my arm softly with his paw.

"Someone at the Gator knows something, Pye. Hopefully, I can find Cristiano and he can shine some light on her murder. I bet he's one of those dart players." I shrugged, reaching over to scratch his tummy. "At the very least, it's a good place to start. I owe Mae."

"Naturally," Pye's soft voice purred.

I smiled. We were going to be just fine.

CHAPTER 23

Pye and I rode into Darkly the next morning under the cover of a foggy dawn. As we bounced along the cobbles of Tataille Street, I avoided the town's busy bodies and rushed into the store, rolling the bike inside and leaning it against the front windows.

Pye scampered from his basket and onto the counter, while I closed and locked the MET doors behind us. I turned on the lights and immediately calmed, as the humming of the fluorescents flowed up the rotunda and lit the galleries above.

"We still doing this?" Pye asked, his eye bright with anticipation.

"We? I don't know about we, but yes. Like I said last night, I owe Mae. Someone at the Gator must know something, and I'm going to find out what it is. But first, we've got some work to do around here."

Pyewacket harrumphed. "We? I don't know about we," he muttered, his long lanky body stretched out along the counter as he rolled onto his back.

I shook my head, scratching my fingers up and down his upturned belly as he began to snore.

"Didn't you just wake up? Oh, never mind."

Creeping out the back door, I scurried down to The Magic Cup and knocked on the service entrance.

After a moment, the door opened, and Azalea stood before me, her hair piled high in a large, braided bun. Her look of concern vanished once she saw it was me, and she grabbed me, pulling me into the shop.

"Avoiding the scandalmongers?" she asked.

I nodded. "But I still need my coffee."

Azalea smiled. "You wait right here, and I'll bring it to you."

"Azalea! Can I ask you something first?"

"Of course, bébé. Anything."

"I know you were good friends with my mom," I said. "What do you know about the dark sorceress Malicent who killed her?"

"Where did you hear that name?" she asked, anger creasing her delicate features.

"Pyewacket."

She calmed. "Windsor, I have no time for this discussion right now. But come see me soon and we will talk. I promise."

With a quick hug, she hurried to the front of the coffee shop.

Obviously, Azalea knew something. But at least she had agreed to talk to me. In fact, she had promised to talk to me.

Waiting for my chai, I studied the flurry of activity going on around me. Two baristas moved back and forth, hustling between the espresso machines in the front and the shiny pastry ovens in the back. Like synchronized swimmers, they twirled and dived, never running into each other.

When my order was ready, one of the baristas handed me a large cup, the aromatic scent of chai wafting throughout the room. I drew in a big whiff. Fuel to make it through this day!

THE MET's opening was only two days away and my anxiety level had risen exponentially as each day ticked off. However, as I looked around, I felt a rush of pride that comforted me immensely.

All the portal books had been repaired, cleaned, and placed along the shelves. Plush chairs and ottomans were scattered about the room and surrounded the stone fireplace. Topping it off, the stained-glass windows gleamed, bathing the room in a soft, warm glow. The shop was comfortable and welcoming, but I realized with a huff that I still hadn't figured out how check-out worked. I made a mental note to ask Pye when he woke up.

The rest of the morning flew by as I tidied shelves, plumped pillows, and dusted and arranged all the vintage clocks and knickknacks on the mantel and tables. Grabbing the broom from the closet, I swept up the floors, apologizing to the shadowmen, who flitted to the top of the cupola when I dusted the corners. I finished up by polishing the wooden bannisters until they shined, and only stopping when I was too tired to take another step into the never-ending galleries.

Around noon, I hung up my broom. Pye was nowhere to be seen, obviously snoozing in one of the many cat beds placed around the shop. I grabbed my bag, slid my sunglasses on my face, and headed to the Green Gator.

When I walked through the door, I was greeted with the sound of tinkling glasses and the low-key hum of patrons. I gave Jess a quick wave as she hustled by with a plate full of nachos, her bright red ponytail swinging like a pendulum.

I grabbed the last seat at the bar, next to an older woman wearing a long, red caftan. While I slid onto my seat, she whipped off the silk scarf tied neatly around her head. I was startled at her appearance. Glossy silver hair cascaded down to her waist; she tossed it back haughtily, tapping one sharp, stiletto nail impatiently on the bar. Bold eyeliner emphasized her dark eyes and pale skin. She turned to me and smiled. exposing the small needle-sharp fangs poking delicately below her upper lip. Ah. A vampire.

"A good martini, dear," she said, leaning into me

conspiratorially. Her voice, husky and low, whispered in my ear. "That's all I bloody want, but Mr. Guthrie here has chosen to deprive me of my basic need." Her eyes rolled skyward as one delicately boned hand flopped onto her forehead.

Carter sighed. "Veronique, like I tell you every week, we have wine and we have ale. Which one do you want?"

She opened one eye. "Oh, fine. Make it a chardonnay then."

Dropping her hand, she turned back to me. "Darkly needs a martini bar, dear. Desperately." She shrugged and accepted her glass from Carter.

"See you round, darling," she cooed at me, disappearing into the crowd.

"Who was that?" I asked, pointing at the woman's receding back.

"Veronique Della Morte," Carter said with a sigh. "She was a famous film star about a hundred years ago."

"Wow," I said, craning my neck to get one more look at the glamorous vampire. "A week ago, I would have said you were nuts for saying something like that."

"Sometimes, I think I am," Carter muttered through strained lips, wiping off the counter in front of me. "Now, what can I get you?"

I stared at Carter for a moment. He was distracted, appearing much more stressed than a martini-obsessed vampire should have made him. His customary blustery goodwill was gone, and I wondered whether he might be ill. His cheeks were sunken and dark circles rimmed his eyes.

"I am so sorry about Maenad, Carter. I know you two were close."

Carter nodded and closed his eyes, as if squeezing back tears. His voice cracked as he said, "Thank you. We were."

I took a deep breath. "Listen, Carter, to be honest, I'm trying to figure out who killed Mae. Do you have any idea who could be behind her death? And why?"

His eyes popped open, and I instinctively drew back. "I know who killed her," he growled and tossed the bar towel into the sink in front of him. "The Mayórs!"

"What?" I exclaimed. "Fernando and Lilith?"

He stared at me with wide eyes, gripping the side of the bar.

"And that son of theirs. With Mae gone, now there's no one to testify against Fernando for killing Dorian!"

I shook my head. "Carter, you don't really believe Fernando killed Dorian, do you?"

Carter stared at me blankly for a moment, wrinkling his brow. The look of pain from a moment before was replaced with one of puzzlement and doubt.

Then he straightened and his eyes grew sharp. "Of course, I do. Mae's death proves one thing. The mayor and his accomplices killed both her and Dorian. Why else would anyone kill her?"

Turning quickly, he raised a hand and gestured to Clobber at the end of the bar. "Take over for me, will you, Clob? Sorry, Win. I'm expecting a delivery for tonight's special. Enjoy your lunch." Without another word, he lifted the bar counter and was gone.

"What the—" I muttered as Clobber hurried over.

"He's been like that all morning," he mumbled, his large green ears wiggling in frustration. "Telling anyone who'll listen that the Mayórs are behind the murders."

"Do you believe they are, Clobber?" I asked, wondering if he would tell me about being in the park with Zelda.

"Jeez, no. I know they didn't kill Dorian." He cocked his head. "Although it is odd, Mae saying she saw Fernando leaving the scene with the blood-soaked glasses. In all these years, I've never known Mae to tell a lie."

"So I hear," I mumbled.

Clobber's big smile returned. "Your regular then, Win?"

"Yep. But let's super-size the sauv blanc. It's been that kind of day so far."

Clobber laughed and turned back to the bar.

A little dazed at the exchange with Carter, I studied the bottles along the wall in front of me, running the conversation over again in my mind. Carter was really worked up today. Although anger and sadness at losing his friend could easily explain the behavior. It was no secret that Carter and Mae were close. But Fernando? According to Zelda, Fernando, along with his family, had been dedicating a new statue of himself in Oakspider Park at the time of Dorian's murder.

I blew a hair out of my face, accepting my glass of wine from Clobber just as a fuzzy black head popped up from the bag hanging on my arm.

"Carter did it."

I stifled a scream and stuffed Pye's face back into the bag.

"What are you doing here?" I hissed.

"I didn't feel like staying at the MET," he said.

"Well, you're wrong. Carter's not the murderer, Pye," I whispered. "And keep your head down. You shouldn't be here."

"Carter despised Dorian."

"Everyone despised Dorian," I countered. "Besides, he adored Mae. There's no way he'd do anything to her."

"Hmm," Pye grumbled. "That is true."

I took a sip of wine just as I felt a slight nudge at my elbow. "Pye, stop—Jess!"

"Hi, hun," Jessamin said, smiling and giving me a hug. "I heard about Mae. I'm so sorry you found her. Any closer to figuring out who is behind all this?"

"I don't know, Jess," I said. "It's so frustrating. I can't see how Mae's death has anything to do with Dorian's unless Fernando is the killer. But, as you know, he has a sound alibi."

"Well, if anyone can figure it out, you can. I better get back to work," she said, reaching into my bag and poking Pye's nose. "And you need to do a better job of not being seen!"

Phenny appeared, placing a huge salad bowl in front of me. I felt Jess hesitate and then lean against my chair. I almost laughed aloud. Nosy fairy!

Phenny patted a stray hair and smiled sadly. "Windsor, dear, I apologize for my husband's rudeness. He just hasn't been himself since Dorian's death. Then Maenad gone on top of that." She shook her head. "I never see Carter anymore. He's always working in the cemetery, scrubbing every stone in that place."

I stabbed at a cherry tomato. "His care shows. I've never seen such a beautiful cemetery."

"Oh, yes," she beamed. "He's so proud that his family has been the official groundskeepers for centuries. They transformed it into the lovely place that it is now."

"Phenny," I began, turning to Jess, who nodded encouragingly, "By any chance, were you here the morning Dorian was killed?"

"Of course," Phenny said. "We had a sizeable crowd, on account of the soccer championship going on that day. All hands on deck, so to speak. Even our backup bartender, Clobber, was working. And, of course, sweet Jessamin."

"Who all was in here with Mae?" I asked.

"My, you sure ask a lot of questions. Well, let me see. Victor. Jesus. Yuliya. Chase. The usual gang for soccer championships."

"At some point, Mae left. Do you know why and what time?"

"I never saw Mae leave, but then again I was awful busy. Last time I saw her, she was beating Victor at darts and yelling about the Portugal win." She laughed. "I already miss that silly old bird."

"Do you know what time that was?"

"Well, I'm not entirely sure, dear. But the championship game ended at one. That I know, because it coincided with our lunch crowd. It was a madhouse," she said brightly.

"Do you remember seeing Dorian in here that day?"

Her face fell. "No. And if I had my way, that man would never have been allowed to set foot in here."

I leaned in closer. "What do you mean, Phenny?"

"All our troubles started with Dorian. Carter should never have brought him in as a partner. We could have figured out a way."

My fork clattered into the bowl as I nearly choked on a Kalamata olive.

"Dorian was your business partner? Here at the Gator?" I finally sputtered.

"Drink some water, dear." Phenny handed me a glass and nodded. "We'd never have been able to buy it so quickly if Dorian hadn't put down the money. Dorian was majority owner, but he let us run it the way we saw fit. However, he always brought in his drinking buddies, expecting their food and drinks to be on the house. Cut into our profits, he did."

I glanced at Jess, who looked as surprised as me.

"Do you and Carter have full ownership now that Dorian is dead?" I asked. Now there was an excellent motive for murder.

"Heavens, no, dear," Phenny said, wringing her hands. "Things are worse off than when he was alive. We have very little money left. I don't know what we'll do when the new owner comes in."

"Who gets Dorian's shares in the tavern?" I asked.

Phenny shrugged. "Someone in the pack. Keir, I'd guess?"

Jess nodded. "Yep. Keir."

"Keir," I whispered, a dark dread flowing through my body.

AFTER LUNCH, I stepped back out into the sunshine. My mind was awhirl with betrayal and death, agonizing over how all the puzzle pieces fit together. I was so engrossed in my thoughts, I didn't look where I was going and plowed straightaway into a man standing outside the tavern.

"Well, well. I was hoping I'd see you today." I looked up.

"Keir," I stammered. "Hey. Um. Are y'all making any progress in the investigation?"

He stuck his hands in the pockets of his jeans. "Not really," he admitted quietly. "Although we're confident she hit her head on that bench next to her body."

"So then, it was an accident?"

He shrugged. "Not so sure about that. We found her shoes on

the other side of the lawn as if she had been picked up and thrown into the bench, leaving her shoes where she was standing."

"Oh, how awful!" I said, my mind shifting into overdrive.

With their strength and agility, a werewolf could easily knock a person across a lawn, especially someone as small as Mae, I thought. Keir disappeared from my side that night in mere seconds, and I still didn't know where he went or what he did.

"Well, I've got to get back to work." I tried to smile normally, but I was sure it looked anything but.

"What's wrong?" His hands reached for me, and when I took a step back, they fell to his sides.

"Are you kidding me?" His eyes widened, and he shook his head. "Now you think I had something to do with Mae's death? Look. I've done everything I can to prove to you who I am." He exhaled, and I saw the hurt on his face.

Had I made a big mistake?

"But I can't do this anymore, Win. Just forget it," he said.

I turned before he could see the tears rolling down my cheeks and rushed back to the comfort of the bookshop.

CHAPTER 24

After I returned to the shop, several townspeople came by to see how I was doing after finding Mae. I halfway thought Keir would stop in to set things right between us, but I thought wrong. By closing time, I was both physically and emotionally drained. As I moved to flip the shop sign to "CLOSED," the door popped open and Chase stuck his head in.

"Shouldn't you be able to do that with your magic by now?" he teased.

"Hey, give me a break. It's only been five days," I protested.

"I was turning my nurse's hair purple before I was even a day old," he quipped, but his usual playful tone was missing.

I tried to grin. "Well, we can't all be magical geniuses like you, can we?"

Chase ambled up to me at the counter and his face grew somber.

"Listen. What would you think about us all getting together tonight? I'd really like to be with my friends." He paused and shook his head. "Mae wasn't the most sophisticated of persons, but she was good, kind, and honest. She would sooner do something for another person than herself. I can't believe she's gone, Win, and I surely can't imagine who would do such a thing."

I came around the counter, wrapping my arms around him as he shook with sadness. After a few minutes, he wiped his eyes and straightened.

"I'm really sorry, Chase."

"At least you were there for her… at the end. I guess it just feels right to do something in her honor. So—tonight?"

"I don't know, Chase. I've had a rotten day myself."

"Honey, I heard," he said with a frown.

"Good grief! People in this town sure do like to talk," I cried. "Why don't people mind their own business?"

"Why, hun, you are our business," Chase wrapped an arm around my shoulder. "Benny the Rat has been taking bets on you and Keir becoming an item since the day you arrived in Darkly."

"I've never heard of anything so ridiculous." I put my hand over my eyes. A headache was coming on and from the current pangs, I could tell it was going to be a doozy. Could this day get any worse?

He tilted his chin and grinned. "I've got bank on y'all getting hitched. I promise you a superb wedding gift from it."

Yep. It could.

"Chase! We're not even speaking!"

"Today you might not be. But who knows what will happen tomorrow?" He threw his hands up in the air like he was Glinda the Good Witch. "It'll all work out."

I shook my head.

"So tonight?" he clasped his hands in front of him. "It's obvious you could do with a get-together yourself, with all your bestest friends."

Pye hopped on the counter, yawned, and then stretched. "It might do you some good."

"Fine," I sighed. "Everyone can come to Fernwood, if you'd like."

Chase flashed his trademark grin. "Good. That's what I already told them."

"I bet you were a heartbreaker before you met Ren."

He leaned back against the counter, his grin growing even bigger.

"Still am, sugah."

After Chase left, my feelings of wretchedness returned. Plopping my elbows on the counter and my chin in my hands, I stared at Pye, who sat rigidly in front of me, staring back.

"I wish things had turned out differently with Keir," he said quietly, rubbing his head against my cheek. "Don't lose hope, ma chérie. Tomorrow is not here, and no one knows yet what it will bring."

I cradled his head in my hand and felt my eyes tearing up. "Thanks, Pye. I love you, cat."

We sat there for a few minutes, listening to the ticking of the many clocks throughout the shop and the hiss and crackle from the fireplace.

"I love you too, Win."

As I lifted the grocery bags from the woven cane basket on my bike, the kitchen doors burst open and Jessamin ran out, arms wide open.

"Oh, Win," she exclaimed, giving me a gigantic hug, almost knocking the bags out of my hands. "I'm sorry I couldn't get by the portal shop this afternoon to check on you. By the time I got there, you'd already left." She took half the bags from my hands. "Are you okay?"

"I'm fine, Jess. You know, I was thinking. As many corpses as I keep finding, there's a good chance I'll be taking you off Boddy's radar."

"I wasn't talking about Mae, hun," she said.

"Oh."

"You watch. The next time you run into each other, you'll talk it over and it'll be like nothing ever happened."

I continued up the walk as Jess bounced along next to me.

"I've known Keir a long time, and I've never seen him so interested in a woman before. Do you know that before you came to Darkly, I saw him in town maybe once every two weeks? A little more often when the Town Elders met. Now, he's here almost every day. The only thing that's changed between then and now? Your being here."

Jessamin kissed my cheek, then bounded up the stairway and into the house.

I followed along behind. With a heavy heart, I took a deep breath and ordered myself not to cry. I was torn. My heart told me there was no way Keir could be a murderer, but my brain listed all the evidence against him. I knew Lucas for years and was wrong about him. I hadn't even known Keir for a week. Could I trust my feelings?

As I entered the kitchen, Chase and Ren were sitting on bar stools, chatting up Jess. "Let me get those!" they said in unison, jumping up and reaching for the bags in my hands.

I handed off the bags as Jess and I moved into the sitting room, collapsing on the velvety sofas. Pye sprang up beside me and curled up on my lap.

"Plantains from the Green Gator!" Chase exclaimed from the kitchen. "Are those for me?"

"Of course," I called back. "Although I was hoping you'd share."

"No way, José!"

Chase was trying hard to be his positive, jovial self, but Mae's death had taken its toll. His face was peaked and drawn, and I was glad I had let him talk me into this. Chase needed it. I guess I probably did too.

Ren walked in, looking at me with a sad smile as he fell onto the couch next to me. He and Chase were an interesting couple. Chase was blond, boyish, and chatty, dressing in light linen suits and jaunty hats; Lorenzo was darkly handsome and quiet, more prone to jeans and t-shirts than Southern gentleman attire. I liked Lorenzo, and he seemed good for Chase.

Chase brought in a heaping tray of plantains, with a side bowl of Hilde's avocado cream sauce. Hilde followed with the rest of our dinner: a smorgasbord of appetizers—mini empanadas, cheese fries, southwestern egg rolls, and stuffed jalapeños.

"Hilde made me share," Chase frowned.

At that moment, there was a sudden loud knock on the door.

I pulled the curtain to the side. Tzazi waved and pulled a funny face at me. I opened the door and gave her a tight hug.

"How's Chase?" she asked, tossing her coat on the coat stand by the door.

"Pretending to be okay," I said.

After we'd filled our plates and sangria glasses, we settled around the sitting room. As we ate, I gave them a condensed version of my dinner with Keir, describing seeing the light and discovering Maenad. I skipped our disagreement this afternoon—although I was pretty sure if Jess and Chase knew, they all knew.

"You didn't see anyone?" Chase asked.

"Not a soul. Although... I think Keir may have. He ran toward a statue of a woman... and I saw a flurry of flying leaves." I looked at Jessamine.

"That's Queen Mab," she said, through a mouthful of chicken, corn, and black beans. "On the northwest corner of the back lawns. Behind her is the road leading to Cradlerock."

"That'd make for a fast escape," Tzazi said, nodding.

"How did she die?" Chase asked, as the room fell silent. He looked down at his drink.

"Chase, no. We don't need to talk about that," Jess said, putting a hand on his arm.

He looked up at us. "I need to know what that fiend did to her. It might help catch the killer." Chase looked at me expectantly.

I sighed. "Okay. All I know is she was lying in the grass when I discovered her. Keir said they believe Mae hit her head on a stone bench. I found a flashlight close by, and her shoes were on the other side of the lawn."

I looked at Chase to see how he was doing before I continued.

"There's one other thing," I said. "She mentioned someone named Cristiano. Do any of you know who that is?"

With any luck, she had given me the name of her killer.

Chase laughed softly. "Cristiano was her favorite soccer player. Plays for Portugal. In fact, the last game I watched with Mae was Portugal and France in the championship. That was the day Dorian was killed."

"She really did like her soccer, didn't she?" I said distractedly.

"Well, have you seen him? Cristiano is gorgeous and Latin. Just like my Ren," he added quickly.

"Chase, what time did Portugal and France play?"

"Eleven in the morning. Why?"

"I don't know yet. There's one other strange thing that happened last night," I said hesitantly.

They all leaned in expectantly, as Tzazi exclaimed, "I knew it! You did the dirty."

"Tzazi!" Jessamin said, giving her a stern look.

Tzazi shrugged and I couldn't help but laugh at Jessamin's expression.

Now that's more like what I expected, and I appreciated Tzazi's inappropriate sense of humor. It seemed to lighten the tension.

"No. Nothing like that," I said. Now or ever, it seemed.

Tzazi's face fell in disappointment.

"Right before Keir arrived at Fernwood, I heard the most horrifying wailing coming out of the swamp. Keir showed up, and it stopped after a few minutes."

Everyone sat silent for a moment and then Jessamin said, "It could have been Clíodhna."

"That's what Keir said."

"No," Ren spoke up. "It's the swamp hag."

"The swamp hag?" I asked, dribbling sauce onto a small section of plantain and placing it on Pye's small plate.

Tzazi rolled her eyes. "Some people believe a witch lives in the swamp."

"Now, don't you go disrespecting the hag, Tzazi Strangeland," Hilde said, bringing in a fresh platter. "You know as well as I do that the hag is real. Your granddad's had his dealings with her, as have I."

"Who is she?" I asked.

"No one knows," Jessamin said. "People have reported sightings for hundreds of years."

I most definitely didn't like hearing that a centuries-old swamp witch was living behind my house.

Wait! Could that be…

"The light," I mumbled.

"What's that, hun?" Chase asked.

I flittered my hand in the air. "Nothing." I looked up to see Tzazi's eyes narrow sharply at me. I had a hard time getting anything past her and had a feeling she was going to bring this up once we were alone.

Chase excused himself and stepped back into the kitchen.

"I have a theory," Jess said, scooting to the edge of her seat. "And I want to hear what y'all think."

She smoothed her long red curls and looked at us excitedly.

"The killer is Solara Nova," she said. "Just hear me out! Solara killed Dorian for revenge and to lure Keir back to her. Mae must have found out, so Solara did away with her too."

"Got this all figured out, huh?" Tzazi smirked.

"Tzazi, you know what Solara's like," Jessamin said.

"I do, Jess," Tzazi said. "I just don't see her running around pushing men off bell towers or tossing women into concrete benches."

"What's all this?" Chase asked, bringing in another huge tray of appetizers. Good grief! I've never seen a man eat so much!

"Jessamin believes Solara's the killer," Ren offered, helping his partner set the tray on the table.

"She has no alibi," Jessamin said. "Win and I checked it out. Solara said she was shopping with Zelda Merryman but forgot to tell Zelda to lie for her."

"Um," Chase said, with a mouth full of plantain, "Solara didn't kill him."

"But she lied about where she was when Dorian was murdered," Jessamin insisted.

"Oh, I have no doubt about that," Chase said, lightly patting the corners of his mouth with a napkin. "That's because she was actually…"

He fell silent. "I can't tell."

"You can't do that!" I said, while the rest of the room exploded with jeers. "Give me those plantains."

"Never!" he exclaimed, moving his plate out of my reach. "Okay, okay. But you can't breathe a word."

He looked each of us in the eyes and made us swear to never tell a soul.

"Solara couldn't have murdered Dorian because she was at the salon when he was killed," Chase said dramatically.

"That doesn't even make sense," Jessamin said. "Why would she lie about getting her hair and nails done? Unless she… oh… Oh!"

Tzazi and Jessamin laughed hysterically. Ren's face blushed red, as Chase smiled smugly.

"I don't get it," I said, looking at everyone. "What am I missing?"

"Solara has a standing monthly appointment for a face and body regeneration glamour," Chase said.

I must have still looked puzzled. "Magical face and body lifts," he explained. "It's like applying a permanent Snapchat filter."

"So that's how she's so absurdly beautiful! Hah!" I don't know why that made me feel so good.

"Not. A. Word." Chase reminded us.

"So there goes your theory, Jessamin," Tzazi said.

"True. But she still could be the one breaking up Win and Keir," Jessamin pouted.

"Nope. That would be me," I said with a sad smile.

"You and Keir will work it out," Jess said. "It'll all be okay."

"That's exactly what I told her," Chase said, taking a big draw on his sangria.

He gave me a wink. "If it isn't, there goes my entire retirement account."

As everyone laughed, Tzazi suddenly stood up. "It's a beautiful night. Let's finish this evening under the stars," she suggested.

"Ooh. Yes. Great idea, Tzazi," Jessamin said, picking up one of the pitchers of sangria. "Win, have you met Greta Garbo?"

"We have not been formally introduced," I said. "And I'd like to keep it that way."

"Greta Garbo?" Now it was Ren's turn to look puzzled.

"The ancient alligator in the pond," Chase supplied.

"Uh, I think I'll pass," Ren said.

"Don't worry, dear," Chase quipped, throwing an arm around Lorenzo's shoulders. "You're safe with me."

Ren chuckled and kissed his partner. "Don't you think it's probably the other way around?"

Chase sniffed and walked outside.

We all grabbed the last of the glasses and followed him to the courtyard between the back porch and the kitchen. Despite Hilde's assurances after my Greta Garbo encounter, I had purposely stayed away from this area of the property. However, as we stepped down the stairs and out onto the flagstones, I was surprised at just how lovely it was.

No doubt fashioned after a traditional New Orleans patio, the courtyard was a haven of banana trees and blue plumbago swaying in the night breeze. Several settees, sofas, and chairs were splayed around a wrought-iron table topped by a green umbrella. Small white lights twinkled underneath its canopy, while strings of bulbs crisscrossed above our heads, providing illumination but not impeding our view of the stars above.

The warm glow, along with the breeze, calmed my nerves, and I settled into a green settee with a fresh glass of sangria.

No one spoke for a few minutes, listening as the crickets and bullfrogs began their eerie love serenades. Fireflies flashed sporadically in the dark, appearing closer and closer.

Finally, Jessamin spoke. "If it's not Solara, then who?"

"That's the million-dollar question, isn't it?" I said.

An idea of what may have happened was forming in my head, but I wasn't ready to voice my suspicions to my friends yet. There was still too much that didn't make sense.

A shout from Jess roused me from my tranquil reverie.

"Look! Over there! What is that?"

Pulsating deep in the swamp was the familiar glowing disk.

Ren said darkly, "Dios mio. It's the swamp hag."

"That is not a swamp hag," Tzazi said excitedly. "C'mon!"

Jess, Chase, and I followed her to the dock, where she untied the boat from the piling holding her.

"Who's coming?" she asked.

I hadn't even heard Ren approach until he spoke.

"You shouldn't toy with the hag," he said, shaking his head.

"Right. I'll stay," Chase said, moving to stand next to Ren.

Jess raised a hand. "Me too."

"I'll go," I said, pushing my way to the front and climbing into the boat.

Tzazi pushed us off and paddled softly through the swamp. The crickets and frogs didn't seem the least dissuaded by the light —or us—as they continued their night song.

I felt a rush of water alongside the boat and when I looked over the starboard side, Greta Garbo was gliding along beside us. Seeing her up close was more soothing than alarming and, at that moment, I realized her purpose was to protect, not harm.

The pond was larger than it appeared to be from the house, but Tzazi steadily moved us forward. The boat had barely reached the middle of the marsh when the light blinked once and disappeared.

"Aww," Tzazi sighed.

We sat in silence for a moment when the boat suddenly began moving backward. Peering over the bow, Greta Garbo's snout was pushed up against the boat and she directed us back to shore.

"This isn't the first time you've seen this light, is it?" Tzazi asked me.

"No."

"How often?"

"Almost every night since I arrived. Even during storms."

Tzazi pressed her lips together, her furrowed brow besmirching her smooth skin. "We're going to find out exactly what that light is. Maybe not tonight. But we will. Swamp hag or not."

CHAPTER 25

To Tzazi's disappointment, the light in the swamp never reappeared that night. After everyone said their goodbyes around midnight, I brushed my teeth, washed my face and collapsed into bed, completely spent from the events of the day. Pye curled up next to me in a silent, bristly ball. The absence of his usual nighttime purring only contributed to my feelings of restlessness and worry.

I tossed and turned for most of the night. My unsettling dreams ricocheted between an image of Mae lying in the grass, her white hair splayed around her head like a diadem, to Dorian in the Gator, laughing as he flirted with Mayor Mayór's wife. Then, him falling backward, impossibly impaled on a metal soccer goal, which gave way to Keir with his cocky smile and his intoxicating brown eyes, leaning against the stone wall of the cemetery. The image dissolved, and a woman with dirty brown hair and pale wrinkled skin pushed herself into my dream and glared at me through broken planks of wood. I screamed and sat up in bed.

Pye immediately jumped up, his back a half moon of cantankerous fur. He hissed and gazed around the room, ready to take off someone's face, no doubt.

I laughed half-heartedly. "Sorry, Pye. Just a bad dream."

He looked at me strangely for a moment and then jumped from the bed.

"Let's get coffee," he said.

"Best idea I've heard all morning."

I slid my feet into fluffy pink slippers next to the bed and trudged behind him to the kitchen. To Pye's immense entertainment, I tried to magic a pot of coffee into existence but gave up after five minutes and made it myself. I watched it percolate as I drummed my fingers on the marble countertop.

When the coffee was ready, I grabbed the largest mug I could find, filled it to the brim, and carried it down to the courtyard—just like Grandmother used to do.

As I relaxed into a deck chair, the moist morning breeze lifted my hair. Tiny wrens chirped cheerily in the hibiscus bushes surrounding me. The sweet scent of frangipani blooms drifted in the air. I could see why Grandmother loved this place so much.

A sudden splash drew my attention, and water began lapping the shore in small rolling waves. I stiffened as two large yellow eyes peered at me from the middle of the pond and Greta Garbo slowly glided toward me, her tail swishing back and forth as she moved.

Pye suddenly appeared in my lap and stretched out across my knee. A feeling of calm and contentment flowed through me, and I settled once again into my chair.

Taking a sip of coffee, I laid my head back and closed my own eyes. The information Tzazi, Jessamin, and I had uncovered swirled in my head, pieces fitting here and there, but no clear picture emerging. More than anything, I wanted Keir to not be guilty, for the evidence to point me in a different direction. I still had so many questions, but who could I ask?

"Pye?"

"Umm?"

"I really wish I could say the evidence pointed to Solara killing Dorian and Mae. But there's just no way she could have been getting her face glamoured at Chase's salon and murdering Dorian at the same time. Even a half-goddess couldn't be in two places at once, could they?"

He rolled onto his back and gazed at me with his one eye.

"So that's what's on your mind? Didn't we warn you to stay out of it?" he grumbled. "But, no, I don't believe Solara, even with her half-goddess powers, can be in two places at once."

"Pye, I just want to solve this to help Jess!" I exclaimed. "And me. And Keir. And Lilith. And anyone else Boddy accuses. Because you know Boddy, bless his heart, won't solve it!"

Pyewacket laughed so hard he rolled off my legs and onto the brick patio. "You said 'bless his heart.' Only a week and you're becoming a Southerner."

"Pyewacket!"

"Okay, okay," he said, leaping back onto my lap and settling on his back. "I meditate best like this. Tell me what you're thinking."

"First there's the mayor," I said. "Maenad's statement against him is sound evidence. She saw Fernando leaving the scene of the crime with an item that was at the murder scene. Every single person who knew her well mentions her honesty."

Pye thought for a moment. "True. But Maenad was a big drinker, Win. Maybe her account of what happened can't be trusted." He batted at an early morning dragonfly that skittered by on the breeze. "Although her murder suggests she was telling the truth."

I nodded and stroked his fur. "I can't think of any other reason someone would have to kill Mae, other than to prevent her from giving evidence against Fernando.

"Plus, the shifter's affair with Fernando's wife Lilith was no secret," I continued. "My first night in Darkly, I saw the way Dorian enjoys being cruel to people. And in front of the whole town, no less. Humiliation. Jealousy. Embarrassment. The mayor's injured ego may have had enough."

I took a long sip of coffee and looked out at the pond. Greta

Garbo moved toward me until her front claws met the edge of the pond. There, she closed her eyes, and remained still.

"The mayor has been in jail all this time, right? So, if he killed Dorian, then who killed Mae? His son?" I gave a shiver. "That would mean there are two killers and one of them is walking free."

"Was Mae's murder a component of the original strategy, or an afterthought designed to lead the investigation astray?" Pye asked.

I shrugged and held my mug out to Pye so he could take a sip. "You talk like a dictionary, you know, but that's a good question."

The pink glow of a Southern sunrise lit the horizon as a pelican dipped low over the pond, looking for its breakfast.

I considered the ledger books hidden in the safe at Greywolf. They pointed to some type of embezzlement going on. Was Dorian stealing from one of his investment properties? According to the newspaper article, he was involved in ventures all over the Charming Isles. That left an awful lot of suspects.

And then there were the Guthries. They had every reason to want him removed as their business partner, but now that he was gone and the Gator had a new owner coming in, would they lose the tavern for good?

Finally, my mind turned to the one issue I was trying most to avoid. What did the DNA test have to do with all this? Everything? Nothing? My mother died at the hands of an evil sorceress before the birth date shown on the DNA test. Why would someone go to the trouble of creating a bogus DNA test for a child who doesn't exist? What the hell was Dorian up to? How did my mother figure in all of this?

I wished Grandmother and Mom were here. I thought back to our conversation, when Grandmother told me about Darkly, its townspeople, my magical heritage, and the importance of friendship.

My eyes opened. Like Chase's friendship with Mae. Could it be? I knew of only one person who could help me figure this out.

CHAPTER 26

To Pye's loud protests, I hurriedly ran into the house, dressed, and ran a brush through my hair. A little lip gloss and some SPF would have to do.

I rolled Grandmother's bike down the back steps as Pye leaped into the basket. Pedaling furiously into town, I waved at Azalea, who was setting up her outside seating area for the morning rush. Leaning the bike against the stone wall, I rushed into the cemetery.

When I finally located Brychen's grave, I parted the trimmed grass and inspected the surrounding ground. I found more of those little blue pieces scattered about. The sharp tip of the tombstone was polished to a bright shine again and someone—Jessamin, I bet—left fresh flowers in the vase. Lilies and purple hyacinth for remembrance.

From the last time I was there, I knew that if I stepped around the mausoleum in front of Brychen's headstone, I'd find the entrance to the bell tower. This thought had no sooner entered my mind when I heard a slight grumbling, and then a scrubbing sound from behind an angel sculpture, enchanted to curtsy and twirl on a tall pedestal.

I crept up to the sculpture and peered around the side. Carter

Guthrie sat on his knees, scrubbing furiously at a footstone, a pail of water at his side.

"Ancestor of yours?" I asked him, stepping out from behind the sculpture.

Carter startled so badly he kicked the pail, sending water flying all over the dancing stone angel, who angrily glared at him and shook water droplets off her long gown.

"I'm so sorry," I said to him. "I didn't mean to scare you."

"No problem, Miss Ebonwood. And to answer your question, no relation to Abimelech here." He stood, straightened the pail, and tossed his scrub brush in. "I just like to keep the cemetery tidy, just like my ancestors have done for ages."

I sauntered over to the pail and gazed down at the scrub brush —a blue one covered in short plastic bristles. The hairs rose on the back of my neck. Blue bristles, just like the ones that rained down on me when I discovered Dorian's body!

Oh, my word! What if Mae didn't say "Kuh" for Keir but "Cuh" for Carter?

Carter's eyes darted back and forth between me and the pail.

"You know, I'm glad I ran into you today, Windsor," he said, rising from where he was crouched. "I haven't welcomed you properly to our little town."

"No problem, Carter," I smiled, edging toward the angel statue, and discreetly glancing around for a weapon. A stick, a tool, a machete. I wasn't picky. "I'm not going anywhere, and I don't want to keep you from ol' Abimelech there. Besides, I'm meeting Keir for lunch. You know how he is when people are late."

I rolled my eyes for emphasis and tapped my watch.

Carter laughed, a low, ill-humored sound that chilled my blood.

"No, you're not. Everyone knows that's over with."

Rats! I swore as soon as I perfected my magic, I was going to tongue-tie every single gossip in this town. On second thought, then who would I talk to?

I dashed behind the pillar of the dancing angel and reached up to tap her leg.

"Think you could help me here?" I whispered when she looked down at me in surprise.

She shook her head and pointed to her pointed toe stuck in concrete.

Double rats!

"I don't know what you think I've done, Windsor!" Carter shouted. "I had nothing to do with those murders! Come on out and let's talk about it!"

I remained silent, not wanting to give away my location, when I felt a sudden rush of warm air, and Carter strolled up from around the statue, a big smile on his face.

I suddenly remembered Grandmother's words and a piece of the puzzle fell into place.

"Heavens! You're an air wizard!" When Dorian was murdered, I'd felt a rush of hot wind and then again when I was with Mae at Greywolf. Too bad I wasn't a vacuum. That'd show him.

"And my father was a fire demon. Best of both worlds!"

I looked into Carter's sneering face and knew if I screamed for help or ran right now, he would instantly smash me against a gravestone—just one more victim to further muddy the evidence. But maybe I could bide my time, catch him off guard, and make a run for it. I didn't see I had any other option.

"But that's not true, is it, Carter?" I said, trying to stand tall, but feeling my legs shaking under the swirling winds. I lifted my chin. "I wasn't positive until I saw you just now. The blue bristles in your scrub brush over there are just like the ones that fell from the bell tower when Dorian was killed."

He cocked his head and grimaced. "Think you've got it all figured out?"

"Not all of it, but definitely most of it. You and Phenny partnered with Dorian to buy the Green Gator. Only you didn't have enough cash for the down payment. Even I wouldn't have been stupid enough to have any business dealings with Dorian Wilde." Oops. Too far maybe?

"Do you think I had a choice? I knew Phenny and I could make a success of the tavern. We just needed the opportunity," he roared.

"That's it!" I said, snapping my fingers, causing Carter's mouth to click shut in surprise. "It was you, wasn't it, who embezzled from the Gator? Not Dorian. You had me fooled with that one."

I shook my head sadly.

"When you went into business with Dorian," I continued, "you didn't count on him draining the profits, did you? For him, it was a lark—a way to show off, hoping to become pack leader. But for you and Phenny, it was everything. That's when you began stealing from the Gator. A little here. A little there. You felt Dorian owed you. But he figured it out and didn't like being stolen from."

Carter leaned against a white marble monument and glared at me. "Dorian came to the bell tower while I was cleaning."

His voice turned gentle as he looked up at the tower. "Mold had grown in between the stones, and I wanted to remove it before it took hold."

I looked at the tower, then back at Carter. Sentimental over stones? Is he kidding?

"Dorian accused me of stealing from the Green Gator," he said harshly, turning his gaze back to me. "Said he had proof. I tried to reason with him. Phenny and I barely had enough to live on. If he kept wasting our profits on his pack buddies, there was no way we would ever afford to have a child. That's all Phenny ever wanted."

I felt a pang of sadness for his wife as tears rolled down his face.

"He threatened to go to the authorities. Threatened to tell Phenny. That idiot, who did nothing but leech off others his whole life, was going to rob us of everything we had worked so hard for, just like he did to Jessamin. I couldn't let him do that to Phenny."

I sighed. I understood, and felt bad for him and Phenny, but the crimes he committed were horrid. Especially killing sweet, trusting Mae.

"So you called up the wind and threw him off the tower," I whispered.

"I didn't mean to," he cried, turning to the gravestone and punching it with his fist, leaving red smears on the white stone. "I just wanted him to shut up." Now was my chance!

I darted behind the large granite mausoleum in front of the dancing angel and then using it as cover, zigzagging between monuments in a frenzied path, one which I hoped was heading toward the exit.

As I ran, a thick, vine-like fog began creeping around my ankles, flowing up around me like a smoky prison. Its putrid smell stung my lungs, causing me to cough and fall to the ground. I could no longer see anything around me, other than the ground directly under my feet.

I screamed in surprise when Carter's head burst through the wall of fog surrounding me. With it came the pungent odor I had smelled on the intruder in Greywolf Manor. Only now I realized what it was. Rosemary.

"Heeeere's Carter!" he said, laughing hysterically at his little joke.

He had me at a disadvantage from the get-go, but now I couldn't even tell where I was or which way I should run. I had to think fast and get rid of this fog.

"But Carter. Why Maenad? She was your friend. She was helping you to... Oh!" I said as another puzzle piece fell into place. "Maenad wasn't helping you. At least, not on purpose. She never saw the mayor leaving the crime scene with Dorian's sunglasses, did she? You placed the glasses in the street for her to stumble across and then planted that false memory in her mind."

I shook my head in disgust. "Poor Mae was always drunk. It

wouldn't have been hard to make her believe she saw something she hadn't really seen. You knew she had trouble remembering what she did an hour ago, much less days ago. But unfortunately, you killed Dorian at the same time her beloved Cristiano was playing in the championship. It made no sense to her that she would have left the tavern during that time."

"Maenad was a good person," he said, remorse tempering his voice. "But she was questioning the events of that day. Watching the championship with Chase. Winning $50 from Victor. Not seeing Fernando. I couldn't let that happen."

"You led her to Dorian's house hoping to incriminate Jessamin for her death."

As the full scope of his horrid plan hit me, I clenched my fists to my side, and a pitiless rage rushed through my veins. "You were willing to destroy three innocent people to protect your own self!"

He looked at me, his face now anything but remorseful.

"You high and mighty Ebonwoods!" he shouted, as the winds blustered again. "Always sticking your noses in where they aren't needed. Believing you're better than everybody else."

"Not everybody. Only people who hurt others!" I screamed into his leering face.

Just as I had hoped, Carter sent a stream of warm air in my direction, clearing the smoke but creating a powerful gale, which threatened to lift me from the ground. I gripped the marker beside me until the winds abated, and then ran for the closest grave marker, a large pedestal supporting a golden pinnacle.

Carter's footsteps crunched through the fallen leaves. Between that and his muttered expletives, I was able to track his position.

I fought to steady my breath, thinking back to Jess's advice for channeling my magic. At just the notion, I felt the magic spark within my chest, answering instinctively to my dire situation.

With a satisfaction I cannot describe, I stilled my mind, concentrated, and felt the magic pulse through me. It streamed from my body, enveloping me in its aura.

As my power built, I listened for Carter's creeping steps, but was unsettled to find all was quiet. My magic pulsed with a need for release, so I stepped around the pillar, arms raised, as a rush of air blew past me. Carter now stood about ten feet away, a murderous look of rage on his face.

Crackling white light arced from my fingertips and, to my dismay, smashed into the pillar of the dancing angel. Carter took a step forward, dipped his head, and directed a surge of wind straight at me. I tumbled backward as the hot gales hit full force, striking my head on a granite tombstone.

I grasped my aching head, a wave of dizziness rising and then subsiding. Blood trickled into my eye, and I wiped it away, as another gust of wind flowed around me. I looked up to find Carter hovering above, his face a crimson mask of anger and fury.

"Carter, this has to stop!" I cried, standing to face the monster, leaves and spent blooms whirling in the air around us. My magic rose within me. It coursed through my veins with a hot vengeance.

He crooked his mouth and smiled, a horrific look that startled me with its viciousness.

"You don't get it, do you?" he hissed. "You don't decide how this plays out. I do. Hey, maybe I'll frame you for the murders. Wouldn't that tarnish the name of the oh-so-perfect Ebonwoods? Flawless Windsor Ebonwood moves to Darkly and takes out her family's secret dysfunctional tendencies on her mother's former lover and the town drunk." He laughed with glee.

"What are you talking about?" I screamed, anger and magic refilling my body.

My fingers seemed to lift of their own accord, targeting Carter's twisted face. White lightning flew from my fingertips with barely a thought, ricocheting from tombstone to tombstone and knocking Carter from the air. He landed with a hard thud on an elaborately carved footstone. I smiled with satisfaction as he grunted in pain.

He sat on the ground and slowly clapped, that horrific grin still plastered on his face. "Very impressive."

Rising to his feet, he screamed, "But you will never beat me!"

As Carter drew back to strike again, I raised my arms and—with a smile I hoped conveyed the serenity and strength I felt—aimed another burst of power straight at his chest. Carter's sneer faltered as a bolt of light —brighter and denser than before—surged through my body and blasted from my fingertips.

This time my aim was on target! Carter catapulted through the air, hit the bell tower, and crumpled into a heap on the ground.

A flash of movement caught my attention, and I glimpsed the dancing angel pirouetting through the gravestones. I laughed as I slid to the ground, realizing my wayward shot must have freed her from her pillar.

Leaning against the base of a grey stone monument, I struggled to maintain deep, slow breaths. My body, aching from the massive use of magic, now seemed as heavy as a boulder and I labored to ready my arms in case of another attack. I kept my eyes trained on Carter's prone body, even as it swam in and out of my vision, like a fog encroaching along the periphery of a terrible nightmare and then receding.

With a jolt, I felt an unnerving tug on the air in my lungs, and Boddy materialized next to Carter's still body. The former reaper wrapped him in golden coils, just as my consciousness gave way. As I fell into oblivion, the warmth of powerful arms wrapped around me and, in my ear, I heard the soft purring of my favorite cat.

CHAPTER 27

When I woke, I lay in a narrow wooden bed, tucked into crisp white sheets and a quilt of golden squares.

I moved to sit up, but a gentle hand touched my shoulder. "Not yet, bèbè." Ileana.

"You're awake!" boomed a gravelly voice across the room. Pye jumped up next to me, rubbing his face against my chin.

I scratched between his ears, and he flopped down, purring loudly at my side.

"Where am I?" I asked, looking around.

Pretty yellow curtains billowed around a window, while birds chirped cheerily outside. A cute squirrel poked its furry head inside and snatched a pecan lying on the sill.

"My home. You've been here a few days now. You had a concussion, and that wind burn was quite severe. Not to mention, your magic depletion took a lot out of you."

Ileana placed a cool hand on my forehead, and I pushed it away.

"A few days! The MET!" I tried to get out of bed.

"No, no, no," she cooed. "Everything's okay. The townsfolk know what happened, and they understand."

"And Carter?"

"He got what he deserved," Ileana said. "We'll never see him again."

"He's not—?"

"No, he's not dead. But he probably wishes he were."

I breathed a sigh of relief and nodded. I felt a soft mop of fur under my hand and a large black dog pushed its way up onto the blanket next to me. It was the Irish Wolfhound I'd seen before Dorian was murdered. "That's Thor."

"He's your dog?"

"Actually, I'm his witch." Ileana laughed as she directed Thor to the ground.

"After you've had some soup and a little juice, do you think you'd be up for some visitors?"

I smiled and nodded. "Definitely."

Ileana's thick, creamy tomato soup was delicious, and normally I would have taken my time savoring every bite. However, I was impatient to see my friends, and Ileana had to keep reminding me to slow down, finally threatening to send them away if I didn't listen.

When I set down my spoon, my mouth still full of soup, I gave Ileana a thumbs up. She laughed, opening the door, then disappearing in a profusion of pink smoke and tiny blossoms.

Jessamin fluttered into the room, landing next to me on the bed. She gave me a big hug and then drew back.

"Oh, no! Did I hurt you?" she asked, a worried look on her face. "I forget myself sometimes."

"Not at all. I don't feel a bit of pain," I said.

"Good!" she said and hugged me again.

Tzazi, Hilde, Chase, and Ren followed her into the room. Tzazi flopped onto the bed next to Jess.

"You look like crap," she said with a smirk.

"No, she doesn't," Jess exclaimed. "She looks like a hero." I laughed at both of them.

"Thank you," Chase said, handing me a vase filled with magnolia blossoms. I set it on the nightstand next to me.

"From my amor and me," he said in his usual melodramatic fashion. "Because if you hadn't taken him out, I would've had to."

Ren rolled his eyes. "Dios mio."

Finally, Hilde approached the bed with tears in her eyes. "I'll be glad to have you home, dear. It's not the same without you."

I lay in the bed and listened to their banter. In a week of crazy realizations, maybe the biggest one of all was the recognition that I was exactly where I belonged.

A hush fell on the room as footsteps echoed in the hallway.

"We'll come back tomorrow," Chase said and gave me a wink as they all filed out of the room.

Keir stood in the doorway holding a large vase full of red roses. He smiled, his beautiful brown eyes crinkling at the edges.

My breath hitched in my throat. "Hi, Keir."

"May I come in?" His deep, lilting voice was a welcome sound.

"Of course." I smiled, extending my hand to the chair next to the bed.

"For you." Keir handed me the roses. I took a big whiff before placing them on the nightstand next to the magnolias.

Keir raised an eyebrow. "Do I have competition?"

"Only if you consider a gorgeous gay man competition."

He laughed, but then grew serious. He leaned forward in his seat, hands clasped between his legs as he stared into my eyes.

"Why didn't you let me know what you were thinking? Ask me to come with yeh?"

He looked away, running a hand through his long, loose hair. My heart fluttered as I recognized his nervousness. He wasn't used to saying words such as this. Then, a few stray locks fell into his face, and I thought I was going to hyperventilate.

"Look," he began before I could answer. "I know I can be difficult, and I'm sorry for the way I overreacted the last time we talked. But I care about you, and I didn't want to see you hurt."

He looked at me with such warmth and affection, I wanted to grab him and wrap him in my arms.

"It happened so fast, Keir. I only wanted to prove to myself once and for all that you weren't the killer. And I'm sorry for ever thinking that! I asked Carter some questions about Mae and then it all suddenly made sense. Once I knew for sure he was the killer, I tried to leave, but he wouldn't let me."

Keir gazed out the window, his hands in tight fists at his side. I reached out to touch his arm.

"I've never felt so close to someone, especially this quickly, and I was afraid I'd never get the chance to tell you," he finally said.

Keir turned and took my hands in his, his lips curling in a moment of anger when he saw my bandaged hand.

"If you're up for it, I'd like us to start over. Get to know each other properly. See what happens."

"I'd like that," I whispered, as I stared into his deep brown eyes.

Wrapping me carefully in his arms, he held me as if his life depended on it.

CHAPTER 28

Two Weeks Later

I smoothed the front of my flowing white caftan and glanced uncertainly around the MET. My hair was piled high in an elegant, messy bun—a la Chase Abernathy-Wyatt—but I still felt ill-prepared and nervous.

The bookcases gleamed with bottled sunshine as fairy lights twinkled above the stacks, tumbling gently back and forth between the distant stained-glass ceiling and the wood floor. Every few minutes a pinwheeling firework burst, bathing the cupola in thousands of colorful prisms. Ileana and Mizizi — neither being fond of crowds nor society in general— sent their regrets but gifted me a spectacular light show for the grand reopening.

Mizizi forgave me for not visiting. However, he hinted that if I didn't get back out there soon, he'd send his own dogs after me. I think he was kidding. Tzazi says he wasn't. I think she was kidding too.

Repaired and shelved portal books stood at attention, ready to take patrons on exciting travel adventures, long-anticipated vacations, or simply visits to cherished girlfriends. Crystal flutes of spiced cider and bubbly champagne lined the front counter, along with rows of sweets, cookies, and pastries from Sugarloaf. The tingle of anticipation hung palpably in the air, like Spanish moss in the Darkly Forest.

I smiled at Tzazi and Jess, who stood on either side of me and reached out my hands to grasp theirs. "Do I look okay?"

"You look amazing," Tzazi said, giving my hand a soft squeeze.

"Everything looks amazing!" Jess chirped on my other side. "And don't forget! This evening we'll have a big celebration! At my house!"

After my encounter with Carter, life in Darkly went back to normal—well, as normal as a town like Darkly can be—with a few notable exceptions. Keir stunned Jess by going against age-old pack law and officially returning all the assets Dorian gained when Brychen died, along with Dorian's shares in the Green Gator and all the other businesses he owned.

The sudden clearing of a throat rumbled from the direction of the checkout counter.

"Enough already!" Pyewacket huffed with a roll of his bright yellow eye. "Open the door!"

Too nervous for a witty retort, I slowly released my breath and turned to the door, where a crowd of people milled about outside, waving and peering through the glass. As I concentrated, the warmth of my magic flowed through me like warm honey and the locks simultaneously clicked, allowing the doors to the MET to swing open. I still had a lot to learn, but each day using my magic got a little easier. (Not to mention, I'd practiced unlocking and opening doors every day for a week now. I wasn't about to take any chances.)

Jess and Tzazi hurried to the refreshments counter, while I stood at the entry, ready to receive my guests. Laughter and quiet chatter accompanied the townspeople as they spread throughout the large room. I beamed with pride, listening to them "ooh" and "ahh" at the gleaming bookcases and endless galleries spiraling upward.

Dewey, Maybelle, and Conny approached me. I crouched to speak to Maybelle in her wheelchair. Her bright floral dress spread around her like a bed of roses, and tiny red toenails peeked out from under the hem.

"I am so glad you came," I said to her.

Maybelle's eyes twinkled. "I love METs on opening days. So much excitement and promise for the future in one short day. Nothing could stop me from being here, dear." As she finished speaking, a magical pinwheel exploded above her head, sprinkling colorful bits of light all around her.

"See what I mean?" she said, reaching out to catch the falling prisms in her hands.

As I stood, Conny enveloped me in her arms. "Minta is so proud," she said, her enormous yellow hat clipping my chin, a matching veil partially concealing her face.

I ducked under the brim of her hat. "Thank you for saying so, Conny. I hope so."

She slipped her hand under my chin and smiled. "I know so."

Conny waddled over to Maybelle's side. With a nod to Dewey, she pushed Maybelle over to the champagne counter, where they each took a flute of bubbly before disappearing up into the stacks.

Dewey stood before me—tall, straight, and dapper as ever in his light blue seersucker suit. Today, a red bowtie sat primly at his throat.

"Miss Windsor, the Darkly MET has never looked better. I believe the MET knows it has a new caretaker, and it approves," Dewey said with a grin. "Now, which way did they go? Last time I left Maybelle alone in the MET, we ended up in Hedonism for a week. Now that's a vacation I'll never forget."

As he followed Maybelle and Conny, my eyes darted to the corner shadows, where I knew Mizizi's shadowmen hunkered during the daylight hours. Did the MET know I was here? Could it give approval? If true, that put a whole new perspective on the relationship between witch and MET. Maybe it explained the strange pull I felt towards the building when I saw it for the first time.

Suddenly, I felt myself being lifted in the air and twirled around.

"Goodness' sake, hun," Chase drawled. "You look lighter than a feather."

Our impromptu pirouette jolted his fedora off his head. It fluttered merrily up into the cupola of the shop.

"Chase Abernathy-Wyatt, put me down," I laughed, playfully slapping his shoulder.

As I came to rest on the ground, he gave me a peck on the cheek.

"You outdid yourself," he said with a serious smile. "Best opening I've ever attended. Granted, it's the only opening I've ever attended."

I swatted him away.

"Congratulations, Windsor," Ren said as he gave me a hug. "Your opening is exquisite."

Chase nodded. "You did the Ebonwoods proud, my peach. Now, is that champagne I see over there by Tzazi?"

So many people joined us for the MET re-opening, Jess had to make two refreshments runs before the day ended! The town had been through hell, and it was good to see we had made it through.

Early in the afternoon, I had just excused myself from a brisk conversation with Veronique Della Morte on the merits of a martini bar in Darkly (I had to admit I was rather keen to the idea), when the bells jingled, and I looked up to see Carter's wife standing in the doorway holding a large tray of plantains, peering around the MET anxiously.

"Oh, Phenny. I'm so glad you came." I hurried to the door and took the appetizers from her, handing them off to Chase, who appeared as if magically summoned. "But you didn't need to bring anything."

Her lips pursed tightly as she glanced behind me at the

gathering townspeople. "I wanted to. I also brought a container of Luna's avocado cream sauce to go with them."

I looked around for Luna and saw her talking to Clobber. She saw me and waved. I blew her a kiss. She responded by raising a fist and shaking it at me. We had such an adorable relationship.

Chase breathed in the delicious aroma. "Good gracious, Philomena. You're going to spoil me!" he exclaimed as he carried his prizes to the counter.

Good luck on anyone else getting any!

Once Chase moved out of earshot, Phenny leaned in close, her hands clenched in front of her plump body. "Win, dear, I am so sorry. If I had known... if I'd had any idea... I would have done something."

"Of course you would have," I assured her. "You don't think anyone blames you, do you?"

Her face scrunched up as if she were going to cry.

"Oh, Phenny! No one blames you in the least." I clasped her trembling hands and gave them a tight squeeze. "You're as much a victim as me and everyone else in this town."

Phenny offered a quiet laugh and slowly shook her head. "I believed in him, Win. I believed in us. Now I feel so alone and like such a fool. I never imagined he was capable of such madness."

"For whatever it's worth, Phenny. I know he loved you."

She sighed heavily, and a tear trickled down her cheek. "Carter hurt so many people—people I care about. I can never forgive that. I thank goodness you're okay. You are, aren't you?"

"I'm fine," I assured her. "A little sore still, but no worse for wear." I smiled but hugged my arms around myself at the memory.

"Very good," she said. "Might I add I am very glad you moved to Darkly? You are fitting right in with this cracked bunch. Minta would be very proud."

I laughed. "And might I add that I and everyone in Darkly are glad you didn't move away? Jess is absolutely thrilled you're staying on to manage the Gator."

"Well, I'd be plum crazy to pass up the offer. A hefty paycheck, a good boss, and a chance to start over," she said, a sparkler bursting in front of her.

She looked around the shop, her eyes widening at the fairy lights and pinwheels cascading through the galleries. "I'd forgotten how fantastic a MET shop is."

"Really? When did you last travel?"

"Oh gosh. I can't even remember." A tiny gleam lit her eyes. "You know, maybe it's time I visited my brother in the Isles. Thank you, Win," she said and with a little wave followed a twirling fairy light up the staircase.

I waved back and turned to look over "this cracked bunch."

After the investigation debacle, Boddy Grim resigned as Darkly's chief lawman, although he continued in his role as island coroner. With his predilection for rules and regulations, Jess took him on as her accountant at the Gator. I couldn't think of a better person, plus he could moonlight as a bouncer!

Infernum Rock, a foreboding, volcanic island fortress in the Charming Isles, was where Carter ended up. The unfortunate inmates of this high-security fortress were guarded by creatures called deathghouls, monstrous fusions of metal-clad skeletal warriors and pustule oozing undead. I almost felt sorry for Carter. But not quite. He had hurt too many people.

The sudden jingling of the bells jarred my thoughts and a large red feather draping down from a yellow captain's hat pushed into the room and announced the arrival of Mayor Mayór. Lilith slid in behind him and gave me a shy smile. Her embarrassment at the rehashing of her affair with Dorian was still apparent on her face. I felt a wave of pity. It couldn't be easy for her with the whole town knowing her business. I smiled and waved.

The mayor snapped his fingers and a staired pedestal appeared before him. He stepped up, turning to the crowds lingering by the refreshments counter and chatting in the entryway.

The room quieted.

"My friends," he trumpeted, his red plume whipping about with each gesture of his hands. "We can say without exception that these past few weeks have been a hardship on our community. An innocent—nay, a virtuous lamb—was detained and nearly martyred! Quite the injustice! However, we rose as one and righted a wrong, we did."

I almost laughed at the mayor's take on recent events, until someone behind me yelled, "Don't you mean Windsor Ebonwood righted a wrong?" A few people clapped, and I turned to find Jaime standing there with a wide grin. He winked at me and turned back to his dad, who scowled at him in response.

"I wasn't forgetting Windsor," the mayor said crisply, his mustache twitching left and right in an agitated dance.

"I doubt that," Jess whispered. I giggled and covered my mouth.

"The village of Darkly owes you a debt of gratitude, especially me," Mayor Mayór said, wiping a tear from his cheek. Stars! Was he crying? Stepping down from the pedestal, he extended his arms in my direction.

What the—? I froze and raised my eyebrows at Tzazi.

"I think he wants a hug," she said with a smirk, giving me a little push in the mayor's direction.

Oh, stars! I stepped forward, bent down, and awkwardly patted him on the back a few times. From the direction of the counter came a loud snort, followed by a round of snickering. My eyes darted in Pye's direction and he quickly busied himself swatting at a fairy light floating above his head.

"That was painful to watch," Tzazi said as I returned to her and Jess. "Like parents kissing."

"Or Tzazi dancing," Jess said, giving her friend a knowing look. Tzazi snapped her fangs in response.

This time I couldn't resist. I broke out in a loud guffaw. Back up on his pedestal, the mayor didn't appear to notice.

"As I was saying," Fernando continued, "the near martyr of an innocent lamb, especially when that lamb is your esteemed mayor—"

"He always finds a way to make it about himself, doesn't he?" a warm, rich voice whispered in my ear.

I was suddenly surrounded by the intoxicating scent of pine and warm spices as Keir stepped up next to me, his arm brushing against mine, causing my heart to flutter wildly in my chest.

"You didn't see the hug, did you?" I asked hopefully.

"Aye, I saw the hug."

"Ugh," I said, turning my head and looking up at his handsome face.

"But I won't hold it against you." He leaned down, lightly kissed my cheek, and then sauntered off to join some of his pack friends. He'd traded in his traditional jeans, army jacket, and tee for a pair of blue trousers, matching blazer, and button-down shirt. My, he cleaned up nicely! We hadn't gone on a second date (yet!), but he had come to see me at Fernwood every few days since Ileana released me from her care.

I was startled from my daydreaming by a sharp "Ahem."

Turning, I found Solara Nova and a man in a three-piece black suit, with chiseled facial features and short blond hair, standing before me. She looked as mesmerizing as always, her hair gleaming as if washed in diamond chips.

Now this I hadn't expected.

"Solara! Sorry, I—"

"Windsor, I'd like you to meet Mason Beckworth." The malicious glint in her eyes caused me to take a step back. "He's an attorney."

The man stuck out a thin, manicured hand. "Nice to finally meet you, Windsor."

I shook his proffered hand and glanced at Keir, who had moved away from the pack and was staring at us with narrowed eyes. As I did a double-take, I noticed the entire pack was quiet and watching. The woman with the curly afro pushed her way to the front and stood next to Keir.

I needed to deescalate this situation quick.

"Well, thank you both for coming—"

"Ah," the man said. "As nice as I find this little soiree, I'm afraid my penchant for grand gestures supersedes. Miss Ebonwood, may I introduce my client, Elspeth Wilde?"

I looked at him blankly.

"Your sister," Solara hissed.

A raven-haired woman with thick ebony eyeliner and pointy nails stepped forward, her stiletto sandals clicking on the wood floors. She gave me a hard look and then her bright red lips curved into a smile. I gasped. It was me. Me with long curly thick hair and sullen jet-black eyes.

Keir was by my side in a flash, followed by his pack.

"Get out, Mason," he growled into the attorney's face, his rage turning his eyes a golden brown. The sound of claws and fangs clicking into place echoed across the room.

Turning to his ex, he said in a dark whisper, "You've gone too far this time, Solara."

Her face crumpled, and she took a step back. I couldn't help but feel a ping of satisfaction.

"Keir, Keir," Mason Beckworth crooned in a placating manner. "You misinterpret my actions. I am not here to cause distress for Miss Ebonwood. I assumed she would enjoy meeting her long-lost sister. They may never have known of each other if Mr. Wilde had not passed."

"I said… Get. Out." Keir growled in a voice that silenced the entire room. I felt Jess and Tzazi slide up next to me, along with Chase and Ren.

"Mason?" Tzazi whispered.

I turned to look at her and was shocked at her ashen face.

Nothing rattled Tzazi. What was going on?

"Tzazi?" I whispered.

She shook her head.

Mayor Mayór pushed his way through the crowd and strutted up to Mason with a bravery that surprised me. He held his head high, red plume leading the way. "Now, see here," he said. "Darkly is not a town for your shenanigans, Beckworth! Go back to the Isles! You aren't welcome here, you aren't!"

Just then, a loud boom reverberated through the MET and a large brown bear charged from the back of the shop. And was that a cat? Oh, my word! A tiny black cat hung onto its shoulder, tail twitching, one eye zeroed in on Solara and her group. Hilde and Pyewacket!

Hilde stopped a hairsbreadth away from Mason Beckworth, rose onto her hind legs until she was twice his size, and huffed a warning, spewing saliva and hot breath in his face. Pyewacket's claws pinwheeled around the attorney's head. Beckworth clambered backward and skidded to the ground, as Hilde shrunk down to normal size and Pye sprung to the floor.

"Don't you come in here starting trouble with our Win!" Even in her human form, Hilde was bigger and more formidable than Mason Beckworth. "Wagging your tongue and not saying anything, just like you did when you were in school. You were an idiot then and you're still an idiot!"

"Get him, Hilde!" someone in the pack yelled.

Keir edged up behind me, protectively wrapping an arm around my waist. "You okay?"

I nodded as his arm tightened around me, holding me steady as my mind dissolved into turmoil.

Mason stood up, dusting himself off with as much dignity as he could muster while the crowd laughed and catcalled. He ran a hand through his thoroughly disheveled hair and turned to me.

"Your sister means you no harm. We arrived in Darkly on other business and heard about your opening." He pulled out a business card and thrust it in my face. "We're staying at the Green Gator, if you should like to see Elspeth."

"Oh, no you're not!" Jess exclaimed. "Boddy, cancel their reservations immediately."

Boddy nodded once. The air sizzled, and with the flash of a black cape, he disappeared.

I reached deep down into my core and pulled out months of anger and fear. A strength I had repressed so long I wasn't even aware it was there —until I moved to Darkly Island.

"Get out!" I took a step toward Elspeth, as magic pulsed from my fingertips, wrapping the room in a dangerous swathe of primal threat concentrated on one person. "And don't you dare take a step into the MET again."

Mzizi's shadows pulled away from the wall and pulsed next to me with a malice that radiated in waves.

Solara and Elspeth raced out the doors, one lone stiletto the only evidence they had been there.

Mason stared at me with wide eyes. He put the card back into the inside of his jacket and let the door slam behind him.

I dropped my arms to my sides, my hands immediately curling into fists. What happened to my mother after she left Dad and me, I didn't know. But if she was still alive, I was going to find out.

THE END

Read on for a sneak preview of the next book, Falling Leaves & Vile Deeds, Book Two of A Darkly Southern Mystery series.

FALLING LEAVES & VILE DEEDS

It's Fall in Darkly! Time for hot apple cider, cozy warm fires, and...*murder*!

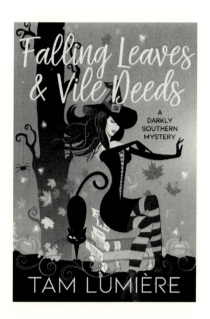

Windsor Ebonwood is looking forward to Darkly Island's upcoming Fall Festival – a weekend of music, autumn ales, and caramel dipped apples. And with hunky alpha shifter Keir Bane on her arm, what could go wrong, right? Quite a bit, Win finds out, when a trip to the local pumpkin farm results in her stumbling onto the dead body of the farmer, suffocated by one of his own prize-winning pumpkins.

If that isn't enough, when the magistrate summoned to rule on Win's half-sister Elspeth's lawsuit is killed, the residents of Darkly wonder uneasily if the murders are connected and, even worse, who might be next.

Win and her friends vow to stay out of it and let Darkly's new lead detective do his job. But when Elspeth is arrested and begs for her sister's help in clearing her name, Win finds she can't resist.

Win may regret her decision, however, when a long-held Ebonwood family secret is exposed and she wonders whether she ever really knew herself—or her family—at all.

If you enjoy paranormal cozy mysteries seasoned with pumpkin-spiced, crisp mornings, don't miss **Falling Leaves & Vile Deeds**, *Book Two in A Darkly Southern Mystery series.*

FROM TAM

Thank you so much for reading TOLLING BELLS & DARK SPELLS. Nothing sells a book better than word-of-mouth from a satisfied reader. If you enjoyed TOLLING BELLS, please consider leaving a review — even if it's just a sentence of two. I would greatly appreciate it!

I also invite you to subscribe to my newsletter where you'll get news, excerpts, special offers, and bonus books that you can only get by being a subscriber!

You can also drop me a line anytime at tam@tamlumiere.com. I love hearing from readers!

Keep your head in the clouds; it's where all the good stories live.

Tam Lumière

ACKNOWLEDGMENTS

I just want to take a second to thank a few people that, without their expertise, TOLLING BELLS might never have come to be the book you now hold in your hands.

First, my magnificent cover designer, Molly Burton of Cozy Cover Designs. Not only does she design the most creative and beautiful covers, she's also a treasure herself. Loving, sweet, caring. I'm so fortunate to have found her.

The second is my editor, Whitney Sivill of MK Editing. Whitney has the patience of a wise, old owl waiting for a juicy little tidbit to pass by. (I think she'd like that comparison!) Her suggestions are helpful and insightful, plus I learned a lot about bookish romantic interaction.

xox THANK YOU! xox

ABOUT THE AUTHOR

Tam Lumière writes funny, sometimes spooky, cozy mysteries full of quirky characters, intriguing locales, and bizarre deaths. A native Texan, Tam received her BA from Texas State University and MSIS from The University of Texas at Austin. She lives in Kingwood with her husband and a home full of animals, including two teenagers. When she isn't dreaming up whimsical and unique ways to kill off her characters, Tam's passions are British mysteries, fluffy socks, and honey lattes in the backyard.

For more fun with Windsor and her friends, visit https://tamlumiere.com/.

Manufactured by Amazon.ca
Acheson, AB